FIRE OVER TRIPOLI

Bullet pulled about six g's leaving the target. Sweetwater was a quarter of a mile in trail. As he picked up this thirty-degree dive angle, he transmitted over tactical, "Kiss a fat lady in the ass, Khadafy." Four thousand feet was the hard deck. Sundance followed right behind. As Sweetwater was passing eight thousand feet, he heard a call from the Hawkeye, "Bogeys inbound."

"Better hit the deck and run for it."

As Sundance pulled off target he made a battle assessment and it appeared to be six MK-83s on target, no survivors.

As Sweetwater was accelerating to six hundred knots, he heard Bullet call, "Feet wet," to signal he was over the coastline. Both Water and Sundance were on the deck trying to get to the water before the MiGs got a lock on. Just as Sweetwater began to catch his breath, he heard a loud explosion.

The left fire-warning light started flashing, so Sweetwater brought the left throttle to idle. His right EGT was high and smoke and fumes started to fill the cockpit. At this point he started to transmit, "Mayday . . . Mayday . . . Mayday."

HORNET'S NEST

Lt. Commander William H. LaBarge, USN

JOVE BOOKS, NEW YORK

HORNET'S NEST

A Jove Book / published by arrangement with
the author

PRINTING HISTORY
Jove edition / July 1991

ISBN: 0-515-10608-9

Jove Books are published by The Berkley Publishing Group,
200 Madison Avenue, New York, New York 10016.
The name "JOVE" and the "J" logo
are trademarks belonging to Jove Publications, Inc.

PRINTED IN THE UNITED STATES OF AMERICA

10 9 8 7 6 5 4 3 2 1

DEDICATED TO MY DAD

We say good-bye to Dr. H. J. LaBarge, whom
we lost on September 20th. For forty-plus years
you served the people of New England with
your healing ministry of medicine. In the laying
of your hands, you helped the poor and cured
the sick. Now free of all your pain and illness
you know only the joys and ecstasies of His
Paradise, which is beyond our human
understanding. I thank you, Dad, for my life,
for teaching me about life, and for the privilege
of knowing you in your life. I will miss you.

ACKNOWLEDGMENTS

The author wishes to express his gratitude to the following persons who have helped in the preparation of this book:

Rear Admiral Raymond W. Burk, USN (ret.), for personal recollections and essential gathering of research material;

Capt. Walter M. Schirra, USN (ret.), for his support and encouragement throughout the writing of this story;

Capt. Frank Dully, USN (ret.), for insight on the characteristics and behavioral patterns of naval aviators;

Capt. Thomas J. Jurkowsky, USN, for expediting the final security clearance of the manuscript;

Cdr. Dale M. Doorly, USN, for personal recollections and essential gathering of research material;

Lt. Cdr. Dana Barclay, USN, for providing key technical information;

Capt. James D. Scott, USMC, for providing key technical information on Special Operations and for editing of the manuscript;

Lt. Gordy K. Cone, USN, for providing first-hand information on Special Operations and editing of the manuscript;

Lt. J. Taylor, USN, for providing key technical information.

TABLE OF CONTENTS

FOREWORD

by
Capt. Walter M. Schirra, Jr.
USN (ret.)
Mercury, Gemini, and Apollo Astronaut

In this modern era of seemingly inexhaustible wonders, such as men walking on the moon or being able to observe pictures of Mars from 23 million miles away, we tend to speak in awe of the complexity and reliability of the fantastic machines that make such feats possible.

This is the first novel of which I am aware that reveals the capabilities of the F/A-18 Hornet, one of the world's most sophisticated carrier-based fighter/attack aircraft, and its vital role in protecting the sea lanes in the Persian Gulf. The freedom we enjoy in this country is due to our strong defense, and if the United States is not there, another world power will be.

We have heard a lot about freedom in recent months. It has come to our attention in the hostage crisis, as we see people forcibly being denied their personal freedom. In general, I think most Americans, as a result of these events, have developed a greater appreciation for the freedom we enjoy in this country. Our personal freedom has taken a special meaning. We appreciate the fact that there is a very real threat to that freedom and we need to maintain a strong defense to continue to enjoy this independence.

Many outside the Defense Department do not see a real threat in the future. However, we must be very careful with large defense cuts. It takes a long time to build a strong military. We must ensure that each and every individual who fights for the freedom of this country knows that they can make a difference, and we must motivate them to continue to build a strong defense.

This novel's authentic account of how we counter the threat is very real, and the decisive role that our aircraft carriers play will make you understand why a strong defense is needed. We will fly our fantastic machines, we will be ready to protect our freedom, and if and when we fight, we will win.

HORNET'S
NEST

Operation Safeguard

The USS *Enterprise* had just passed the international date line and was headed towards Guam, where she would operate for the next several days. The ship had left Stateside six and a half weeks before for an eight-month Western Pacific deployment. The *Enterprise* and her air wing would be involved in Operation Safeguard near the Mariana Islands before pulling into the Philippines for the crew's first liberty.

As the mighty warship sailed over the Mariana Trench, Captain Frost, her commanding officer, gave the order to the officer of the deck, "All engines stop."

The OOD passed the word to the helmsman, "All engines stop," and the helmsman rang up ALL STOP on the engine-order telegraph, stopping all engines. As her four propeller shafts came to rest, 90,000 tons of cold steel continued to cut through the water like a razor-sharp knife. Twenty minutes later and five miles of sea behind her, the *Enterprise* finally came to a standstill.

Captain Frost reached for the 1-MC microphone, a public address system which could be heard throughout the ship, and made the announcement, "Swim call, swim call, I now say swim call."

Lt. Cdr. Matt "Sweetwater" Sullivan and his room-

3

mate, Lt. Cdr. Thomas "Sundance" Karnes, had just sat down for lunch in Wardroom One when the swim call announcement came over the 1-MC. Sweetwater jumped up and said, "Holy shit, holy shit! I can't believe the old man is really doing this!"

"What do you mean, Sweetwater?" Sundance asked.

But just as Sweetwater started to explain, another announcement was made over the 1-MC, requesting Sullivan's presence on the bridge. "I can't believe it," he said.

Sundance said, "What the hell are you talking about?"

"I made a bet with the skipper, that if he would have a swim call on this deployment, I would dive—not jump, but dive—off the flight deck to start swim call."

"You dumb shit, Sweetwater! Do you know how far it is to the water from the flight deck?"

"Yeah, about sixty feet."

"Have you ever dived that far?"

"Hell no," Sweetwater said, "I'm scared of heights."

"Scared of heights?" barked Sundance. "How in the fuck can you fly airplanes if you're scared of heights?"

"It doesn't bother me when I'm in the cockpit. But on a ladder, or looking over a steep drop, my testicles start tingling and I break out in a cold sweat."

"Then why in the hell would you make a bet like that?"

"I figured the old man would never stop the ship long enough to have a swim call. I hadn't seen a swim call in four deployments, so I figured the odds were on my side."

"Well, they weren't, so you better get your ass up to the bridge and take your medicine like a man."

"You're right, and this ain't going to be pretty."

Sweetwater stopped by his stateroom on the O-3 level to get his cover. It is proper protocol to wear your hat when on the bridge. By the time he got to the O-9 level, he was out of breath. After gathering his composure, he opened the door to the bridge and asked the OOD for permission to enter.

"Come in," replied the OOD. "The captain is awaiting your arrival."

Before he stepped through the door, Sweetwater mumbled to himself, "I just bet he is."

As he walked towards the captain's chair on the left side of the bridge, Captain Frost spotted him coming and the smile on his face broadened. Sweetwater extended his hand to grasp the captain's, already extended, and said, "Good afternoon, sir," as they shook hands.

"Well, Sweetwater, it looks like you lost your bet. The ship's crew will be awaiting that first dive to get this show under way. We only have two hours. The ship is a little ahead of schedule, and since one doesn't get to swim in the deepest part of the Mariana Trench very often, I decided to have a swim call on this beautiful warm afternoon."

"Yes, sir. I can't think of a better place myself," Sweetwater gulped. "Well, sir, I'd best get my swimsuit on and get this show on the road."

"Say, Matt, have you ever dived from this height before?"

"Oh, yes sir, we used to dive off bridges back home all the time."

"Make your dive off the starboard side on Elevator One. We'll lower Elevator Two to the hangar deck and drop a cargo net to the water, so all swimmers can get back aboard. I'll have several Marines in the catwalks with rifles in case we see some sharks. But I don't think there's much to worry about. The water is so deep here, and sharks tend to feed on the outskirts of the trench.''

"Will you be joining us for a swim, sir?''

"I'd love to, Matt, but I don't think I could make it up that cargo net. I'm not as young and daring as I used to be.''

"Thank you, sir, for allowing me to be the master of ceremonies at this gala event.''

"Oh, you're quite welcome, Sweetwater,'' the Captain replied with a big sadistic smile across his face.

As Sweetwater said his good-byes, he thought to himself, What a bullshit mess I have got myself into now.

He knew he'd better get his suit on and get it over with as soon as possible or he might chicken out. Sundance had his trunks on and was waiting for Water when he entered their stateroom. "Hey, Sundance,'' he said, "keep an eye on me and if I don't come up soon, get your ass in and pull me to the surface.''

"Didn't you tell the old man that you were scared of heights?''

"Hell no, I couldn't back out, the bridge was full of sailors.''

"Are you going to dive or jump?''

"I'm going to dive, but I better hurry up, because I ain't feeling so hot.''

"Okay, Sweets, remember how those cliff divers do it in Acapulco. When you dive off the deck, make sure your arms hit the water first. Form a fist to break the water entry. You'll have to dive straight out, so as to make a vertical entry. What ever you do, don't land on your back. Have you got the picture?''

"Yeah, I think so. Let's go before I ruin my image on this ship."

Sweetwater and Sundance left their stateroom and headed for the O-4 level, which would allow them access to the flight deck. They came out a hatch that led onto the starboard catwalk just forward of Elevator One. When they climbed up on the deck, there were quite a few sailors already gathered for swim call. So far, none of them knew about the bet with the captain. But the cat was about to be let out of the bag.

As soon as the captain saw Sweetwater hit the flight deck, he quickly came up on the 1-MC and made the announcement that swim call would commence with Lieutenant Commander Sullivan's dive from the flight deck into the world's deepest swimming pool, the Mariana Trench. Now there was no turning back.

The ship's safety department would monitor the swim call. After the historic dive, no one else could dive or jump from the flight deck. Elevator One would be lowered to the hangar deck and the men would jump or dive off Elevator One and swim over to Elevator Two and climb up and out of the water on the cargo net hanging. The distance from the hangar deck to the water would still be a healthy thirty feet or so.

As Sweetwater walked to the elevator's edge, he looked up to the bridge were the captain was seated, gave him a sharp salute, and dove off. The fall to the water made him feel what most suicide victims must feel when they first jump: "Do I really want to do this?" But, of course, it is too late, and you are hostage to the forces of gravity.

The fall seemed to take forever. But it was nothing compared to the collision with the water, which felt like hitting a cement wall. Sweetwater's arms felt as if they were both dislocated. His head and neck felt like they had been driven to his asshole and he was certain he had broken his back.

Realizing, against all expectation, that he was still conscious, his main concern was to surface and get out of the water. He paddled furiously, pulling toward the surface. When he finally came up, blood was streaming down his face and he could hardly catch his breath. As he rolled over on his back, he could barely focus on the waving hands and cheers from the flight deck. By the time he got over to the cargo net, safety had sent a swimmer in to assist him.

It took Sweetwater almost ten minutes to get up the cargo net. By the time he reached the top of the elevator, the captain had made his way down to see if he was all right. Blood was pouring out of Sweetwater's mouth when the captain came over to shake his hand.

"Are you all right, Sweetwater?" asked the captain.

"Yes, sir, I just forgot to shut my mouth before water entry and put my teeth through my bottom lip. A few stitches and I'll be as good as new."

By this time Sundance was waiting to congratulate him and help Sweetwater to medical. "Say, Water," he asked, "how was it?"

"It was like standing still and letting a fucking freight train hit you head on. I won't be pulling that stunt again for a while, believe me."

Within thirty minutes Sweetwater had his lip sewn up and was out on the deck watching his shipmates enjoy swim call. Fortunately he had no dislocations or broken bones, but he would be sore for a day or so.

Swim call was a big morale booster for the crew, and as usual, fun was had by all. A couple of enterprising sailors drafted up a logo for a T-shirt which read, "I

SWAM IN THE DEEPEST PART OF THE MARIANA TRENCH
AND SURVIVED. WESTPAC 87.'' It included a sketch of
sailors jumping off the carrier. Once in the Philippines,
they would get several hundred shirts made up and sell
them to the crew who actually went swimming and
make a little extra spending money for the rest of the
cruise.

After the evening meal, Sweetwater and Sundance
went for a walk on the flight deck to look at their aircraft and see how the maintenance was coming along
on a couple of birds. The following day was the beginning of Operation Safeguard, and the aircraft needed to
be ready to respond if called upon. Captain Frost was
out jogging and stopped to see how Matt was feeling.
As he approached the two of them, Matt and Tom
greeted him with, ''Good evening, sir.''

The captain asked how Sweetwater was feeling, and
he said fine, and told him that he never figured to have
a swim call in a million years.

Captain Frost smiled. ''Well, Sweetwater, I never
like to be predictable. But to be honest with you, when
this Safeguard mission was laid on us, we had some
time to kill and we were in the right place at the right
time. Anyway, I am glad you're okay. It took some
balls to dive from that height, Matt.''

''Yes, sir, and I don't think I'll be doing it again,
ever.''

The next morning, briefs for Operation Safeguard began. Their mission was to assist a naval extraction team
on the recovery of a missile being launched from Vandenberg Air Force Base. The missile was scheduled to
splash down in one of the atolls near the Marshall Islands. The payload was top secret and it would not be
in the best interests of the United States if it were to

end up in foreign hands. Intelligence reports predicted that the Big E was going to have visitors and its job was to keep them out of the area until the payload had been retrieved.

Sweetwater's F/A-18 squadron, VFA-114, the Fighting Aardvarks, would fly on the first day of Operation Safeguard. Cdr. "Slick" Morely, the executive officer for the Fighting Redcocks of VFA-22, would fly on the second day. The mission required them to fly in and around the recovery area to ensure no unwanted vessels or aircraft interfered with the retrieval of the missile.

The naval extraction team was prepositioned around the atoll and if everything went as planned, the target would splash down at 0900 Wednesday morning. Once the missile's sensitive material was recovered, the *Enterprise* was cleared to proceed to the Philippines.

Sweetwater and Sundance had been scheduled to fly on the first event in support of Safeguard. But the following morning, Sweetwater's bell was still ringing from the dive, so he was grounded for the day. Captain "Bullet Bob" Baland, the air-wing commander (commander of the air group, or CAG), decided to fly the mission with Sundance. Sweetwater volunteered to be the tower representative for his squadron, since he couldn't fly that day. His duties while in the tower were to interact with the air boss and liaison with his aircraft while they were airborne.

The aircraft scheduled for the Safeguard mission were to launch at 0800 and recover at 1000. The Aardvarks would fly two more events in support of the operation and their sister squadron, the Fighting Redcocks, would assume the duty the following day. CAG Baland and Sundance were spotted on Catapults One and Three.

The morning was crystal clear and the temperature was in the mid eighties.

Sweetwater entered the tower at 0745, and at the stroke of eight o'clock, CAG and Sundance were blasted off the ship. Sweetwater didn't have to spend the entire day in the tower, but he was required to be there for the launches and the recoveries. If at any time one of his squadron airplanes had a problem while airborne, his presence would be required in the tower then, as well.

Primary, which is how the tower is known, was a great place to observe flight-deck operations, and since the air boss was an old squadron mate of his, Sweetwater decided to spend some time with him after the launch.

"Say, boss," asked Sweetwater, "what makes these flight-deck men tick?"

"They do amazing things out there on the deck and never get the credit they deserve."

"They are certainly a rare breed and, professionally, I would match them against any sailor in the Navy. They may not be as polished as some, but I guarantee, they will outwork any two sailors in a given day."

"Look up on the bow, Sweetwater," replied the boss. "Tell me what that flight-deck director is telling the *other* yellowshirt down by Elevator One."

"Hell boss, I can't read lips from this distance."

"You don't have to. Look at the hand signals he is giving him. What does it look like he is doing?"

"It looks like he's trying to roll down his sleeves and dribble a basketball at the same time."

"Pretty good analogy, Sweetwater. But what that one director is actually telling the other is, 'Don't sweat the small stuff, keep the ball rolling.' See how they are trying to move that aircraft from Elevator One up to the bow?''

"Yes, sir," replied Sweetwater.

"The director on the bow is more experienced and saw that the younger director down by the elevator was getting a little frustrated with the move, so he gave him a little sign language to pump him up and take a little pressure off him."

"How do you know that, boss?" asked Sweetwater.

"Well, Water, after several months watching these men operate on the deck, you learn their lingo. That's what makes these guys so special. They can react to any situation and get the job done effectively and professionally under the most adverse conditions. Every day these men amaze me. Sweetwater, this air-boss job is the best-kept secret in the fleet. If you have to go to sea after your command tour, remember, there are only two jobs on this ship that have windows that are worth waiting twenty some years for, and one is the air-boss job and the other is commanding officer of the ship."

Sweetwater laughed and said, "You know I like to be where the action is and this air-boss job certainly fits the bill."

By this time CAG and Sundance were on station, looking for intruders. The ship was seventy miles away and once the pilots got to the atoll, they would split up and sanitize the area. On the day of the recovery, the ship would pull within five miles of the splash point and have alert aircraft ready to launch, if called upon by the extraction team.

CAG and Sundance spotted several ships within a twenty-mile radius of the atoll. But close scrutiny revealed that they were just merchant ships transiting the shipping lanes north and south of the atoll. No targets of interest were spotted and both aircraft recovered aboard the ship without incident.

The rest of the day's flights yielded no contacts. Commander Morely and Lt. "Gunny" Leonard were scheduled to fly on the first event for the Redcocks the following day.

At six-thirty in the morning, a call had come in from one of the naval vessels on the extraction team that they had visitors in the area. Sundance and Sweetwater were awakened by the 1-MC blaring "Launch the Safeguard aircraft, launch the Safeguard aircraft." The hornet nest came alive in a hurry. Luckily the flight-deck and aircraft crews were up and made this scramble look easy, although they would be launching an hour and a half early.

Slick and Gunny manned their machines and were headed for the catapult within twenty minutes from the call. The flight-deck crew only had one cat ready to shoot, so they both went off Cat Three. As they were taxiing to the cat, strike operation, an information center, said, "Your surface targets of interest are bearing zero-one-zero and one-four-five from the ship. Locate and report their position."

Twenty-five minutes after the call, both aircraft were airborne and headed for the targets. With the speeds they were traveling, the F/A-18 Hornets would be on station within ten minutes.

En route to the targets, Slick told Gunny over the tactical frequency, "I'll take the target up north, you get the one down south." Two clicks on the transmit button located on the throttles came from Gunny's Hornet, acknowledging the request. Slick's radar locked on a surface target just north of the atoll where the missile was to land. Gunny got a lock-on at the mouth of the atoll.

Slick dropped down to two hundred feet at a speed of three hundred knots as he came in on the bearing line. As he flew past the stern, he pulled his Hornet into the vertical, and on the back half of his loop picked up a 30-degree dive and rolled 180 degrees in the opposite direction, coming back at the target.

On his second run, he took pictures of the vessel and climbed to four thousand feet, circled overhead of his target and contacted Gunny over tactical, to see what he had found. "Redcock 207, this is 202, did you find anything?"

"Roger, I have a Russian trawler, it appears to be a Balzam."

"Does it have two large white radar balls on the superstructure?"

"Sure does."

"Well, it looks like we have two of them out here. I also have one up north. Make one more photo run and I'll meet you over the atoll at five thousand feet. I will be in a left-hand turn at three hundred knots. Join on me and we'll head back to the ship."

"Roger," replied 207.

The rendezvous was made expeditiously. Once they had joined up, they headed back to the ship. As soon as they deplaned, Slick and Gunny went to the intelligence center to debrief the mission. Slick reported their findings and Gunny sent the photos to the lab to be developed.

The intell people were concerned about the two Balzams in the area. This was very unusual, since the Balzam was the Russians' most sophisticated intelligence-gathering ship. It seemed odd to have two of them in the same area. There was more to this than met the eye.

Captain Jurkowsky, the ship's intell officer, called Rear Admiral Mitchell's office to brief him on the findings. Admiral Mitchell was the battle-group commander for the *Enterprise*'s task force.

Jurkowsky was asked to come down to the admiral's office immediately. The flag spaces were just down the passageway from the intelligence offices. By the time the captain was ready to brief, the pictures had been developed and were assembled in the briefing package. Jurkowsky laid out the findings to the admiral, who agreed that something was up.

The admiral then called CAG and ordered aircraft in the air around the clock until the missile section was safely on board the recovery ship.

Captain Baland, the air-wing commander, called a meeting with the COs of the squadrons in his air wing. He passed the word that he wanted air support around the clock on these Russian trawlers, with fighters and antisubmarine aircraft. Three aircraft would be in the air at all times until the missile section was recovered. Concluding the brief, he said, "Okay men, we have about twenty hours of continuous flight ops, so get your aircrews lined up and let's get them airborne."

The Redcocks had their second crew all manned, so they launched as planned. The Fighting Redtails of VS-21 launched one S-3 to look for a submarine that might be involved in this puzzle. With two highly sophisticated intell-gathering ships around the splash point, it was felt that a sub may be in the area to assist in picking up the missile section.

Since there were only a few hours left until nightfall, Captain Frost brought the carrier within ten miles of the atoll, to be close by for the morning recovery. As the Redcocks were manning up for their third event, the word was passed to launch an additional two fighters. There was one aircraft to be intercepted. Sweetwater and Sundance were in the alert status for the Aardvarks, so they got the call.

Lt. Cdr. "Ralphy Boy" Petriccione was flying for the Redtails, while Slick and Lt. "Psycho" Smith were flying for the Redcocks. Because of the inbound aircraft and escort duties required, a KA-6 tanker would also be launched. Lt. Cdr. "Boots" Costello would be flying the tanker mission.

The Redcocks were to watch the trawlers, Ralphy Boy was to do a ladder search around the atoll for subs, Boots had extra gas if required, and the Aardvarks were to intercept the aircraft inbound. The vector to the inbound aircraft was 350 degrees at 165 miles.

When the Big E was in international air and sea space, it was not unusual to have this sort of encounter with the Russians. It was obvious that, in this instance, their intelligence knew about the missile shoot. If they could beat the U.S. team to the missile and recover it, the information they might gain would be damaging to national defense. What had been routine had suddenly become urgent.

Sweetwater and Sundance were at twenty-five thousand feet about eighty miles northwest of the atoll, when Sweetwater's radar locked up on the intercept. They were flying in formation when Sweetwater told Sundance to get into a loose-deuce position. This gave them better coverage for each other. As they closed on the contact, Sundance spotted the target at ten o'clock low. The target aircraft appeared to be cruising at a slightly lower altitude when Sundance called a tally on him. As the two got closer, Sweetwater could see that it was a Russian May. This plane is similar to the United States' P-3, which is a four-engine turboprop aircraft. Their closure rate was about six hundred knots.

Once the intercept was made, Sweetwater and Sundance flew aft and to the right of the Russian May and escorted him as he headed towards the atoll. As the Russian aircraft got within five miles of the splashdown area, he descended to one thousand feet and started a left-hand turn. Then he flew directly over the southern spy ship at the entrance of the atoll, and continued up to the other intelligence ship, steaming to the north. After both Balzam ships where flown over, the Russian aircraft headed for the S-3 conducting search patterns around the coral island.

The atoll was twelve miles in circumference and two hundred feet deep. Ralphy Boy was at the western tip of the lagoon at an altitude of two hundred feet. His mad boom, used in detecting submarines, was extended out of the tail section of his aircraft. The boom was about sixteen feet in length and fifty inches around. The May abruptly dropped down to five hundred feet, which put it on a collision course with the S-3.

Sweetwater came up on tactical. "Redtail 702, this is Aardvark 102."

"Go ahead 102."

"We have a Russian May aircraft headed toward you at about your one o'clock position. Do you have him in sight yet?"

"Negative, can't see him yet."

"He is being pretty aggressive. He's at five hundred feet, so don't make any evasive maneuvers down that low. We don't want you in the drink."

"Roger, thanks for the heads up. Tally ho, 102. I

have him. Jesus Christ he is low," Ralphy Boy shouted to his copilot.

The May flew over the top of the S-3 and started a slow turn back to the right, making what appeared to be another run on the S-3. By this time Sweetwater had accelerated alongside the May until he was even with the cockpit. Sundance circled overhead at one thousand feet. As Sweetwater rolled into position, he dropped his gear and flaps, so as to stay level with the Russian at his slow airspeed.

When he was far enough forward alongside the May that the pilot could see him, he gave the Russian a climbing motion with his hand, signaling for him to climb. In reply, the Russian turned his aircraft into Sweetwater's Hornet. Sweetwater hit his afterburner and made a climbing left turn. "Hey, Sundance," he called over tactical, "did you see that dumb sonofabitch? He tried to run into me."

"No, I missed it."

"We best keep our distance until we figure what he's up to."

"Roger," replied Sundance.

"Redtail 702 this is Aardvark 102."

"Go ahead 102."

"You better haul in your boom and get some altitude. This crazy Ivan almost ran into me."

Just as Ralphy Boy started to key his mike, his copilot started yelling, "Mad man, mad man."

Petriccione passed the word. "Aardvark 102, I have a possible sub down here, keep him off me."

That's all Sweetwater needed to hear. Now things started to fall into perspective. It appeared the Russians were indeed trying to sneak a sub into the area.

Sweetwater climbed up overhead and joined Sundance. "Okay, Sundance," he said, "we are going to give this crazy Ivan the old thump maneuver. You fly out to his left and I'll approach him from down under." While all this was going on, 702 had firmed up what appeared to be a hot sub contact. The Russian aircraft had completed his turn and was headed back towards 702. Sundance rolled his Hornet over on its back, let the nose fall through, and headed for the reconnaissance aircraft.

Once Sundance was clear, Sweetwater hit afterburner and made a wide circle so as to get behind the Russian. The May was about three miles from 702 when Sundance pulled up alongside. When Sweetwater saw that Sundance was in position, he dropped a hundred feet below the May and came screaming in at four hundred knots. As he passed under the Russian, he pulled his Hornet into a five-g vertical and climbed straight up in front of the four-propeller aircraft. His wake turbulence and wing-tip vortices made the Russian plane roll hard right and dive for the deck.

When Sweetwater reached the top half of his loop, he rolled 180 degrees to an upright position and topped out at 7,000 feet. Sundance did a 360 and stayed on the Russian's six while he headed for the northeast corner of the atoll. The sun was was setting in the west and the glare off the water was blinding, so Sweetwater decided to stay high and observe for a while.

At this point Lieutenant Commander Petriccione had a flashback and realized what was going on. It was the oldest trick in the Russian playbook. Ralphy Boy had hot contact all right, because the sub was trying to stick an antenna up to communicate with the May and Balzams. By using the sun to camouflage his antennas while they were out of the water, the sub captain felt he could go undetected long enough to pass and receive intelligence that needed to be transmitted. But Ralphy Boy's sub-hunting techniques ruined their opportunity to communicate. Sweetwater, along with Sundance, kept the May from interfering with the S-3 while it was tracking the sub.

Sweetwater had enough fuel to stay on station for another thirty minutes, then he would have to tank or return to base. Sundance had about fifty minutes of fuel before he had to RTB. Ralphy Boy was on a double cycle, so he would track the sub for a couple more hours before being relieved. The May circled the atoll several times, and when he realized the sub wasn't going to attempt a radio transmission, he headed home.

By now the sun had set and Sweetwater joined on Sundance and they headed home to the nest.

Because of the aggressive escort etiquette by Sweetwater and Sundance, they missed their recovery time by twenty minutes. The second wave of Hornets was headed for the atoll when they rolled in behind the ship. Feeling good about their accomplishments, Sundance and Sweetwater were smokin' coming into the break. At four hundred knots, Sundance broke at the fantail. Five seconds later Sweetwater broke. To pull this off and get aboard with an okay three wire, you had to have your shit together. Sundance made a combat-groove approach with about four seconds on the meatball before he trapped. It was necessary for him to do that, otherwise he would have fouled the deck for Sweetwater. They both got aboard looking like pros.

After the Hornets were parked, chocked and chained down, the two pilots walked off the flight deck and headed for the intelligence center. CAG and Captain Jurkowsky were waiting for them when they entered.

"Well," CAG said, "by the looks of that break, you had a good afternoon."

"Yes, sir, we did," Sweetwater said. "The aircraft inbound was a May and he was there to pass or receive info from the sub."

"What sub?" CAG and Jurkowsky chorused.

"Wasn't the word passed that Petriccione had hot contact on a Russian sub?"

"No, what class sub was it?" Jurkowsky asked.

"Not sure," Sundance replied, "but I thought I heard Foxtrot."

Just as Captain Jurkowsky picked up the phone to call down to the antisubmarine-warfare module, a call came in on the other line to confirm the sub contact and that it was a Kilo sub and not a Foxtrot.

Jurkowsky said, "The pieces of the puzzle are falling into place now. The intell ships were there to pick up any info from our battle group, the sub was the main recovery platform and the aircraft was a detractor. Information was to be passed and received this afternoon in preparation for tomorrow's recovery, but the Russians seem to have run into a Hornets' nest."

"Okay, gents, thanks for a job well done," CAG said. "And let's not hotdog it into the break quite so fast. If some of the junior officers try that shit, they might end up in the drink. Get cleaned up and get some chow."

"Sounds good," the two aviators replied, as they headed out the door.

Captain Jurkowsky briefed the admiral on what had occurred, and the admiral told him to pass the word to the extraction team to proceed as planned. As night settled in, the three extraction ships went to work.

One of the ships blocked the entrance to the atoll

with a wire-mesh cage. This would stop any subs from entering the lagoon. The other two ships laid out netting around the splashdown coordinates to assist in the extraction of the missile. The section of the missile that would be recovered weighed around fifteen hundred pounds. A parachute would lower it to a safe water-entry speed, a procedure similar to that used with the Mercury space capsule. Once everything was in position, the ball game was in Vandenberg's ballpark.

The Balzam intell ships were close by all night, watching the preparations for the recovery. But what they didn't know was the surprise in store for them on recovery day. As the morning sun came up in the east, a five-plane event was about to be launched. It involved two Hornets, an S-3, a tanker and an E-2 Hawkeye. These planes were to fly around the atoll until thirty minutes to splashdown. Then they were to go to their designated holding points until the missile section was in the water.

An hour prior to splashdown, intell got the word that bogey aircraft were inbound. CAG and Slick got the call for escort duty. They manned up and were airborne within fifteen minutes. They flew the same profile as Sweetwater and Sundance did the day before. The bogeys were coming from the same sector. Both aircraft were Russian Mays and they were pretty predictable. Five miles from the atoll, they descended and headed for the center of the lagoon. Messages were transmitted to the Russians that they were entering a danger zone and should evacuate the area, but the messages were ignored. Once they hit the center of the atoll they split up and started to circle the reef.

As splashdown approached, the rest of the aircraft went to their holding positions. CAG and Slick remained flying escort. Within ten minutes the E-2 made the call over tactical, "Safeguard's in the chute." At this point, CAG and Slick hit afterburner and went to the north and south sectors of the atoll to watch the show.

The chute opened at four thousand feet and was heading for the splashdown point. It appeared to be right on target. By the time the missile section was down to two thousand feet and floating towards the atoll, the Mays were flying straight toward it, with a thousand yards between them. Each aircraft was towing what appeared to be a large grappling hook on the end of a cable. CAG and Slick again hit burner and trailed the Mays as they attempted to grasp the missile out of the air. The first Russian aircraft just missed hooking the floating chute. The second picked it off.

CAG and Slick flew on either side of the grappling aircraft, taking pictures all the way. When CAG got even with the cockpit, he transmitted over a common frequency, "Smile, you're on candid camera."

Operation Safeguard had worked. It was a total scam—a dummy missile shoot to make the Russians show their retrieval techniques, so that the United States could update its intelligence on their procedures.

The Shadow

As the Russian Mays flew out of our escort range, all aircraft returned to the nest. A "mission complete" message was sent from the carrier to the extraction-team ships, releasing them from the atoll and clearing them back to their home port in Guam. The Russian spy ships and submarine also left the area once the dummy missile had been grappled.

As the yellowshirts were parking CAG and Slick, one could feel the excitement building in the expression and movement of each flight-deck director. All hands knew that the mission was complete and the ship was cleared for the Philippines, home away from home for the *Enterprise* and its company. CAG was doing a post-flight inspection of his aircraft when a young blueshirt (a man who chocks and chains the aircraft down to the flight deck) stopped him and asked, "Is the Philippines as great as they all say it is, sir?"

"Well," CAG said, "let's put it this way, shipmate. It's like Fantasy Island. Once you've been there, you'll never forget it."

A big smile crossed the young sailor's face as he charged over to Slick's aircraft to put a twelve-point, intermediate tie down on his bird.

As CAG passed Slick on the flight deck, he told him he would meet him in the intelligence center after he stopped off in flight-deck control, the heart of flight-deck operations. CAG liked to visit the handler and flight-deck crew whenever he had a chance, since he used to be an aircraft handler years ago. The visits always brought back old memories.

Flight-deck control handles all movement of aircraft both on the flight deck and on the hangar deck. It can become a real hot spot during heavy flight operations. A miscalculation in positioning one aircraft on a final recovery, with a full flight deck of aircraft, can put a pilot and his plane in the water. It takes a strong-willed, thick-skinned officer to be an effective aircraft handler. Some can't cut the mustard under the pressure and end up being carried out in a little white jacket.

CAG opened the hatch to flight-deck control and started to enter. Once the handler saw who it was, he called attention on deck and everyone came to attention. This was done out of professional courtesy to the air-wing commander and any senior ranking officer. CAG immediately put everyone at ease and told them to carry on. "Goddamn it, Handler, I told you not to be locking your men up when I come in here," he joked. "Remember, I used to sit in that hot box a few years ago myself."

"I know," replied the handler, "but we like to make an old handler feel welcome whenever we can. You want some coffee?"

"Sure, as long as it isn't made with salt water."

This was an ongoing joke. The last cup of coffee the handler had given CAG had been made with sea water. A young flight-deck sailor forgot which faucet produced the fresh water and made up a real nasty batch of coffee. Unfortunately for CAG, he got to test the first cup.

"Well, are you and your men ready to pull into port?" CAG asked.

"You bet, CAG. They've been busting their butts since we left the States and they need to get their batteries charged. We're going to scrub and paint the landing area over the next few days, so we won't have to work quite so hard while in port. That way, I can give my men max liberty in the P.I. You know how aviation bos'n mates think. I never met an AB who didn't think liberty meant more to him than his paycheck."

"Things still haven't changed, have they, Handler?"

"Nope. They still like their liberty."

"Hey, I best get down to the Carrier Intelligence Center [CVIC]. The boys in intell are waiting for me to debrief this mission. Thanks for the coffee. Not a bad cup."

The handler smiled as CAG left.

CAG entered the intell center and went directly to the war room. Slick had already filled out all the brief sheets and turned the film over to the lab for processing. By the time CAG got all his flight gear off and reviewed his notes, the admiral and his staff had arrived. The intell officer, waiting at the door, called, "Attention on deck."

"Be seated, gentlemen," the admiral said. Then, turning to CAG, he asked, "Well, Bob, how did it go?

CAG briefed the mission as it unfolded. "Admiral, I feel the Russians had no idea that this was a setup. We got excellent photos of their Balzam spy ships. The S-3 recorded a lot of tracking information off their sub and we got the whole grappling extraction on film. In my estimation, the mission was a complete success. We compiled the data we needed on their procedures and we now know how they retrieved the items from the other missiles we couldn't locate.''

"Excellent work. It looks like we're going to have an exciting Westpac. I'll pass the word to the captain that he can start steaming towards the Philippines. If there are no more questions, that will be it, gentlemen.''

CAG raised his hand.

"Yes, CAG,'' the admiral said.

"I'd like to send a couple of pilots on ahead early to plan for our low-level missions while in the Philippines.''

"Sounds like a good deal. Can I go?'' Several snickers rang out across the room.

"Sure, Admiral, you can do anything you want,'' CAG laughed.

"Wish I could, but I have a battle group to run. But whoever goes in early, have him get me a tee time for the afternoon we arrive. Admiral Barclay is coming in from Japan for our in-chop brief and I need to get some of my money back. That sonofabitch is about a two handicap and he took me to the cleaners the last time we played.''

"No problem, Admiral. We'll make that happen.'' The men came to attention as the admiral departed and then they headed for their respective offices.

As CAG was gathering his flight gear and heading for the door, Slick stopped him to find out whom he planned to send to the beach early.

"Why do you ask, Slick?''

"Well, CAG, I have a couple of hard chargers and I would like to get them a little early liberty.''

"Give me one name, I already have the other pilot picked."

"Leonard. Lieutenant ('Gunny') Leonard."

"Consider it done, Slick. Tell him to be ready to go with Sweetwater. Launch time will be noon tomorrow. The ship will be a day out, and it'll give them a little more than twenty-four hours head start on the rest of the crew."

As Commander Morely was leaving, he thanked CAG and asked, "How did Sweetwater get to go in early?"

"He's planning the low level for you F/A-18 guys, and I asked him to get that old junk car running for my men. We stash it by the BOQ and pass Old Betsy down to each air wing when it comes through. She's getting pretty old and needs some work, so I figured if anyone could get her running, it had to be Sweetwater. When you give that man a mission, you can rest assured he'll do his best to make it happen."

"You're right there, CAG. Okay, thanks again. I'll tell Gunny he's flying in early."

Sweetwater was up at the crack of dawn, ran two miles on the flight deck and had breakfast before reveille sounded at seven. After breakfast he met with Gunny Leonard to go over the flight. "Gunny, we'll blast out of here at twelve noon, fly to Clark AFB and refuel. Once we have a full bag of gas, we'll fly the low-level route I have mapped out, and check the terrain for logging wires and obstructions. After the route check, we'll land at Cubi Point and get stupid."

"Get stupid?"

"Yeah, you know, light our hair on fire and take no prisoners. We have missions to accomplish once we arrive."

"Like what?" asked Gunny.

"We have to arrange a tee time for the admiral, I've got to get Old Betsy running and you're going to set up a welcoming party for the ship. I'll give you more details after we get to the beach. Get your liberty bag packed and be ready to kick the tires and light the fires at noon."

This was Gunny's first deployment, so he was all geared up for the unknown. Sending Sweetwater in early was like letting the fox run wild in the henhouse. However, this was his fourth Westpac, so he knew the area and personnel like the back of his hand and could get missions accomplished that some admirals would have trouble completing.

At eleven o'clock both pilots were in flight-deck control with their weight sheets for the catapult officer. These sheets told the cat officer the weight of the aircraft, so that he could select the proper steam pressure to launch the birds safely. It was the responsibility of each pilot to drop off his weight sheet before he manned up. Sweetwater had given Gunny a solid brief an hour before, so they were ready to preflight and launch. The flight to Clark was about two and a half hours and the low-level route would take them a little over an hour to fly once they had refueled at Clark. So, if all went as planned, they would be at Cubi Point by five.

As Sweetwater's F/A-18 rolled into position to launch, the catapult officer could see Sweetwater smiling from ear to ear. While the cat crew was waiting for the steam to build, Sweetwater hooked up his oxygen mask and gave the cat officer a thumbs up, to tell him that all systems were go and that he would see him on the beach.

Gunny was behind the jet-blast deflector and would

launch after Sweetwater. Since Gunny and Water were the only two launching, Catapult One was used for the launch. Once Sweetwater was off the cat, he would get his gear and flaps up, accelerate to 250 knots, then make a wide left-hand turn, in order to be back at the bow of the ship as Gunny launched. This would expedite the rendezvous and give the flight-deck crew a little show to help boost morale.

The running rendezvous worked as briefed. Sweetwater positioned his aircraft perfectly and the cat crew got Gunny airborne just as Water's bird passed the bow. It was a beautiful sight. The flight to Clark Air Force Base went without incident, and the refueling took about an hour once they were on deck.

After a head call and a short snack, the two were back in the air circling over the Zambales Mountains. This was where the low level would start. Sweetwater would fly the route two hundred feet above the actual runs to check for any obstructions. Gunny would fly a combat spread with a five-hundred-foot step-up behind Sweetwater's bird. He would also be looking for any unusual flaws in the flight path. The route would take them up by Baguio over to Cabarruyan Island and down the coastline back to Cubi Point.

This type of flying was the last of the good deals. You could get down in the weeds and do some real barnstorming without getting a flight violation. Although most of the route was over unpopulated areas, there were some spots that took you over villages. The locals always knew when the crazy American fly-boys were back. The big iron birds roared over their countryside like a giant roller coaster, scattering water buffalo and villagers. They knew work in the rice paddies would not be normal for the next four to five days.

Sweetwater and Gunny hit the mouth of Subic Bay at ten to five. At 2,000 feet and three hundred knots, Sweetwater called the tower requesting a carrier break. The air traffic controller said, "Welcome back to the Philippines. Carrier break approved."

Sweetwater told Gunny, "Tuck it in. Let's look sharp."

Two clicks over the mike meant he acknowledged and liberty was only a landing away.

Both aircraft landed safely at Naval Air Station Cubi Point and were parked. Sweetwater and Gunny buttoned up their birds and checked in at base operations. Once all the administrative paperwork was filled out on their arrival, the two called for a taxi and headed for the BOQ at Cubi. As they were riding up the hill to the BOQ, Gunny asked Sweetwater, "What does Cubi Point mean?"

Sweetwater explained, "Cubi Point got its name from a Seabee unit called 'Construction Unit Battalion One.' They were the outfit who built the airfield and buildings around the base. When they couldn't come up with a suitable name, it was simply called Cubi Point after the unit that built it."

"Interesting piece of history," replied Gunny.

Sweetwater said, "Not many sailors know how the name came about."

As they got out of the cab, Sweetwater said, "Hurry up, Gunny. We need to get a do-me before they close up for the day."

Gunny looked at Sweetwater as if the heat had over-temped his brain. "What in the hell is a 'do-me'?" asked Gunny.

"Don't worry, just check us in and get us two rooms

and meet me down at the barbershop at the end of the corridor to your right.''

''Roger that,'' Gunny said, as he walked up to the front desk at the BOQ. Sweetwater headed for the barbershop.

As he passed through the swinging double doors, Sweetwater sighed in relief. The barbershop was still open. He walked in and Jesse, who had cut his hair for many years, was sweeping the floor.

''Jesse,'' Sweetwater said. ''How are you doing?''

''Oh, Mr. Sweetwater, it's good to see you, come in, come in.'' Jesse never forgot a face or a nickname. He had been cutting hair at that barbership for twenty years and knew most of the pilots, who came in for a do-me whenever they were in the Philippines.

''How long you in for, sir?''

''Same as always, Jesse, just a couple days.''

''Well, you ready for your regular treatment?''

''You bet,'' replied Sweetwater. ''You know, Jesse, I wait many months to come back for your special do-me. Say, are you here alone?''

''No, no. I have my nephew working with me now. It is our night to stay late, the others leave at five. Ben will be back, he went to get some clean towels.''

''Jesse, I have a young lieutenant with me who has never had your do-me, so when he hops in the chair, give him the royal works.''

''You got it, Mr. Sweetwater.''

The do-me includes a shampoo, a haircut, a facial, a shave, a manicure, a pedicure, boots shined, and an hour-long massage, all for the price of twelve dollars. So when an officer walks into the barbershop at Cubi Point and says, ''Do me,'' they know that you want the works.

By the time Gunny arrived at the barbershop, Sweetwater was having his facial and couldn't talk. Gunny looked sheepishly around, not real sure if that was really Water under the mud pack. "Come on in, Lieutenant," Jesse said. "Are you ready for our special do-me?"

"Well, I don't really know. Have you seen Lieutenant Commander Sullivan?"

"Sure, he's right here," Jesse said, as Sweetwater waved his hand from under the white and blue drape. Gunny thought to himself, What the fuck is he getting done?

Jesse realized Gunny was uncertain. He said, "Sit down, Lieutenant. Ben will polish your boots and do your nails while you wait to get into the chair."

Gunny looked at him with concern, but Jesse said, "Don't worry, son, it's all part of the do-me special."

As Gunny relaxed in the chair, while Ben polished his boots, he could see the price breakdown of all the services offered tacked to the wall. At this point he put two and two together. However, getting a manicure and a pedicure along with a facial seemed more on the feminine side and he didn't want any of his squadron mates to see him getting the works for fear they would rib him to death. He didn't realize that all the old veterans who had been there before fought to get signed up for the do-me before they departed the Philippines because it was such a treat to be pampered.

After Sweetwater got out of the chair, Gunny couldn't wait to hop in and get the works. Sweetwater sat back while Ben did his boots and nails and pointed out to Gunny how sweet it was to beat the herd to the beach. Gunny now was realizing what a good deal he was getting, even if he had no idea what was yet to come. The hour massage was the grand finale of the do-me, which made the eight weeks of shipboard living all worth it.

The massage rooms were near the pool at the back west end of the BOQ, and Rosie ran the time schedule for the rubdowns. Once the ship pulled in, it was difficult to get a massage, since it was so popular. The massage was handled very professionally and it sure felt good after a hard workout or a round of golf.

After Gunny completed his haircut, facial and pedicure, he and Sweetwater paid Jesse and headed to their rooms to change out of their flight suits. Then they headed to the bar for a couple of Cubi Specials before they were to get their massages. This drink went down as smooth as a frog's hair, but kicked like a mule after three or so. One couldn't stay at Cubi and not drink a Cubi Special, they were that good. The tickets for the massage could be purchased at the bar, since Rosie's was just out the door.

While Gunny was at the head, Sweetwater signed them up, and told Rosie to come over in a half hour and escort Gunny to the massage room. Rosie always liked new clients, especially ones who had never experienced a massage before. Gunny was in for a real treat.

After a couple of Cubi Specials, Rosie came in and said, "Is Lieutenant Leonard here?"

Gunny said, "I'm Lieutenant Leonard."

Rosie smiled and said, "Come with me, sailor. Have I got a deal for you."

Gunny looked at Water, who gave him the high sign and off they went. Gunny knew of the massages from all the talk on the ship, but he was now about to experience one. While he was getting his rubdown, Sweetwater went to the front desk and asked for Old

Betsy's heart. That was the code to get the key to start her up.

As he walked to the back of the BOQ, Water could see Old Betsy sitting there in her rusted Datsun shell. He hadn't seen her for several years and the wet, humid Philippines weather had taken its toll. He opened the driver's door and just about shit when two monkeys jumped at him. He shut the door and stood back and watched. After a minute or so a mother and two little monkeys came out under the car by the trunk and sauntered off into the jungle.

He knew right then he had his work cut out for him. If a family of monkeys had taken up residence inside the car, he wondered what else might be living in the back of her. Water slowly opened the door and the smell hit him like that of an outhouse in midsummer.

After a couple of deep breaths, he hopped into the front seat, put the key in the ignition and lit off Old Betsy. To his surprise, she started purring like a well-tuned race car. Since she started right up, Sweetwater figured he ought to take her for a short spin to ensure she was drivable. He put her in reverse, but when he stepped on the gas she didn't budge an inch. He checked to make sure the emergency brake was off, hit the gas again, and still nothing. At this point he shut her down and took a walk around to see if she was hung up on anything. When he couldn't find anything wrong, Water headed back to the bar where Gunny was to meet him after his rubdown.

As Sweetwater walked through the door to the bar, Gunny was talking to Rosie. "Hey, Gunny," he yelled, "how about giving me a hand with this car?"

"Be right with you, Sweetwater," he replied. Within a couple of minutes, Gunny joined him and they walked toward Old Betsy. Water asked him how his massage went. Gunny said he felt like a clam at high tide and that he signed up for a massage every day they were in port.

"I thought you could only sign up twenty-four hours in advance," Sweetwater said.

"Well, that's supposed to be the rule. But a little green stuff dealt in the right direction helps scheduling."

"Yeah, right," Sweetwater laughed. Then, in a fit of inspiration, he asked, "Say, Gunny, do you know anything about cars?"

"Not much, but I've worked on a few in my day. Why, what's the matter?"

"Well, I got Old Betsy started, but she won't budge."

"Sounds like something is bound up. Let's take a look."

Nightfall was starting to settle in and visibility was getting poor. As Gunny inspected the car, he decided the rains had caused the wheels and brakes to rust up. The whole car looked like a rust bucket anyway.

"Well, what do we need to do to get this old girl moving?" Water asked.

"We need to get her to the garage and unfreeze these wheels with some lubricant."

"Okay, let's call the gas station and have her towed in. I've got to have this old bastard running by two tomorrow."

Sweetwater and Gunny returned to the BOQ's lobby and Sweetwater made the call. "This is Commander Sullivan with the *Enterprise* air wing. How are you this evening?"

"Fine sir," replied a Filipino, whose English was very good. "What can I do for you?"

"Well, sir, I have this car whose wheels are frozen with rust and I need to get it in working order by noon tomorrow. Could you come up and tow it to the gas station?"

"Oh, no sir, we are short of help and the earliest we could tow it would be tomorrow morning."

"Are you sure you can't come and get it tonight?"

"No can do."

"Okay, thank you," and Sweetwater hung up. "Goddamn it," he said.

"What's the matter?" Gunny asked.

"Oh, they can't pick her up until morning."

"Well, if they can't, then she'll just have to sit one more night."

"Bullshit!" Sweetwater barked. "There has got to be a way to get that piece of junk into the shop tonight. Let's get a drink and think on it."

While the two were sitting having a drink, they discussed some of the items that had to be accomplished before the ship arrived in port. "Gunny, tomorrow I'll work the car problem and get the tee times for the admiral and I want you to—wait a fucking minute, the admiral, that's it."

"What are you talking about, Sweetwater?"

"The admiral, the admiral, that's our ticket to getting this car fixed. A while back, when I did a chief of naval operations survey, Admiral Barclay was my sponsor while I was over here in the Philippines. We got to know each other well, and he told me I could use his name anytime I wanted as long as I didn't intimidate any sailors."

"Oh, no Sweetwater," Gunny said, "I know what

you're thinking and I don't want any part of it. We'll get our asses kicked.''

"Hey, I'll call public works, civilians not sailors, and tell them that I'm Admiral Barclay and that I need to get this car running before the ship pulls in tomorrow. If they buy it, we're home free. If not, we'll get the gas station people to move it in the morning.''

"You no more look like an admiral than the man in the moon.''

"I'll put on my flight suit, pull a ball cap down over my eyes and be smoking a cigar. If you stand around and call me Admiral, we might be able to pull it off. Don't worry, I'll take the hit if we get caught. Besides, they may commend us for our ingenuity. Shall we go for it?''

"Why not?'' replied Gunny. "What can they do, make me a lieutenant forever?''

"Let me make the call.''

Sweetwater dialed the trouble desk at public works. "Good evening, this is Admiral Barclay and I have a car I need to get operating by tomorrow, could you come take a look at it?''

"What seems to be the problem with it, Admiral?''

"The engine runs fine, but I believe the brake shoes have locked with rust due to all the rain we've had.''

"No problem, sir. Where is the car located?''

"In the flag spaces behind the Cubi Point BOQ.''

"Okay, we'll be up in twenty minutes.''

"I'll have my aide outside waiting for you. I have a dinner engagement that I'm already late for.''

"No problem sir. Where can we reach you when we get the car serviced?''

"I'll call you in the morning and see how things are going.''

"Okay, sir. Have a good evening."

"Thank you." Sweetwater hung up. "Okay, Gunny, we've done it. I'll pose as the Admiral's aide."

Gunny was suitably impressed. "Say, that was good thinking. We should be able to pull it off with no sweat now. You stay dressed the way you are and I'll get into my flight suit."

Sweetwater and Gunny were standing by the car when the wrecker and two public works mechanics arrived. "Okay," Sweetwater said to Gunny, "look official."

The two men looked the car over and both agreed that they needed to haul it down to the shop to fix it. Not offering much conversation, Sweetwater and Gunny stood by while the mechanics hooked Old Betsy up and pulled her out of the parking spot. After they secured the car with a safety chain, the driver told Sweetwater to tell the admiral that they would have her running by noon. Water acknowledged and headed for the back door to the BOQ, as the wrecker towed Old Betsy away.

"Goddamn it, Gunny," Sweetwater exclaimed, "I think we'll pull this one off. Let's get a beer and I'll explain your mission for tomorrow."

"I can't wait."

"Hey, this'll give you a chance to excel."

"I'll bet," Gunny replied.

"Hey, Gunny, if you can't hack the program, you shouldn't have signed up. We have to have a little show for the ship when it ties up tomorrow. A good friend of mine, named Snake Bouldin, handles all the refueling of the planes down at the field. He has a couple of guys who work for him who'll be perfect for this joke. One of the men who you need to get is called Tiny. He stands about six-ten. And the other guy is called Stretch. Naturally, he stands about four feet even. Get them dressed up in those white decontamination pullovers and get a bullhorn. We want them to look like the hosts that used to met the guests on Fantasy Island. We'll get them to stand on the pier and call out, 'The ship, the ship!' and 'Welcome to Fantasy Island,' as the Big E pulls in. The crew will shit. Snake owes me a couple of favors and he'll be glad to help out. I'll buy Tiny and Stretch a case of beer for their trouble.''

"Sweetwater, you're a great one," replied Gunny.

"Well, I don't know about that, but I like to make people happy. This will get our in-port stay off to a good start. Do you think you can handle it?''

"No sweat, Water. Consider it done.''

"Great, let's get some sleep. We've got a big day ahead of us. I'll meet you for breakfast at 0800.''

"Roger that, Admiral.''

"Fuck you, Gunny,'' Sweetwater laughed, as he headed for his room. As Sweetwater unlocked his door, he realized that he had missed his massage. Oh well, he thought, I have four more days to get one.

They met for breakfast and got their game plan in order. Sweetwater had already gotten the tee times and alerted Snake that Gunny would be down to set up the gag for the ship's arrival. While Gunny was getting the guys fitted and explaining to them what they had to do, Sweetwater went to base operations to lay out the canned low-level route and flight plans for those who were going to fly the mission. He and Gunny would meet back at Barnacle Bill's, the restaurant at the BOQ, at eleven.

Before Sweetwater left base operations, he called public works to see how they were coming with Old Betsy. He was told that they had lubricated the wheels so they operated correctly and cleaned out the inside of the car. The car would be ready around one o'clock, but they still had to patch a rust hole in the trunk. That answered the question of how those monkeys were getting in and out of the car.

Sweetwater told the supervisor to contact him, he being the admiral's aide, at the Officers' Club when it was ready, and he would make arrangements to have the car picked up. The ship was due in at two, so he had time to get the car and watch the show on the pier before he turned the car over to CAG. If he could pull this off, he would be a hero in the eyes of his air-wing commander, which might get him another good deal down the road.

Sweetwater and Gunny rendezvoused at Barnacle Bill's at a little after eleven. Sweetwater asked Gunny how it went with Tiny and Stretch.

"They were fired up and really ready to get into it," Gunny said. "They even hammed it up. Snake appreciated the case of beer for the guys. It made the request easier. When they see the ship pass Grande Island and start into the bay, they'll head for the pier."

"They know the ship is tying up on the Subic side, don't they?"

"Sure do."

"Good," replied Sweetwater. "The car will be ready by one, so we need to be over at the Officers' Club by twelve-thirty. That's where I told them to contact me. Things are beginning to fall into place, Gunny. When you fly in early, this is the results you want. Fuck up one thing and no matter how many other items you did correctly, you'll be remembered by that one detail that slipped through the cracks."

By twelve-thirty they were seated in the bar at the

club. At one-ten, the call came for Admiral Barclay. Sweetwater looked around to see if he knew anyone in the club and then answered the page. As he walked to the phone, he told Gunny they were to page his aide and not the admiral. "Stand by and run interference if anyone starts to approach me while I'm on the blower."

When he got on the phone, Sweetwater cleared his throat to sound older, then said, "Admiral Barclay."

"Yes, sir, this is Ray at the garage. Your car is ready."

"Thank you, Ray, and tell your men I appreciate their efforts on this matter. I'll send my aide down to pick the car up."

"Okay, sir, and who shall we bill for the work?"

"My aide will have all the details."

"Very well, sir. Have a nice day."

Sweetwater hung up and said, "Shit, shit, shit!"

"What's the matter?" Gunny asked.

"Ray, the supervisor at the garage, wants payment for the work on the car."

"What the fuck are we going to do?"

"Let me think a minute. I've got it. I'll get into our flight packet, and fill out a standard Form 44."

"Can you do that?"

"Hell, I'm an admiral, aren't I?"

"Shit, we're going to jail."

"Don't worry, Gunny, I'll cover our six. Let's get over to the BOQ. I need to get that form. You know, I'm going to fill that sonofabitch out and charge it to CAG. He's the one who wanted that car running in the first place."

"Hey, good idea. Sweetwater, you never cease to amaze me."

"That's why I get to go in early. 'Performance, not excuses.'"

They took a cab down to the public works motor pool where the car was being worked on. When they arrived, Old Betsy was sitting outside looking like a million bucks. Sweetwater filled out the Form 44 and without a hitch closed the deal. They started her up and headed towards the pier on the Subic side of the bay. By this time, they could see the *Enterprise*'s massive island structure filling the skyline as the tugboats pushed her alongside the pier.

Captain Frost, the commanding officer of the ship, had the crew man the rails for port entry. This simply meant that the officers and men of the ship stood at parade rest and outlined the edge of the flight deck in their summer white uniforms. It's Navy protocol for entering a foreign port for the first entry on that deployment. This helped give Tiny and Stretch a big audience.

By the time Sweetwater and Gunny had parked the car and gotten on the pier, they could hear the bull-horn bellowing, "The ship, the ship!" then "Welcome to Fantasy Island," over and over again. The crew loved it and when he looked up to the bridge, Sweetwater could see the skipper, the navigator and the admiral laughing their asses off. It appeared the welcome mat had been laid out in style. Tiny and Stretch looked and played the part to a T. Water suspected they might have gotten into that case of beer a little early.

After checking to make sure the welcoming party had done its thing, Water and Gunny hopped in Old Betsy and headed for the club at Cubi Point. It wouldn't be long before the herd would be at the water hole. Weeks without a drink tend to make the desert pretty dry. By three o'clock most of the aviators were up at the Cubi Point Officers' Club. The ship drivers, or "black shoes" as the aviators call them, were all down at the Subic Bay Officers' Club partying.

By eight o'clock the club was rocking and rolling. Sweetwater gave CAG the keys to Old Betsy and told him that the repair work had been charged to his office.

"No sweat, Sweetwater, good show," CAG said. "Let me buy you a drink." At that point a message came over the club's intercom paging Admiral Barclay.

Sweetwater knew Admiral Barclay was playing golf with Admiral Mitchell, so he figured he had better answer the call. Especially if it was concerning the car. He told CAG he was drinking scotch and that he'd be right back.

What he failed to notice was Captain Frost sitting at the end of the bar near the phone. Sweetwater picked up the phone and said, "Good Evening."

"Admiral Barclay, this is Ray at the garage."

Sweetwater felt a sudden sinking in the pit of his stomach. He thought, What the fuck is this guy calling here again for? He swallowed hard before answering. "Yes, Ray," he said. "Is there a problem?"

"Not really, sir. But the guys forgot to put the spare tire back in after they repaired the hole in the trunk."

By this time Sweetwater had the feeling someone was watching him. Captain Frost was standing about a foot away, taking in the whole conversation. Water's heart started to pound. "Okay, Ray," he said, "I'll have someone come down in the morning to get the tire. Thank you for your concern."

When Sweetwater hung up, Captain Frost said, "Well, Sweetwater, I didn't know you made admiral in the last few days."

"No, sir, but I can explain."

"I'll bet you can and will, *Swamp*water."

Oh shit, Sweetwater thought, I don't like the tone of that last remark. He didn't know whether the captain was kidding or pissed off. He told him the story and Captain Frost just shook his head and said, "Sweetwater you are going to give me a goddamn ulcer before this cruise is over. I'll brief the admiral in case someone should bring this car thing up. It'll be better if he knows about it."

"Do you want me to explain what I did, Captain?"

"No, Sweetwater. I will. You've done enough already, don't you think?"

By the time Sweetwater got back to where CAG had his drink waiting, he saw the two admirals enter the club. Sweetwater watched as they walked up and stopped right next to Captain Frost. He knew it wouldn't be long before the scam was out on the street. He could see himself spending the next two port calls on the ship the entire in-port period. Oh well, he thought, shit happens. He figured he'd better have fun now, because it might end rather quickly. After a couple more drinks he slipped out the side door and headed back to the BOQ. It was about time for his massage, and he had never been more ready for one.

After a hot sauna and a magnificent rubdown, Sweetwater headed out the door for his room and ran smack into Admiral Barclay and Admiral Mitchell.

"Excuse me, sir," he said.

"That's quite all right, son," replied Admiral Barclay, not recognizing Sweetwater, until Admiral Mitchell said, "Hey, Dave, there goes your shadow, Sweetwater."

Headhunters

Sweetwater went back to his room in the BOQ to get cleaned up for dinner. Slick, Gunny and a couple more squadron mates would be joining him. Sundance was the air-wing duty officer and he had to stay aboard until morning. There was nothing worse than having the watch the first day in port. But Sundance volunteered for the duty in the Philippines so he wouldn't have to stand watch in one of the better ports scheduled later in the deployment.

After dinner, the group planned on playing some shuffleboard. It was a nice way to relax and stir up some competition between the squadrons. Sweetwater and Sundance usually were the kings of the board, but since Sundance had the duty, Sweetwater had to pick a new partner. Gunny teamed up with Sweetwater, but he wasn't in the same class as Sundance, and they only lasted two games before getting beat. After a couple hours of shuffleboard, the guys decided to cross over Shit River and head for town.

The bridge over Shit River linked the base to Olongapo City. The locals gave the river its name because of the raw sewage that was dumped into it. On any given night, the passage to and from town would clean one's sinuses, and on some occasions, the smell was so ripe that you didn't want to observe the "water show." The water show was driven by the sailors throwing pesos into the river for the children to dive after. The local women would put on a show for the sailors as they crossed the bridge into town. The women would stand in banca boats floating by the bridge and, for several pesos, would flash their breasts. If you could stand the smell, you got quite an eyeful.

Across the bridge, you hit Magsaysay Drive and Rizal Avenue in Olongapo City. The stream of neon lights, bars and restaurants made this island paradise look like Hollywood and Vine. Some of the better nightclubs along this strip were Hot City, Cal Jam, and T's Tavern. Before the night was over, Sweetwater and the boys would hit them all. The more energetic would dance until the early morning.

Just as Sweetwater's body went into a deep sleep, he was startled by someone banging at his door. He wondered who in the hell it could be at such an ungodly hour. He ripped the sheet off his clammy body, staggered to the door and opened it, only to see Sundance, all bushy-tailed and full of piss and vinegar.

"Hey, roommate, it's party time," Sundance said.

"Bullshit," Sweetwater snapped, as he headed back to bed.

"Come on, Sweetwater, it's eight-thirty. The sun's out and I got us a tee time for nine-fifteen."

"You go ahead, I feel like shit. I'll see you at the pool later."

"Okay, let me drop off my gear and I'll be out of here."

"Roger that," replied Sweetwater. "And don't let the door hit you in the ass on the way out."

"Ha-ha-ha! I'm leaving," Sundance mumbled as he closed the door.

By one o'clock Sweetwater made it out to the pool. As he walked through the gated entrance, the setting reminded him of a scene from *Caddyshack*. The pool area was packed with sunburnt bodies, a game of water basketball was being played at center pool, and all the recliners and chairs were occupied.

"Hey, Sweetwater," called some of the guys he had been killing brain cells with the previous night. "Come in the kiddy pool. It's the only seat left."

"Let me get some water and I'll be with you shortly," he said.

It wasn't five minutes after he got settled in the knee-deep pool that he was recruited to play water basketball. The guys in the kiddy pool were waiting their turn to play the winners of the game that was going on when he arrived. His body wasn't up for the torture, but he couldn't let on that he couldn't hack it.

The game was to twenty by ones. The Marines had won four straight and were playing jungle rules. This meant anything goes, splashing in the eyes, dunking and holding. After a broken toe, a couple of shiners and a cut lip, Sweetwater's team came away victorious.

When he climbed out of the pool, he headed for the kiddy pool to lick his wounds and recover.

As the sun-baked bodies started to leave the pool, chairs and recliners became available, so he transitioned to a more suitable mode of relaxation, a recliner. The guys who spent the first day shopping started to drift by the pool to see what was up and show their wares.

A few minutes later, Sundance sauntered into the pool area with a big shit-eating grin on his face. Sweetwater knew the golf game had gone well and his roomie had some money in his pocket. As he approached the side of the pool, two squadron mates jumped him and they all ended up in the water. Sundance came up swinging, and swearing like a real sailor.

The guys decided to really piss him off. They took his clothes off and put them in a chair beside Sweetwater. By this time, everybody's attention was directed to center pool. Sundance had a few more choice words, then became real humble. Sweetwater threw a towel over to him and he got out of the pool.

"Well, roommate," Sweetwater said, "how did the golf game go?"

"Real good. And I won some money to boot."

"Great! Who did you play with?"

"Captain Frost, Admiral Mitchell and your shadow, Admiral Barclay."

"Oh shit," Sweetwater said, as he came to attention on the recliner. "What were they saying?"

"They thought it was pretty funny that a junior officer would have the balls to try something like that. They said you only saw stunts like that pulled back in Pappy Boyington's era."

"Then they weren't pissed?"

"Didn't seem to be."

"Looks like I cheated death one more time. Sundance, I signed us up for a massage at five."

"Great, let me take these wet clothes back to the room and I'll meet you in the sauna."

"Okay. I'm going to relax a few more minutes and I'll see you in a flash."

As Sweetwater lay back on the recliner, he thought he had better cool it for a while. His name was too fresh in the minds of the higher establishment. Just at that instant a mature coconut landed right by his head. "What the fuck was that?" he said, leaping up off the recliner. He thought some of the guys were getting smart, but as he investigated, he spotted a large bull monkey in a palm tree above the pool. The monkey either dropped the coconut while trying to get some food or threw it because he was pissed. They can get real mean if confronted. Sailors were always warned to walk the other way if they ran into one.

A crowd started to gather to look at the assailant. Sweetwater picked up his gear and headed for the sauna. A foot closer and he would have needed a very large aspirin to cure the headache he would have received.

After a twenty-minute sauna and an hour massage, Sweetwater felt like a new man. Sundance finished up just ahead of him and they met back in the room.

"Let's go to the club for dinner, Sundance, and turn in early. We have a bounce period at ten o'clock and some are going to fly the low level after the FCLP period."

"Sounds good, let's get cleaned up and we'll hit it."

Since the ship was in port for five days, the aircrews had to keep their flying skills up. Each squadron had a period at the airfield where it would practice field carrier landings which simulated landing on the carrier. A section of the runway at Cubi Point Naval Air Station was painted like a carrier deck and you had to fly the optical landing system, or "meatball," to touch down, just as you would at the ship. A landing signal officer would observe your landings to ensure you were still up to speed and could get aboard the ship safely.

After the landing practice was over and the planes were refueled, some of the pilots got to go on the low-altitude-navigation route. This really tested one's ability to fly at high speeds and navigate at low altitudes.

That evening after dinner, Sweetwater and Sundance went into the bar and played shuffleboard for an hour or so and then turned in. The two were up at seven the next morning, had a hearty breakfast and headed down to the hangar for their brief. The weather was less than optimal: monsoon season had arrived and the low clouds and rain could last for days, depending on how large the front was.

VFA-114 would fly first. They would have six planes in the landing pattern at one time, each pilot would get six passes and then they would hot refuel and change pilots. After they finished up, VFA-22 would follow the same procedure. This would go on each day and night in port, until all squadrons and aircrews got refreshed. As a result, the first and second days in port are the only real days off for the aircrews. The rest of the time is spent practicing and getting in training which you can't always do when on deployment.

The Philippines is the only place to get warm-ups after being in port. Most of the other ports don't have an airfield available for practice.

After the bounce period was over, Sundance and Sweetwater got lunch and talked about the low level. Sweetwater wouldn't get to fly the route, since he was the one who mapped it out. However, Sundance and Lieutenant Bill "Burner" Delaney from the Aardvarks would fly the low level first. Slick Morely and Lieutenant "Sidewinder" Sasson from the fighting Redcocks of VFA-22 would launch thirty minutes after the Aardvarks launched. The route took about one hour and fifteen minutes to complete. The low-level route was to be utilized as much as possible, so everyone whose mission required low flying got the chance to practice.

Low-level flying imposes significant demands on the pilot and reduces his margin for error. One miscalculation in this treacherous environment can cost the pilot his life. While vision is the most important perceptual sense when flying, sun glare and height or distance mis-estimations can cause a pilot to get closer to the ground than he may realize. Therefore, he must recalibrate his judgment accordingly.

Sundance and Burner got a good brief prior to manning up. They studied the route well and elected to fly it at 360 knots and two hundred feet above the terrain. At thirteen hundred hours, they were on the runway ready to run up their engines for a section takeoff. Sundance was the flight lead, so he was giving the signals to turn up. When he looked over to Burner for his thumbs up, Delaney was shaking his head that he wasn't ready.

Sundance came up on the tactical frequency and said, "What's the matter, Burner?"

Delaney replied that his inertial measurement unit had dumped and was malfunctioning. The IMU contains a gyro stabilizing platform, which is used in navigation and operates attitude and heading sources. This made his aircraft unflyable and he would have to return to the flight line to get it fixed.

They both taxied off the duty runway and headed back to the flight line. Sundance called ground control and asked them to alert their maintenance people that they were returning to the line with an IMU failure in aircraft 100. If they only had to change the box, it would be an easy fix and they would be on their way in ten minutes. A troubleshooter met them on the line with a replacement for Burner's IMU. He switched boxes, and within a few minutes Burner got a good alignment and they were ready to go.

The takeoff and climb out were uneventful. But as they flew north, the ceiling and visibility were dropping. The weather was still acceptable for the mission, but if it continued to deteriorate, Slick and Sidewinder might have to wait until the next day. The plan was for the two aircraft to circle over the Zambales Mountains, take a four-minute interval, and fly the route. They would join up by Dasol Bay and fly back to Cubi in formation. Sundance would go first and Burner would follow four minutes later.

The lighting conditions were perfect. There were no shadows and Sundance was feeling good. He was turning and burning, hitting his navigational checkpoints on time and with accuracy. Four minutes had elapsed and Burner was on his way. Since this was his first low level overseas, he was more concerned with the scenery than pinpoint accuracy on his navigation.

As Burner approached the San Quintin Trench, south of the Baguio Mountains, he started to feel uncomfortable. Things weren't quite right. Towns and roads were not matching up according to his route of flight. He checked to see if his navigational platform was on-line and functioning properly when there was a loud explosion and the plane yawed and started to go out of control.

"Holy shit," he shouted, "I've hit something." He reduced the throttles and started to climb. The aircraft had hit a logging cable and just about cut the Hornet's tail section off. The plane was barely controllable. Warning and caution lights were flashing like a broken pinball machine in the cockpit. Burner was trying to get the aircraft in stable flight but couldn't. He entered the clouds and became disoriented.

It was time to give his aircraft back to the taxpayers. He made one Mayday call and pulled the lower ejection handle. He heard the explosion as the canopy jettisoned and felt the seat start up the rails as his legs were being pulled back under his seat by his leg restraints. As the wind blast hit him in the face, Burner was knocked unconscious. Fortunately, the ejection sequence worked as advertised and he got a good chute.

Sundance didn't hear Burner's Mayday transmission, and continued on to the rendezvous point at Dasol Bay. After fifteen minutes of circling with no radio contact from Burner, Sundance started for home. He was getting low on fuel. Thirty miles out, he contacted Cubi approach control. He asked if they had heard from Aardvark 100, but there had been no contact since he left.

The weather at Cubi had dropped to the point where he had to shoot an instrument approach. Slick and Sidewinder's flight had been canceled due to weather.

In ten minutes, Burner's flight would be overdue and the search-and-rescue helicopters would launch and start looking for him. By the time Sundance got back to the line, there was still no contact with Burner, so the SAR helo was scrambled.

Cdr. Tom "Garters" Kistler, the commanding officer of HS-6, was the duty pilot for the day and he was getting a brief from Sweetwater as to Burner's route of flight. Sundance entered the briefing room just as they were ready to walk. He updated the crew on exact times and starting points and confirmed that he had heard no

Mayday call. The rain had started and they only had a couple of hours before nightfall to locate Delaney.

By the time Garters had launched, the word was out that there was a possible plane down. Other helo crews arrived to assist in the search-and-rescue effort. The visibility and ceilings were dropping to the point that a helicopter was the only bird that could operate safely.

Rain began to fall all over the Luzon area. Burner came to when water started to run down his face. He was hanging in his parachute straps about thirty feet from the jungle floor.

He checked himself over for any major injuries and when everything appeared to be in the right place, he started thinking about survival. His oxygen mask and helmet had been ripped off during the ejection, so he had to be careful not to injure himself getting out of the trees. He tried to swing over to a group of trees but was unsuccessful. Then he remembered his seat pan.

The seat pan, which hung just below his butt, had his survival raft in it, and a seventeen-foot-long dropline. Delaney firmly pulled the release handle on the right side. This released the lower half of the seat pan and the raft and dropline fell free. Burner pulled the line up to where he could tie it firmly to his chute, then carefully got out of the upper coke fittings that attached him to the chute and rappeled down the lanyard to the jungle floor.

He tried to pull the chute free but was unable to. The chute could have been used for many things, such as a shelter, a signaling device, or extra clothing. The seat pan had an AN/URT-33A radio beacon locator which activates during the ejection, so Burner knew they would be looking for him soon. By this time the rain had begun to fall in sheets, so Burner tried to find cover.

He cut his one-man raft free and used it as a roof over his head. He had already made up his mind that he would be spending the night in the jungle, so he got mentally prepared. The weather was too nasty for the rescue crews to find him before nightfall. As he sat there, he tried to imagine what had happened and where he was in relation to his planned route. He could plainly see that he was in a mountainous area.

After collecting his thoughts, Burner inventoried the items he had in his survival vest. His PRC-90 survival radio was the most important piece of gear he had. However, he didn't want to wear the batteries down until he heard a plane or helo close by. His signaling mirror had shattered during the ejection, but he still had his signaling flares. These flares were shot out of a pencil-like holder and could go as high as one hundred feet. The actual cartridge that housed the flare was a basic .38 caliber shell. It was a deadly weapon if pointed at someone. He had a couple of containers of water, a compass, a whistle, a survival knife and some beef jerky that he carried for the unexpected.

Commander Kistler was just north of San Nicolas, heading toward Baguio, when he started to pick up a locater beacon signal. The direction-finding equipment in his helo indicated the signal was coming from the Baguio Mountains area. But the visibility and ceiling had dropped too low and he had to discontinue the search. He plotted his position on the map and reluctantly headed for home. En route, he contacted the other helo that had joined in the search and told it to return to base. The weather was closing in fast, and they would have to resume the search at first light in the morning.

When Garters got back to the flight line, it was already dark. He went to the hangar where they were basing the rescue operation and briefed CAG on his findings. Master Chief Bobby Newton was standing by to assist in the search. He taught jungle survival to the men and women on the base. He knew the jungle and its predators like the back of his hand. After Kistler pointed out on the large topographical map the area where he felt Burner went down, Newton spoke up. "Gentlemen, I don't mean to make things worse, but the Igorot and Ifugao tribes who live in the Baguio Mountains still practice cannibalism. If that young lieutenant survived the ejection, he has bigger problems than he realizes. I'm sure the headhunters are looking for him as we speak. I have several Negrito friends who hunt in those mountains. I'll get word to them tonight through one of the men who works at the Baguio Hotel. They have ways of communicating with others in the mountains. If that plane went down up there, we will know about it in the morning."

Before night settled on the jungle floor, Burner figured he had better find more protection. He took his survival knife and dug out a small area alongside the hill and used some bamboo shoots to support the raft for a lean-to. Then he camouflaged the raft with leaves and brush to hide from predators.

Burner didn't get much sleep during the night. The uncontrollable shaking of his body awakened him in the early morning. He knew he had to get on the move to stay warm, so he looked at his compass, figured out which direction was south and started walking. The weather was still bad but the rain had stopped and he was confident he could walk to safety. After an hour or so, his clothes started to dry and the jungle came alive with noise.

Because of the mountainous terrain, the jungle wasn't very thick or difficult to maneuver through. Burner came up on a ridgeline and had stopped to rest when he saw smoke curling up the treeline. An emotional surge hit him, thinking he was found. But he still moved down the sloped terrain with caution to investigate. As he got closer, the air became very pungent and almost nauseating. For the life of him, he couldn't figure out what that smell was. He could hear voices as he moved in, but the language was none he had heard before.

Laying down on his stomach, he crawled the last few yards to get a better look. As he moved the brush aside, he couldn't believe his eyes. There were three men squatting by a fire that had a familiar shape on a spit over the fire. The smell was human flesh burning.

The adrenaline started pumping as he eased his way back from the cannibals. Once he was far enough away, he started to run and must have gone five miles before stopping to rest. He had heard stories about the cannibals in the Philippines, but hadn't believed the stories were true. Now he was a believer. His whole mode of survival flashed back to his SERE school training at Warner Springs. SERE stood for search, evade, resist and escape. Any aircrew that would be in a possible hostile environment had to go through this training before going overseas. It was originally developed for the Vietnam War aircrews. But one still had to be SERE trained before going to a combat squadron.

Burner knew he had to stay off beaten paths and get to an area where he could signal for help and get picked up. He first planned to go down the mountainside, but when he went, the foliage became much more dense and the jungle canopy over his head blocked all views. He headed for higher ground, eating some fruit along the way to keep his strength up.

By this time the rescue helos were en route to the Baguio Airport, up in the mountains. Master Chief Newton's friend was to meet them there with several Negritos who hunted the area. It was hoped they would have some favorable news.

The weather was still poor and the ceiling was up and down along the route of flight, and it took Garters and his wingman several tries to get into the small mountain airport. Burner could hear the helos off in the distance, but had no visual on them. He kept climbing for the high country.

Master Chief Newton could see his friend standing by the small terminal building. He hopped out of the helo and headed toward him. "Hey, Burt, how's it going? Did you find out anything?"

"The plane went down on the southeast side of mountain."

"How did you find out that information?"

"After you called last night, I got these Negritos to pass the word to the closest tribe that lives in these mountains. They sent runners and signals to the other friendly tribes who live in the hills. Early this morning, the word was passed back as to the whereabouts of the 'big iron bird.' "

"Can we get to it?"

"We can't," Burt answered, "but these Negritos can. One catch, though: they want to be compensated for their work."

"No problem. How much do they want?"

"They want flight boots, survival knives and blankets."

"We can make that happen. Tell them we will have a dozen of each item here tomorrow, same time." Then as an afterthought, Newton asked, "Will they get in the helo and direct us to the crash site?" "Wait, while I talk with them." Burt went over to the two men to communicate with them in their native tongue. He had to use some sign language to get the point across during the brief talk.

The Negrito live in the jungle around the Navy bases at Subic Bay and Cubi Point. They are hired by the U.S. Government to help their security forces protect the bases from intruders.

Burt and the two Negritos agreed to fly in Kistler's helo and direct the rescue crews to the crash site. The Negritos would point the way to Master Chief Newton and Newton would transmit the directions to the pilots. Burt sat in the back with the crewman. This technique was kind of cumbersome, but without their directions, it could take days to find the crash site.

Master Chief Newton briefed Burt, who in turn briefed the Negritos on the flight. They weren't especially happy about riding in a machine that had twenty thousand parts all going in the wrong direction, but they climbed in reluctantly. They were in the air fifteen minutes, which took them thirty miles west of the airport, before they reached the crash area. The weather was still overcast and they were only a few hundred feet below the ceiling. As they circled over the crash site, they saw that most of the plane appeared still to be intact due to the low impact angle.

Looking down at the cockpit, Commander Kistler

could see the telescopic rail that the ejection seat rides up on before the seat leaves the airplane. It was broken off. This told him that there had been an ejection. Now they would have to set up a search pattern and hope for the best.

Burner's heart started pumping with the sound of the helos getting closer. He got his pencil flares out along with his PRC-90 radio. He tried to transmit on guard, the emergency frequency, but got no response. He then switched to the beacon locator, but the helo didn't seem to home in on him. He was now convinced that the radio was a piece of shit and the Navy needed to get a replacement. At one point he got a glimpse of one of the helos across the ridge from him and fired a flare, but they never saw it. As the day progressed, the helos got close several times and Burner used up four of his six flares trying to get their attention, but they never saw a thing.

As the afternoon drew to a close, the helos went away. Burner knew he had to find a clear area and wait for the weather to break if he was to get out of there alive. He started moving up the mountain before it got too dark to navigate. With all the activity in the area he knew he was probably being hunted. He reached the bottom of a ravine and could hear running water. His water supply was gone and he needed to refill his containers. As long as water was running down a stream, the chances of it being pure were pretty good. He knelt down, took a long drink, and filled up the plastic containers he carried in his survival vest.

When he stood up and turned around, he was charged by a wild man, dressed in a loincloth with some sort of animal skin draped over his shoulder. Burner shoved the smaller man aside and reached in his vest for his pencil flare. The man got up, pulled a large knife, and headed for Burner. He couldn't believe this was happening to him. He tried to stop the man with hand signals, but he kept coming. Burner waited until he was a few feet away and shot the flare right between the sonofabitch's running lights. It dropped him dead in his tracks.

Burner didn't wait around. He crossed the stream and headed up the ridge. It was almost dark, but he kept moving. It was an hour or so before he decided to stop and find a safe place to spend the night. The jungle was alive with noise, and the aftershock of the attack had started to wear on Burner's nerves. He was tired, scared and running out of ideas. However, the will to survive was still strong. He found a rock formation and wedged himself in between the rocks. Despite his anxiety, within an hour he was fast asleep.

The rescue crews went back to the Baguio Airport, where they would spend the night. At first light, they would resume the search. A third helo would fly up in the morning and bring the items the Negritos requested. If the weather broke, two S-3s would be brought in to assist in the search. They could cover a much larger area in less time.

Burner was awakened by the roar of a helicopter flying close by. He gathered his senses and popped up from the rocks. The weather was much better, and to his amazement he was in a relatively open area alongside the ridge. He got his radio out and started making transmissions in the blind. He also loaded his last flare into its holder. He could see the helos off in the distance, but he wanted to wait until one appeared to be headed in his direction before he expended his last flare.

He was afraid to expose himself too much, for fear the cannibals would spot him. They had to have found their fellow headhunter and "lunch" by now.

Several hours passed and no helos or S-3s came close enough to signal with the last flare. Burner started to become uneasy and let his emotions take over for a few minutes. He got control of himself when a helo started toward him. He positioned the flare at the helo and fired, but nothing happened. What the fuck? he thought. What else can go fucking wrong?

Delaney recocked the firing mechanism and fired it again. It fired, but the helo had just started a turn and missed seeing the flare. Now he was out of signaling devices and would have to get out in the open to be seen.

The sun started to break through the clouds and Burner instinctively started looking for his sunglasses. In the bottom left-leg pocket of his flight suit, he found his mirror Ray-Ban sunglasses neatly stored in their case. With all the excitement and no sun, he had forgotten he had them. When he saw those teardrop mirrors, he felt a surge of adrenaline boost his morale.

He got the sun to reflect off the lenses and create a flash on the opposite hillside. Burner tried to remember the Morse code he was taught in flight training, but he had forgotten even the most basic SOS signal. He kept flashing the glasses, hoping someone would see the reflection in the sky.

Within a few minutes the clouds covered the sun again. "Come on, come on, sun," Burner repeated, over and over again. Then it hit him: "NKX," the three-letter identifier for Miramar Naval Air Station. Each military air station has a three-letter identifier along with a Morse code to identify the airfield over the radio. Miramar's code was dash dot, dash dot dash, dash dot dot dash. From all the times he had flown into Miramar he knew that was the code.

"Come on sun." He was ready now. It took a half hour or so, but the sun finally came out and he started signaling.

Redtail 700, which was an S-3, spotted a flashing object on the western side of the ridge. He called it into Indian 605, which was the helo's call sign. "Indian 605, this is Redtail 700."

"Go ahead 700."

"I have a flashing signal on the western side of the ridge, off to your right. Can you see it?"

"I will investigate it."

As the helo headed for the reflection, its occupants felt confident that they had found their downed pilot. Burner knew they had spotted the flashing, so he got out of the rock pile and stood up. Commander Kistler flew the helo over Burner and put it into a hover. The crewman got a thumbs up from Burner, meaning he was all right and did not need any assistance getting hooked up. The crewman dropped the horse collar down the cable.

Burner let it ground out before he wrapped it under his shoulders and was hoisted up into the helo. As he was being pulled up, he looked around to see if any headhunters were making one last run on him. He saw nothing, and just kept repeating over and over as he was going up the hoist, "They won't believe it, they just won't believe it."

When he got inside the helo, the crewman wrapped him in a warm blanket and asked him how he was doing. Burner gave him a thumbs up and said, "It's great to be alive."

The crewman handed Burner a headset and told him Commander Kistler, the commanding officer, was flying the bird. "Hey, skipper, thanks for the lift. How did you like my Morse code?"

"An S-3 saw the first flash and directed us toward you. As we rolled in we figured out 'NKX' by the dots and dashes, but it meant nothing to us."

"It meant nothing to you?" asked Burner in an excited voice. "Shit, Skipper, that's the three-letter identifier for Miramar, Fighter Town USA. Haven't you ever been to Miramar on Wednesday night?"

"Sure have, but my wife won't let me go there anymore."

"Why's that?"

"Last time I went with my wife, a couple of junior officers took her shoes off and started licking her toes."

"Shit hot, wish we were headed there now."

4

King Neptune's Party

The helicopter ride from the Baguio Mountains to the naval hospital at Cubi Point would take a little over an hour. Commander Kistler told Burner to sit back and enjoy the ride. The aftershock of Burner's odyssey began to show. The crewman noticed that Lieutenant Delaney was restless, excited and showed some grayish discoloration. The crewman had the pilot lie down with his feet slightly elevated and wrapped him in another blanket. Then he informed the aircraft commander that he needed to put some turns on, and alert the hospital that Burner might be in a state of shock.

The helicopter would land at the emergency helo pad on the hospital grounds. As Commander Kistler put his bird into a hover, he could see the emergency medical team waiting to off-load Burner. Within seconds after landing, Burner was on a stretcher and headed for the emergency room. Kistler lifted off and headed back to the flight line. As he taxied into the line, he could see what appeared to be half the air-wing personnel waiting to find out Burner's condition.

The *Enterprise* was getting under way at 0900 the next day, so a lot of the air-wing personnel were down at the hangar. After Commander Kistler shut down the helo, he made an announcement to the troops that Lieutenant Delaney was safe and was at the hospital under observation.

The ship would stay in the area for several days until all pilots were refreshed and requalified to land at night. Whenever a pilot had gone five days without a night carrier landing, he needed two day landings before he could go at night. So it usually took a day or so to get everyone night qualified.

Burner would probably join the ship on the third day, if all his tests were negative. The Redcock squadron would leave a five-member accident team behind to complete the investigation on the downed aircraft, and once everything was complete, the team would rejoin the ship. The battle group had to be in the Persian Gulf by late March. There were rumors in port that something was going down, but no one knew what.

Sweetwater and Sundance had just landed after finishing up their final field carrier landing practice. They received the news that Burner had been picked up when they entered maintenance control. They both wanted to see him, as did many of his squadron mates. They decided to get cleaned up first and stop by before dinner.

Once the doctors examined Burner and verified that he was stable, an IV drip was started and he was cleared to have visitors. The first to talk with him were the accident investigators. They needed the facts leading up to the ejection.

Lieutenant Delaney didn't try to hide anything. He told the accident-board members the facts as they happened. He explained that, as he approached the San Quintin Trench at 360 knots, his checkpoints weren't matching up to his route of flight. The next thing he felt was a rapid deceleration and the explosion. At that point he knew he had hit something.

The flight surgeon on the accident-board team asked Burner, "What altitude were you at?"

Burner said, "I was at two hundred feet."

The flight surgeon said, "Are you sure?"

"The last time I scanned my altimeter, I was right on."

"You may have experienced speed blur."

"What?"

"You may have had speed blur. It's one possible result from a combination of high speed and terrain proximity that exceeds the fixating capacity of the eyes. This stop-action or stroboscopic flash sensation can cause you to go fifty to one hundred feet lower than you think. This visual misrepresentation may have caused you to hit whatever it was that made the aircraft uncontrollable."

Burner continued on through the whole ordeal, and after a two-hour session, the accident-board members were stunned by his frightful adventure. As they were leaving Burner's room, Sweetwater and Sundance arrived on the scene. The air-wing commander, Delaney's commanding officer and Slick were all waiting to talk with him, so Sweetwater and Sundance decided to eat and see him after the smoke settled.

At seven o'clock, Sweetwater and Sundance returned. No one was visiting Burner at the time, so they were able to get in to see him.

Sundance gave him a big hug and said, "What the fuck happened, Burner?'

"I don't know, but I hit something that really fucked up my day."

"Well, you cheated death once again, Burner. Have

a beer.'' Sweetwater slipped him a cold Bud from under a jacket he was carrying.

"Hey man, the word is out that you smoked some goddamn headhunter. Is that a no-shitter?'' asked Sundance.

"It was either him or me. So I blasted him with my pencil flare, right between the peepers.''

"Holy shit!'' the visitors said in unison.

"Looks like they are going to keep you another day, Burner. The ship gets under way tomorrow, so you should be back with us before we go through the Strait of Malacca. Shit, you will arrive just in time for King Neptune's Party,'' Sweetwater told him.

"What in the hell is that?'' asked Burner.

"You'll see,'' replied Sundance. "How about another beer?''

"I was wondering how long it was going to take you guys to offer me one. By the way, how many beers did you bring.''

"Between Sundance and me, we have a six-pack.''

"Shit hot, boy, it's great to see you guys. I was scared shitless my last night out there. I began to run out of ideas, plus I figured it would only be a matter of time before I was the main course for those cannibals. I didn't realize there was a tribe in Baguio.''

"No one else did either, shipmate.'' Just then, Burner's night-shift nurse walked in and caught them with the beer. The encounter wasn't a pretty sight. She was junior to Sundance and Water, but you never would have guessed it. She came at them like Nurse Rachett, and read them the riot act.

They were out of Burner's room and out the front door of the hospital in a heartbeat.

The two pilots headed back to the club for a few

drinks before they turned in. Both were scheduled to fly out to the ship at noon and flight ops would go until midnight. The junior pilots would walk aboard that night and get under way with the ship in the morning. The more senior pilots would fly the planes out the next day, get their two-day landings, swap out with the gents who walked aboard and they would finish up the day work.

Night operations began one hour after sunset, and those who qualified during the day got their night landing as well. The entire air wing got refreshed and was back up on the step in two days. As the battle group steamed toward Singapore and the Strait of Malacca, a US-3 aircraft out of Cubi Point brought Burner aboard on the third day. The following day the *Enterprise* went through the Strait and there was no flying. The air-wing commander asked Burner to give a brief on what had happened and what he had to do to survive. There was standing-room only during both of his briefings.

During the briefings, the ship's supply department was getting ready for King Neptune's Party. This ceremony has lived on for thousands of years. It takes place when a ship crosses the equator and the slimy cargo of landlubbers, beachcombers, cargo rats, sea lawyers, lounge lizards, park-bench warmers, crossword-puzzle bugs, and all other living creatures from land who masquerade as seamen, get to meet with Neptunus Rex, King of the Raging Main.

As the *Enterprise* prepared to cross the equator en route to the Indian Ocean, the ship and her crew awaited King Neptune's arrival. By tradition, a visit by King Neptune requires that all trusty shellbacks on board carry out a ceremony so ancient that its origins predate written history.

The early ceremonies were to determine whether the pollywogs, or novices, could endure the hardships of life at sea. Having "crossed the line," appeared before the Royal High Court of the Raging Main as presided over by King Neptune, Ruler of the Deep, been tried in an initiation by trusty shellbacks (as veterans of such a crossing were called), and proven themselves worthy, the pollywogs became sons of Neptune, or "shell-backs."

During the night before the crossing, Davy Jones, Royal Scribe to King Neptune, will come aboard the *Enterprise* to meet with Captain D. L. Frost, the commanding officer, and the crew and air-wing squadron members to provide them with details of King Neptune's visit the following morning.

King Neptune is portrayed by the most senior shellback on board. His Royal Court is selected from a talent contest and the heaviest man on the ship would win the honors of being the Royal Baby. The ceremony usually lasts about five hours, depending on the number of pollywogs that needed to be initiated. The whole ritual was voluntary and done in fun. However, the medical and safety department had observers walking around to ensure nobody got out of hand.

Sweetwater and Sundance had been over the line back in 1975, so they were salty veterans of this solemn order of the deep. But their close and senior friend Commander Slick Morely, executive officer for VFA-22, had spent most of his naval career on the East Coast and never had the opportunity to become a trusty shellback. As one might imagine, Slick was in for a long day.

At 0515, Sundance went to Slick's stateroom, got him up, and brought him to flight-deck control, where Sweetwater was waiting for him. They stripped him down to his underwear and chained him to the "aircraft handler's" chair, which traditionally was an old barber's chair. Then the air bos'n covered him with arresting-cable grease from head to toe and had him sit there until the ceremony started at seven. At five minutes to seven, Sweetwater and Sundance dressed him over the grease and escorted him to the hangar deck where the show began.

All pollywogs had to crawl wherever they went, because they weren't worthy of walking. Accordingly, it behooved them to have extra padding on their knees and hands, due to the abrasive nonskid on the hangar and flight decks. Sweetwater and Sundance made sure Slick had a set of foam kneepads and a pair of old flight gloves. Having trusty shellbacks as friends on initiation day helped in some areas.

Safety was always the rule, and if someone appeared to be in physical distress, he was attended to. The hangar deck was the staging area for the pollywogs to ride the elevator to the flight deck. Once the elevator was at hangar-deck level, the pollywogs were loaded on it, face down. Before they were allowed to pass before King Neptune and his Royal High Court, they had to have their slime removed. So thirty feet above them, on the flight deck, several trusty shellbacks armed with fire hoses hosed down and cleansed the slimy landlubbers before allowing them up on the flight deck.

If you were an unruly pollywog while down on the hangar deck, a trusty shellback could give you a subpoena. The summons meant that you had to appear in front of the Royal High Court of the Raging Main and face charges brought against you. Most pollywogs got to pass by the Royal High Court of King Neptune, but the more senior officers and senior crew members got a summons whether they did anything wrong or not.

If your action caused the trusty shellbacks a lot of time and effort, you would probably get the coffin. This was the worst form of punishment. It was a wooden box constructed like a coffin and filled with a week's garbage. As a pollywog awaiting trial, you were put in this nasty, rancid-smelling box until it was your turn to meet with Neptunus Rex. Naturally, Sweetwater and Sundance saw to it that Slick spent several minutes in the coffin. What are friends for, after all?

Sundance and Sweetwater escorted Slick to the coffin. The smell was so bad that Sweetwater started to gag and almost puked. After three minutes of lying in this decomposed food waste, Slick was brought before the Royal High Court. He was not there one minute before he was sent to the royal barber for having his hair too long. The royal barber wasn't supposed to cut anyone's hair, but Sweetwater prevailed on him to make an exception for Slick. The royal barber gave him the best flattop anyone had seen since the early sixties. Slick went bullshit and was ready to kill Sweetwater. He knew his close personal friend had set him up. But it didn't come cheap. Sweetwater had had to slip the royal barber a double sawbuck, and promise to take all the flak.

They knew that the Big E would be in the Persian Gulf for at least sixty days, plenty of time for Slick's hair to grow back, so they went for it. Slick was more than a little vain when it came to his hair. He was the type that had to have each hair in place at all times.

After an hour or so for fun, Slick finally got to the

end of the initiation line. He stripped off all his clothes and threw them overboard. As he walked off the flight deck, the venomous look on his face would tell even a blind man he hadn't heard the end of this.

While all the festivities on the flight deck were coming to a close, Burner was sitting up in the tower eating a bag of popcorn, thanking his lucky stars he got an exemption and was made an honorary shellback. Besides, he had almost met with the highest-ruling court—death. A message had been sent from the senior member of the accident board, confirming that Burner had in fact hit a logging cable. The findings were conclusive, and Burner would not lose his wings. It had been a costly accident, but fortunately Burner had survived relatively unscathed.

It took most of the afternoon to clean up the flight and hangar decks. All hands helped and by six that evening the ship had been rid of all slimy pollywogs and was back on the line as a mighty warship. As night began to fall, the ship entered the Indian Ocean.

After the evening meal, Captain Frost came up on the ship's intercom. "Gentlemen, I want to thank you for a safe crossing-the-line initiation. No one, I repeat, no one was injured, and I want to commend you all for a job well done. We are now getting ready for two months of intensive flying. Some of you have been up in the region before and you know what we are facing. Be aggressive, be professional, but most of all be safe. That's all."

Sweetwater and Sundance went down to the ready room to look over the next day's flight schedule and watch the evening movie. The flight schedule was an aggressive one. Most of the pilots had two hops, so after the movie they decided to turn in. While getting ready for bed, Sundance said, "Did you see the look on Slick's face when the royal barber started to cut his hair?"

"I sure did," laughed Sweetwater, "but did you see the look he gave us when he left the flight deck? We haven't heard the end of this, believe me."

Sweetwater was the first to hit the rack and a loud *sonofabitch* came out of his mouth as he slipped between the sheets. Sundance said, "What's the matter?"

As Sweetwater rolled the sheets back, Sundance began to laugh uncontrollably. The bed was full of peanut butter and jelly.

"Hey, don't laugh, shithead. You better check yours."

Sundance rolled back his sheets, and let out a loud, "Fuck me."

Slick had the last laugh.

5

Gotcha

Sweetwater was just falling asleep after a long day of flight operations when his stateroom phone began to ring. As much as he wanted to ignore the ring, he knew it must be important or it would have waited until morning.

"Lieutenant Commander Sullivan?"

He recognized the voice. "May I help you, sir?" he asked.

"Lieutenant Commander Sullivan, this is Admiral Mitchell's aide. The admiral would like to speak to you."

"Roger that. I'll be there in five minutes," he said, putting down the phone.

As he threw on a fresh set of khakis he was thinking, Finally, they're going to rip those terrorists a new ass-hole. Or, maybe the Rolling Thunder mission on Bandar Abbas is going to be activated. Whatever the hell it is, it must be important to get us up at this hour.

Within five minutes, Sweetwater was at the admiral's stateroom. A razor-sharp Marine corporal was standing watch outside. "Good evening sir," the corporal said. "May I see your ID?"

"Sure, Corporal. How's it going this evening?"

"Fine sir." He checked the ID, then handed it back. "You may pass. The admiral is expecting you.

"Thanks," he said, as he knocked on the admiral's door.

"Enter," came a loud bark from behind the finely polished teakwood door.

Sweetwater stepped inside and said, "Lieutenant Commander Sullivan, reporting as ordered, sir."

"Have a seat, Sweetwater," replied the admiral. "Would you like some coffee?"

"Yes sir, I'd love a cup."

The admiral nodded to his steward and Sweetwater was served a cup of coffee on the admiral's fine china, embossed with the Naval Seal.

"That will be all," said the admiral, and the steward left the cabin.

The air-wing commander, Capt. Bullet Bob Baland, was sitting across from the admiral. Sweetwater acknowledged his presence and then focused on the admiral. The admiral took a deep breath and took off his reading glasses.

"Sweetwater, I've known you since your first cruise on the *Enterprise*. You are a superior officer, and a hell of a good stick. Maybe the best pilot I have seen in the F/A-18 Hornet. Your natural instincts are very sharp. For this reason, CAG and I feel you're the best qualified pilot on the Big E for this very special mission. In fact the mission is classified top secret and to discuss it much further will require a commitment on your part."

Without hesitation, Sweetwater said, "I'm in."

"You know, I pay off on performance, not excuses." The admiral chuckled. "I knew you would attack this mission with that old 'play to win' attitude of yours."

Little did Sweetwater know that this play-to-win attitude was going to make history. But he started to get an idea when the admiral put a sheet of paper in front of him and said, "Read this, but don't sign it."

Sweetwater read what initially appeared to be a typical classified-assignment briefing sheet. But he could tell this one was unusual. He kept running across sentences like, "You will be exposed to technology critical to the security and operational success of a special U.S. military element," and "You are strictly prohibited from discussing anything you see or do with this element at any time for the rest of your natural life."

Sweetwater looked up from the form and said, "I understand the requirements of this document and I'm ready to sign."

"No, you aren't," replied the admiral. "Let me expound on this agreement for a minute or two. By signing this document, you will never be allowed to travel abroad without it being cleared through the CIA. For the rest of your life, the counterintell gurus will have to know where you are anytime you travel outside Conus. If you discuss the technology involved in this mission with anyone outside the special element, you could possibly face life in prison for treason . . . or it wouldn't surprise me if The Company would just take you out. It's that important."

Sweetwater began to get a lump in his throat as the admiral continued. "Think about it and be back here at 0630 to join me for breakfast. Discuss this with no one. Comprende?"

"Yes sir," he snapped. "See you at 0630, Admiral. Should I be packed, sir?"

The admiral smiled and repeated himself with an I'm-not-shitting-you tone. "Sweetwater, think about the commitment and discuss it with no one. Now get your ass out of here and get some sleep!'' He slapped Sweetwater on the back.

"Good night, CAG,'' Sweetwater called as he left the admiral's stateroom. Walking by the Marine, he said, "You're looking sharp this evening, Corporal. Keep up the good work.''

The corporal answered, "Thank you, sir. Have a good evening.''

Water replied, "Roger that,'' then started back to his stateroom.

When he got back to the room, Sundance was awake and asked him what was up.

He said, "Nothing important. The admiral just wanted to ask me some questions regarding a possible mission over Iran.'' Sweetwater was the operations officer for his squadron, so he was involved in the planning of missions which would go into enemy territory. "Hey, I've got to get up early, let's get some sleep.''

Sundance bought the story for now, but he had that look in his eye, the one that said he knew Water wasn't telling the whole story. Sweetwater set his alarm for 0530 and hit the rack.

"See you in the morning, Sundance.''

"Okay.''

The sleep was a restless one for Sweetwater. He tossed and turned thinking about what he was getting himself into should he accept the mission. At 0530, his alarm went off and he got up and headed for the rain locker. By 0615 he was ready to meet the admiral for breakfast. He had already made up his mind that he would accept the commitment and sign the document.

As he approached the admiral's stateroom again, the

same Marine was at the door. "Good morning, Commander. Short night."

"You bet."

"Go right in, sir. The admiral is waiting for you."

Sweetwater opened the door and the admiral was just coming out of his office as he entered. "Good morning, Admiral," he said.

"Good morning, Matt. How did you sleep?"

"Not very well, sir."

"I expected as much after what we talked about. Well, what is your answer?"

"I'm in, sir. Where do I sign?"

"You know what this means . . . ?"

"Yes, sir, I do, and I'm ready for the challenge."

The admiral smiled and pushed a copy of the document across the breakfast table. "Good! Sign here and have a seat."

The steward took their orders and the admiral got down to business. "Matt, you will be flying cover for the special element, but what special element, I don't even know myself. You are to be briefed by a Marine major by the name of Jim Lott at the U.S. embassy in Bahrain tomorrow at 1400. We will fly you off the ship at 0600 tomorrow morning. You have hotel reservations at the Gulf Hotel next to the embassy. Check in when you arrive and someone will be in touch with you. After you finish breakfast, carry on your daily routine and try not to let on where you're going. Your skipper has been briefed and will handle the rest of your squadron mates if too many questions arise. Pack only civilian attire. Lieutenant Commander Petriccione will fly you in tomorrow morning in an S-3. Change into your civilian clothes in the plane after you land and leave all flight gear behind. Ralph will be back to pick you up at the same time he drops you off in two days. Any questions?''

"No, sir, but is that all you can tell me?''

"Not only is that all I can tell you, Sweetwater, that's all I know. Shit, when you come back from that briefing, I'll be working for you.''

Sweetwater smiled and said, "I don't think so, Admiral.''

"No shit, Matt, you will only be able to tell us need-to-know information to pull off this mission. I'll be debriefed later on, after whatever you'll be doing, by a higher source.''

After breakfast, the admiral shook hands and told him to be strong and pay attention to the details. "Your life, and the lives of many others, may depend on it, son.''

"Yes sir, Admiral, I won't let you down.'' Sweetwater took his leave and headed back to his ready room.

When he got there the commanding officer had an all officers' meeting in progress, and Sweetwater discovered he was the main topic of discussion. He walked in and took his assigned seat, up front and to the left of the CO's seat. The CO was briefing the squadron on Sullivan's position and warning them not to bug him for information, because of the high-security priority put on him. He also made it clear that anyone overstepping the boundary would pay a personal visit to the admiral, which would not be in his best interest. Everyone knew where the line was drawn and left it at that. The meeting was terminated and business went on as usual.

Sweetwater worked most of the day on the week's schedule and got his bag packed for the upcoming trip.

The support in the squadron was strong and everyone honored the request not to pry into the mission's plan.

That night Sundance said, "I knew there was more to that visit than met the eye last night."

Sweetwater said, "I wish I could brief you on the mission, roommate, but my hands are tied."

"Not to worry, we're behind you."

The alarm went off at 0500 and Sweetwater was in flight-deck control at 0540, ready for the flight to Bahrain. Ralphy Boy Petriccione met him for a quick brief, and they manned up for an 0600 launch. The flight to Bahrain only took forty-five minutes and everything went like clockwork. A car was waiting at the airport for him, his reservations were in order at the hotel, and at 1400 he was contacted at the hotel to confirm the meeting. The rest of the day was his own and he took full advantage of being off the ship.

Sweetwater spent most of his time by the pool watching the ladies and having a few well-deserved drinks. Of course, like any lucky man in his situation would do, he thought about his poor shipmates still on the ship, who wouldn't see dry land for several weeks. And he had a drink for them, too.

At 0900 he reported to the U.S. embassy, as instructed, in civilian attire. He was met at the front gate by a security guard and escorted to the secure briefing room. The whole area was swarming with Marine guards.

Once inside the briefing room, he was fingerprinted and mug shots were taken. He was starting to feel very much like a felon. Within twenty minutes two men entered the room, a Navy captain and a Marine major. The Navy man was an intell type and had the SEAL team insignia pinned over his left chest pocket. The Marine was wearing a flight suit and carrying a slide tray.

The captain introduced himself, then introduced Major Jim Lott, who, as it turned out, was a Marine helicopter pilot. Once all the introductions were complete, the captain left the room and let Sweetwater and Lott get on with the briefing.

Major Lott just finished slipping the slide tray into position when Sweetwater interrupted to ask, "Did the captain say you're a helo pilot?"

"That's right, Commander. Any problem with that, sir?"

"Not really, but anyone who flies a machine with twenty thousand parts all going in the wrong direction must have a death wish."

Lott bristled, until Water said, "Just kidding, Jimbo. Let's get on with the show."

Realizing he'd been had, Lott flashed him a grin. "Roger that, Sweetwater. By the way, what do you have planned for tonight? Anything?"

"Nothing really, why?"

"I've been seeing this Gulf Airline stewardess who has a friend you may be interested in. She's the head nurse at the hotel where you're staying. Maybe we all can get together tonight before you head back to the ship."

"Hey, that sounds like a deal. What does she look like?"

"Many a man would drag his balls through miles of broken glass to have a date with her."

"That good, huh? I guess that tells it all. I'm a player. We'll talk about it later. Let's get on with the brief."

Major Lott reviewed the security agreement and asked Sweetwater if he had any reservations. He had none, so the brief began.

"Sweetwater, what I am about to brief you on is America's greatest secret unit. The unit is named Spectre, an acronym that stands for 'special operations tactical response element.' It's a Marine composite-helo squadron, based in California in a secret hangar near the Salton Sea. The classified aspect of the unit is not only that it does not officially exist, but it has helicopters with state-of-the-art technology. They're always under heavy guard and are only flown at night.

"The helicopter is called Night Train and is officially designated as the Special Attack Helo 7. Only ten SAH-7s exist. They're manufactured in the Arizona high desert. They are a cross between a McDonnell Douglas MD-530F and the German-made BK-117. They have two silenced jet engines that turn a six-bladed manual-folding rotor head. The blades are rigid and are made with specially shaped tips, so as to make the rotor system nearly silent. A patent called BERP, which stand for 'British Experimental Rotor Program,' was used to design the tips. The SAH-7 is fully aerobatic and is the fastest and most maneuverable helicopter in the world. There is no tail rotor. It uses ducted air from a fan unit to vector thrust and control the yawing torque created by the main rotor. It has dual controls and is manned by two pilots who fly with night-vision goggles and forward-looking-infrared, or FLIR, cameras. This helo can carry three thousand pounds of ordnance in any combination: guns, rockets, or missiles. The helo is streamlined and is made of composite materials. It is invisible to radar. It will fit in a C-130 or a C-141. With selected ordnance, the helo can carry eight commandos.''

Sweetwater interjected, ''How do I fit into this plot? I'm a Hornet driver, not a goddamn helo puke.''

Major Lott said, ''Now, take it easy, Commander. You and a few others will be the only aircraft support from the *Enterprise*.''

''What others off the ship, and why aren't they here for the brief?''

''The fewer people who know what this special unit has and does the better. They'll be passing info to you, then you in turn will pass it on to us. You'll brief them prior to the mission. Okay?''

When Sweetwater didn't object, Lott continued. ''The President has ordered us to capture an Iranian mine-laying ship in the act of dropping mines. We need to show the world that these terrorists, with Soviet help, are in fact the ones who are laying the mines in the Persian Gulf and the Gulf of Oman. This mission is critical to the political relationship that we are developing with several Arab nations. By proving our ability to keep the sea lanes open and free from mines, we'll introduce new stability to the world oil market and also protect the supertankers going in and out of this area.''

''I'm not sure we ought to be risking American lives for Kuwaiti tankers,'' Sweetwater argued, ''even if they are reflagged by the U.S.''

''Wrong, Poncho!'' Lott blurted. ''Those tankers, all of them, are owned by a conglomerate in Philadelphia, PA. They are registered in Kuwait to avoid taxes and hire Asians for minimum wage to crew them. Wake up, Sweetwater! This is big business in a dynamic world.

We are riding shotgun on America's big business. It's that simple."

"Well, kiss a fat lady in the ass," Sweetwater laughed, as he leaned back in his chair. "You learn something new each and every day, don't you, Jimbo?"

"You got that right. But this mission is not as easy as it sounds. We want to capture this mine-laying ship and its crew, without sinking it. That's where Spectre comes in. We can be on them before they know what hit them. We also need to get good photo evidence, which will bring world press coverage. We only have a week or so to catch these bastards."

Major Lott continued with the slide show. "These are the areas in which we should catch them in the act. Intell tells us their next mine-laying mission is going to be near the Strait of Hormuz. Once intell has dates that look good for catching these terrorists, we'll have twenty-four-hour E-2C Hawkeye and SR-71 Blackbird coverage for photos and positioning, until the mission has been completed. After the mining has been confirmed and the ship identified, then you and I go into action. Spectre will be able to hit them totally by surprise. However, if they should get a distress call off before we capture the crew, then you and your wingman will have to keep the unwanted guests away until we get out of there."

That caught Sweetwater's attention. "Who are the unwanted guests?"

"Boghammers . . ."

"What in the hell are boghammers?"

"Small gun boats that sometimes hang near these ships while they're laying the mines. If they make a run on us, your job is to vaporize them." When that sank in, Lott continued. "The only people involved on the *Enterprise* will be the E-2, one tanker and two F/A 18s. When you brief this mission, refer to it as 'Mouse Trap.' Do not mention Spectre or our part in the mission. Only tell them need-to-know information. That concludes my brief. Any questions?''

''How will we know when to launch and where?'' Sweetwater asked.

''Within two days after you get back to the ship and brief the others, you and your players will be put in an alert thirty status. A flash message will be sent to your admiral, who in turn will start operation Mouse Trap once everything has been confirmed. Things will happen fast after the mouse has been caught in the trap. So, brief your people well.''

''That I will, Major.''

''Now, let's get a beer and figure out what we should do about tonight.''

''Sounds good. Where should we go, any ideas?''

''The embassy has a little pub in its basement and the beer is real cold. Let's hit it.''

After a couple of beers, it was decided that Major Lott would set up a dinner date for 2000 in the hotel's restaurant. He would contact Laurie, his friend, who would check with Nancy, the nurse, and would let Water know if he'd have a date for dinner or be alone with Jimbo and Laurie.

As Sweetwater was getting ready to go back to the hotel, Jim said, ''I'll call you by 1800.''

On the way back to his room, Sweetwater started to realize that this was a highly visible mission and the security involved was not to be taken lightly. One screw-up and he could be splitting rocks on a chain gang somewhere in Bumfuck, Egypt.

The mission had his attention, and he knew Lott was a team player due to the responsibility that he handled. Sweetwater and the Major were basically trained in the same mold; they both paid off on performance, not excuses.

Mouse Trap

Sweetwater had a couple of hours before Jim was supposed to call and let him know if Nancy would be joining them for dinner. He decided to work out at the weight room in the hotel and swim a few laps in the pool. He was back in the room by five-forty and no calls had been received by the front desk, so he hit the shower. At six on the nose, Jimbo called to say things were set for eight and Nancy was really looking forward to the evening out. If this woman was as good-looking as Jim claimed, he knew he'd best have his act together. Sweetwater was at the stage in his life where he was looking for a meaningful relationship. Who knows, he thought, this could be the start of something nice. After that ordeal with Ginny a year ago, he'd had to reevaluate who he was and where he was going. He still wasn't sure, but time was wasting, and he didn't want to be an old man before he knew the answers.

At seven-thirty, he was dressed and ready for action. He had on some of his finest cologne, a mixture of Kouros and Royal Copenhagen. His habit of mixing fragrances had earned him his nickname, and made him the butt of more than a few jokes. But he had the last laugh. This combination got women's attention, even if he didn't.

Sweetwater figured he would have a drink before they arrived. This would give him a good view of them from the lounge as they entered and a chance to evaluate Nancy before they met. The lounge was hopping when he got down there. Happy hour was still in progress and everyone seemed to be having a good time.

As he was going up to the bar to get a drink, a woman ran smack into him, spilling her drink down the front of his shirt. She was very apologetic, and tried to clean up the gin-and-tonic stain with her napkin, but it would be several minutes before the wet spot dried and he didn't have time to wait. He politely excused himself and made a dash for his room. By this time it was almost eight and there was no way he would be changed and back down in the lobby before they arrived.

He fancied himself sort of a fashion plate, and was very particular how he dressed. Everything had to match. The habit went back to his prep-school days, and it meant his whole outfit had to be changed. When he came out of the elevator, he saw Jim standing in the lobby looking for him. Nothing pissed him off more than being late for an engagement.

"Hi, Jim," he said. "Sorry for being late, but this dumb broad in the lounge spilled her drink on me and I had to change."

"No problem, Sweetwater, I figured you had a good reason for being late."

"So, where are the ladies?"

"They're in the lounge, waiting for us."

"Well, let's go check out these hot spots."

"Hot spots? What the hell does that mean?"

"On the carrier, when a woman is on the flight deck,

the aircraft handler will say over the 5-MC—that's a loud speaker that can be heard all over the flight deck— 'Check the hot spot near Catapault One,' or wherever she's standing. He gives the location so every one can get a look without the lady knowing she's under the microscope.''

"Hey, I like that,'' Jimbo laughed.

Feeling a little apprehensive, they walked into the lounge and Laurie, Jim's friend, walked toward them. She was an attractive woman and carried herself well. After the introductions, Sweetwater asked where Nancy was and Laurie said, "She's over there,'' and pointed her out. Nancy was talking with some people she knew.

"Let's go over and break the ice,'' Laurie suggested.

As they got closer, Sweetwater almost shit his pants. Nancy was the woman who'd spilled her drink all over him. When she turned around to meet him, her face went flush. He thought she was going to faint. After the formal introductions, and the second round of apologies, were finished, they got a table in the lounge and had a drink before dinner.

Nancy was truly a knockout and Sweetwater couldn't keep his eyes off her. All through dinner, he had the feeling that this lady was special and wanted to get to know her better. But he didn't want to let her know he was *that* interested. After dinner they went dancing for an hour or so, and then called it an evening. He and Nancy made arrangements to meet for breakfast, then she dropped him off at the hotel before driving home to her apartment. Jim and Laurie wanted to dance some more so they stayed on at the nightclub.

Sweetwater met Nancy at 0730 in the hotel's cafe. During breakfast, they exchanged addresses and discussed the possibility of getting together when the ship pulled into Australia. Sweetwater had to meet with Major Lott before he left for the ship and there wasn't much time to get romantic. Besides, he wanted to play it cool with Nancy. He figured he probably wouldn't see her again, anyway. She was so good-looking that someone else would have her under his wing before a meaningful relationship could be established between them.

Despite this apprehension, the time together was most enjoyable and both of them felt something special had happened. Uncharacteristically, Sweetwater felt total respect for this woman, even though he hardly knew her. That fact alone had to make her extraordinary.

"Listen, Nancy, I need to get over to the embassy, so I better say good-bye for now. Thanks for the special time, and watch out who you run into."

They exchanged platonic kisses, then Sweetwater left the cafe. Just before turning the corner, he looked over his shoulder to see if she was still watching. She was. A short wave and lingering eye contact made the departure an upbeat one.

Major Lott was going to drive Water to the airport and give him some last-minute details, if needed. As he entered the main lobby, Lott was standing there waiting for him.

"Ready to go, Water?"

"You bet. Let's head 'em up and move 'em out."

The drive to the airport was only ten minutes. Jim went over the game plan once again and reiterated how important it was to ensure that the secrecy of the special unit and the mission be preserved. Sweetwater fully understood his parameters and conveyed his concern.

As they pulled up to the area where the pickup was to be, his airplane was taxiing in. "Hey, good timing," Jimbo said.

"Take care of yourself, Jim. I'll be covering your six in a few days. With the technology we have, they won't know what hit them."

"Just keep those attack boats away, Sweetwater. We'll get the mouse out of the trap and be gone before anyone's the wiser."

"Thanks for the lift. Tell Nancy I'll write. See ya."

Sweetwater climbed into the aircraft, put on his flight gear and was airborne in ten minutes. As they flew back to the ship, Ralphy Boy asked him how the brief went and if he got his ashes hauled.

"The brief went well, and I didn't get laid, but I met this nurse who will turn your head. Time well spent. She has real potential. By the way, how far are we from the ship."

"It'll take us a good hour to get back. The ship is operating in the lower sector of Cash Box." That was a term they used for the operating location of the carrier. It was used like Yankee Station in the Vietnam War and Camel Station in the Iranian hostage crisis. These locator terms give the people making the decisions a geographic shorthand for the ship's location on a particular day. Cash Box got its name because they were in a combat zone and didn't have to pay taxes on their pay checks.

As they approached the ship, Sweetwater checked in with Strike, a controlling agency, and informed them of the plane's position and fuel state. Strike switched them over to Marshall, who gave them landing instructions. Five minutes later, they were lined up for an arrested landing on Hotel 65. Ralphy Boy made the call, "Viking Ball, two-point-one."

The landing signal officer responded, "Roger, Ball." This meant that the aircraft, an S-3 Viking, had visual contact with the optical landing system and there was 2,100 pounds of fuel remaining. "Viking Ball, 2.1" tells the landing signal officer (LSO) that the plane is within the three-degree glide slope and has plenty of fuel, in case you bolter or had to be waved off for some reason. If the pilot calls "Clara," it tells the LSO that the plane is out of the three-degree glide slope and that the plane is either high or low.

Ralphy Boy made an okay three-wire pass and the aircraft came to rest just forward of the island structure. The yellowshirt—one of the flight-deck directors—taxied the aircraft out of the wire and parked him on the foul line, on the starboard boundary of the landing area. The aircraft was shut down and Sweetwater, Ralph and the crewman left the plane. Sweetwater thanked Ralphy Boy for the ride and headed straight for the admiral's briefing room.

The admiral, CAG and Captain Frost were waiting for him. As Sweetwater entered the room, the admiral, along with the others, greeted him.

"How did it go, Sweetwater?" asked Admiral Mitchell.

"Very well, sir."

"Have a seat and give us a brief on as much as you can."

"Let me get out of my flight gear, and I'll be right with you."

The admiral nodded. "Steward, would you please bring some coffee and iced tea for our guests?"

"Yes sir," replied the steward, "coming right up."

After everyone was seated, Sweetwater explained what was going to take place. "Admiral, Captain Frost, CAG, we only have a few days to prepare for this operation. It'll be called Mouse Trap. We'll need E-2

Hawkeye support, an A-6 tanker and two F/A-18s. Our mission is to catch the Iranians laying mines and capture the boat and crew in the act. Starting tomorrow night the E-2s will run night ops until dawn every night until Mouse Trap has been completed. The tanker and F/A-18s will be on alert thirty. I don't have to tell you a thirty-minute response time is tight.''

Sweetwater waited for questions, but the officers just leaned forward expectantly as he continued. ''An SR-71 will also be up starting tomorrow, during night hours, taking photos of the boats suspected of laying the mines. Our mission from the carrier is to give support to the team making the assault on the mine-laying ship.

''Intelligence information has it that the terrorists are going to start laying mines tomorrow night near the Strait of Hormuz. Once the pictures are taken and the E-2 has a good lock on the target of interest, Mouse Trap goes into effect. Evidently, these minelayers have fast attack boats in the area while they're mining. Our job will be keeping them off the assault team while it's doing its thing.''

CAG Baland interrupted. ''Will two 18s be enough firepower to keep these boats away?''

''Yes, sir. The whole idea of this operation is surprise. The assault team will be on the terrorists before they realize what's happened. That's basically it, CAG. If you can let me know who the other players are going to be, I'd like to brief them at 2100 tonight.''

The admiral said, ''Use the war room for the brief.''

And CAG added, ''I'll have the aircrews here by 2100.''

Sweetwater turned to the CO. ''Captain Frost, if you position the carrier at the northern operating area of

Cash Box, it will put us within optimum striking range.''

''We have the technology to make that happen, Matt.''

''Well, that's all I have, Admiral. Are there any questions?''

CAG asked, ''How is this assault team going to get in there without being detected?''

''I can't answer that, sir. That part of the operation is highly classified, and I'm not authorized to talk about it.''

''Understood.''

''Okay, gentlemen, see you at 2100.''

Sweetwater gathered up his flight gear and took it down to his paraloft, where his squadron kept all of its flight gear, near their ready room. Then he would go see his commanding officer and brief him on as much as he could about the operation. After his brief with the skipper, Water went to his stateroom. Sundance was doing some sit-ups in the middle of the floor when he arrived.

He stopped grunting long enough to ask, ''Hey, hotshot, how'd it go?''

''Real good. Got a chance to sniff some pussy and drink a little whiskey.''

''No, come on. You didn't.''

''Not really. I spent most of my time in the brief, but I did meet this nurse who has my attention.''

''Does she have any friends?''

''Not sure, but I'll ask in my next letter.''

''Can you brief me on what's going on?''

''Nope. But I can tell you we're going after some terrorists who are laying mines in the area.''

''Am I going to get to see some action?''

"CAG will make that decision. Let me take a shower and get cleaned up and we can get some chow."

As 2100 approached, Sweetwater got his briefing material together and headed to the war room. When he entered, CAG, along with the aircrews he had selected, was waiting for him. Sundance wasn't there.

"The admiral can't make this brief, Matt," CAG said, "so get started when you're ready. Commander Brown, the E-2 squadron CO, will be handling all the E-2 briefings for his men. Commander Slick Morely, executive officer for the Fighting Redcocks, will be flying this mission with you, Sweetwater, and Lieutenant Commander Boots Costello will be flying the tanker."

Surprised, Sweetwater said, "CAG, I thought *you'd* be taking this mission."

"I would, but I have an ear block and I'm grounded."

It was time to get started. Sweetwater took a deep breath, and began. "Okay gents, I don't know how much you know about what's been going on, but I can tell you this is a top-secret mission and very sensitive. It'll be code-named Mouse Trap. One of our most powerful enemies on this mission has destroyed more men than all the wars fought by all nations. Widows know this enemy, to their everlasting sorrow. It's in the air and on the sea. It is relentless, merciless and cruel. It will give you nothing and rob you of everything. This enemy, gentlemen, is *carelessness*. We can't afford to make mistakes on this mission. Does everyone understand the importance of this mission?"

A firm "Yes sir" came from the men. "Now the rest of the tasking is pretty straightforward." Sweetwater reviewed the mission once again with the aircrews involved and felt assured everyone knew his responsibilities. "Tomorrow night we go on alert, so get your rest and let's catch some terrorists in the Mouse Trap."

At sunset the following day, the E-2 launched and climbed up to thirty thousand feet and made contact with the SR-71. The E-2 would swap every five hours, the SR-71 had its own schedule, and the rest of the team wasn't privileged to its ops. At 0345 the E-2 got a contact near the Strait, pictures were taken, but they proved to be nothing. At sunrise, the E-2 recovered aboard the carrier and the day's normal flight schedule began.

Again, at sunset, the E-2 launched and climbed to its cruising altitude. Contact was made with the SR-71 and the waiting game began. At 2330, the E-2 got multiple contacts near the Strait. Pictures were taken which showed that the "mice" were out. Operation Mouse Trap was put into action when the code words *mouse trap* were sent back to the ship.

Sweetwater had just pulled the covers over his head when he heard, "Mouse trap, mouse trap, mouse trap," followed by "General quarters, general quarters, general quarters. All hands man your battle stations." He jumped out of the rack, put on his flight gear and headed for the flight deck.

The alert planes were all prepositioned on the fantail of the carrier, better known as the Fly Three area. Three aircraft needed to be launched. Two F/A-18s and a tanker. The tanker was to go off first, climb to ten thousand feet, and wait for the Hornets to come up and top their tanks off with fuel before going on their mission. Getting the three aircraft off on time required the co-ordination of several hundred crew members. Catapult Three was the alert cat. Crews were manned and ready to go within fifteen minutes.

The night was black as the ace of spades, with no visible horizon and a thin cloud cover at two thousand feet. The KA-6 tanker taxied to the cat first and was fired off the deck at twenty minutes from the call. The Hornets were a few minutes behind.

Sweetwater and Slick climbed up to ten thousand feet over the ship, spotted the tanker and joined on him. Sweetwater was leading the section on the night's mission, with Slick on his wing. All communications with the tanker were done with flashlights. Both pilots received a full bag of gas and headed for their combat air patrol station. The E-2 had already passed Night Train the vector to the target over the secure voice radio. The F/A-18s would continue to circle their CAP station until the assault team boarded the mine-laying vessel.

Major Lott and his copilot spotted the vessel a mile away on their FLIR. They got a good visual on where the engine room was located. The heat the engine room gave off projected a white image on their tactical scope. Lott armed his rockets, hit his master arm switch to ARM and squeezed the trigger on his stick. A pair of six-foot rockets left the rails on the side of Night Train and raced to their impact point.

"Bull's-eye," shouted his copilot, and Lott brought the helo into a starboard hover. There was total chaos on the mine-laying boat, mostly disbelief as to what had just happened. They were hit totally by surprise. There was a small firefight as the helo hovered over the deck while the assault team boarded the vessel. Calls were made that the team had boarded the mining boat.

Sweetwater and Slick were overhead at fifteen hundred feet. A CH-46 was inbound to pick up the prisoners. A couple of Iranians tried to escape in a Zodiac boat but were shot before they got away. Sweetwater and Slick were in a combat cruise formation when the E-2 called, "Targets moving in from the west," which would have been off the port bow.

Slick picked them up first on his radar and rolled in on the first target. By this time Sweetwater had also picked up the targets. At 350 knots and 800 feet they made their first strafing run.

"Take the one on the right, Water. I'll get the left," was the call over tactical.

Sweetwater gave two clicks on the mike switch, acknowledging the request. Slick and Sweetwater peppered the area with their 20-millimeter guns, pulled up into the vertical, did a half Cuban eight and came back for another run. They sanitized the area once more and the E-2 confirmed the targets had disappeared. They headed back overhead of the minelayer.

Within five minutes after their return, all prisoners were on board the CH-46. Night Train loaded the rest of the assault team aboard and headed back to its home-plate. The mission was so secret, the F/A-18 aircrews didn't even know what amphib-carrier Night Train was working from.

Trapped was the code word for Slick and Water to sink the minelayer and return to their ship. They used a lay-down method of MK-82 bombs to sink the boat. It only took four and the minelayer was on its way to the bottom. As he and Slick were climbing up to altitude on their way home, Lott came up on their tactical and said they had three confirmed dead Iranians and eight captured. There were no casualties on Lott's team.

He sounded ecstatic. "We caught them with their pants down. Good show! See ya on liberty."

All players made it back to their carriers without a scratch.

The next day, press releases hit the wires with pictures of the Iranian ship laying mines, along with photos of twelve Soviet-made antishipping mines on the deck of the captured boat. After the news releases, the Arab oil states sided with the United States and the Middle East was stabilized for the time being.

7

War at Sea

On April 14th, the USS *Samuel B. Roberts* struck two mines while on routine patrol in the Persian Gulf, and was severely damaged. The *Roberts* was patrolling the waters in preparation for the safe passage of merchant ships in early May.

When the ship hit the first mine, a loud explosion rang through the air like thunder coming from a racing freight train. As the officers and men ran to the area of the explosion, they could only see a dense blinding wall of smoke filling the passageways of the ship.

"Mines, mines, mines. Port side. All hands brace for shock!" an overhead loudspeaker intoned. Then the ship hit the second mine, which caused another thunderous explosion. The *Roberts* moved to the right several feet, knocking down the men near the impact area. After the second explosion, it was a fight for survival. The crew of the *Roberts* was fighting the fires to stay alive. There was no place to go. They had to extinguish the fire or perish.

The damage-control working parties gouged holes in the bulkheads and walls of the ship to drain the water. The ship was listing eighteen degrees starboard and the drainage would help to level her. An initial count listed fourteen men dead and twenty-seven injured.

The mines had ripped a ten-foot hole in the side of the ship. Within minutes after the first mine was hit, the forward part of the ship filled with smoke and flames. At that time, six men were catapulted into the sea by the impact and were never recovered. The heat from the fires was estimated to be around 2,700 degrees Fahrenheit, hot enough to ignite the ship's combustibles and melt structural materials in the forward section.

Several other ships in the battle group came to the *Roberts*'s rescue when the distress call was sent. But there wasn't much they could do until the fires were out, except stand by in case the crew had to abandon ship. Damage-control working crews fought the fire for nearly twelve hours before it was under control and the ship was safe from sinking. After the ship was stable again, she was towed into Bahrain, where she would undergo repairs.

At that point, the USS *Enterprise* was bustling with anticipation. The entire crew was thinking it might see some action. The whole battle group was in alert status, ready to go to war within a moment's notice. The warplanes on the *Enterprise*'s flight deck upgraded their launch from thirty minutes to five minutes. This meant the designated attack and fighter aircraft had to be airborne within five minutes if a threat appeared or was detected on any of the battle group's ships' radars. Aircrews were now sitting, strapped into their aircraft and ready to launch, if needed. There was no more waiting around the ready rooms or staterooms.

CVIC came alive with planning teams. Each squadron in the air wing had designated pilots who were known as strike leaders. These pilots were the more senior ones, some of whom had combat experience and others who were knowledgeable in tactics. The code name for this particular operation was to be Preying Mantis. The plan called for a retaliatory attack against the Iranians.

CAG, Sweetwater, and Slick Morely, Executive Officer for VFA-22, had seen the most combat among the planners. The admiral's staff and CAG's staff had several contingencies laid out for the strike planners to develop. One was the complete takeover of all shipping in and out of the Persian Gulf; another was the destruction of Bandar Abbas, the Iranians' major airfield; and the final option was to destroy two Iranian offshore gas-oil separation plants. The GOSPs were being used by the Iranians for targeting information and troop staging. The Iranian ships doing the shooting were also to be destroyed. Once the plan had been developed, and the admiral agreed with it, the Joint Chiefs of Staff had to be the final approving authority.

Rear Admiral Mitchell, the carrier-group commander, made the decision to have two strikes. He wanted combat-seasoned pilots leading each attack, and he and CAG would decide who would be on the first and second attacks, once the target had been selected.

Planning went late into the night before a consensus was reached. The plan to hit the GOSPs and two Iranian frigates was the one finally sold to the admiral's staff. This was the best of the three options and it would send the strongest message to the Iranian government. If this didn't get their attention, then the U.S. would hit their airfield next.

The admiral wanted CAG Baland to lead the first attack and Commander Morely to lead the second. Slick was pissed when he got the news that he wouldn't be on the first attack. However, being the professional he was, he dug in and helped refine and complete the tactics to be used on the first raid.

The rules of engagement were reviewed. Each flight leader and crew had to know what could and could not be hit. Any deviation from selected and approved targets could mean a court-martial, as CAG reminded everyone. "The practice is over, gentlemen. The real ball game is about to start and you had better know the rules!" But, rules aside, they could fire on any hostiles firing at them, and protect any downed aircrews, no matter what it took.

April 16th was a busy day for the ship. By this time all hands knew that a strike was planned against the Iranians. The strike planners went back to their squadrons and briefed the aircrews who would be flying the mission. Fifteen aircraft would make up the first wave and ten more would be used on the second attack, if needed. The first strike would have eight F/A-18s, four A-6 bombers, two KA-6 tankers and one E-2 Hawkeye.

Sweetwater briefed his squadron while Commander Morely did the same with his. Sundance was sitting in the first few seats near the entrance to the ready room. You could hear a pin drop as Sweetwater began his brief. "Okay, men, this is a no-bullshit mission. We're going in and kick some terrorist ass, and show them what we mean when we say, 'Stop mining the Gulf and shooting up defenseless ships!' I want each and every one of you to give me your undivided attention, because your life may depend on it. The operation we are going to be involved in is code-named Preying Mantis. If we use the follow-up attack it will be named Rolling Thunder. The skipper, Sundance and I will fly on the first strike. Goldie, Sidewinder, and Snake will be on the second attack, if launched. Commander Morely, from our sister squadron, will lead the second attack. There will be fifteen planes on the first go and ten on the second. This will be the first time the F/A-18 Hornet has been in combat, so review your weapons manuals and know your aircraft systems well.'' Sweetwater looked to the back of the room and asked the ordnance officer to ensure all the small arms that the pilots would be carrying in their survival vests were checked and ammo made available.

"I want all flight suits and personal gear sanitized for combat operations. I mean I want all, not some, but all patches, nametags, etcetera, removed. Review your search-and-rescue cards. Remember, the answers you put down will be the responses the rescue helo crew will expect to hear before they attempt to pick you up, should you get shot down. Commit them to memory and don't forget them. Your life may depend on it. If you don't know the answers, buddy, you got a long swim. We can't run the risk of getting suckered in and shot down by the terrorists. I will brief the maintenance troops on as much as I can. They need to know the importance of this mission so they can put the proper emphasis on their maintenance actions. Any questions?''

When none was forthcoming, Sweetwater ended the brief.

Work started at 0400 on the 18th. The ordnancemen were working like little bees. The flight deck was wet from the night's rain showers. Lights were kept dim while ordnance was being loaded on the attack aircraft: Harpoons, MK-82 bombs, Sidewinder missiles, Rock-eye and 20-millimeter ammo was being staged and loaded onto the birds.

Operation Preying Mantis had been approved by the Joint Chiefs of Staff and by Commander Task Force Middle East. The green light to sink SAAM-class frigates and destroy the GOSPs had become a reality.

All aircrews for Preying Mantis gathered in Ready Room One for their final update brief. Rules of engagement were reviewed once more, targets and sector responsibility were gone over, and one last piece of scuttlebutt was passed out to the aircrews. The briefing officer said, "Some of you may or may not know that the skippers of the Iranian frigates like to add insult to injury after they destroy or sink a ship." The aircrews leaned forward as he explained how the Iranian captains would pass a message or signal to the ship in distress as they steamed away. The message simply stated, "Have a nice day." When the outrage died down, the briefing officer concluded, "Let's show those terrorists what a nice day looks like from the bottom of Davy Jones' locker." The pilots broke into a loud cheer.

Before the aircrews walked back to their respective ready rooms to sign for their aircraft, CAG went over a few last details. "Some of you haven't been in combat before, so make sure you review your ejection and survival procedures. Have a game plan in case you should get shot down. Know your limitations and know your enemy. Remember, 'She ain't over until the fat lady sings.' " The ready room exploded with cheers as the pilots departed.

After checking the maintenance logbook and signing the white acceptance sheet for the aircraft, Sweetwater made one final trip to the head for a nervous relief, before heading to the flight deck. After dropping off the weight sheet in flight-deck control, Sweetwater began to realize this wasn't just another training mission, this was the real thing. Like CAG had said, "Practice is over." As he walked toward his aircraft, his gut started to rock 'n' roll. He had almost forgotten what the feeling was like, but it was coming back real fast. He felt more confident because of the experience he had obtained during his last combat missions.

His aircraft was parked near the fantail of the ship, better known as the Fly Three area, back around the arresting wires. A carrier's flight deck is broken up into three sections: Fly One, which is from the bow of the ship to the front of the superstructure, or island; Fly Two, from the superstructure to the junkyard, which is where they park tilly and some of the crash equipment; and Fly Three, which begins just forward of the Number Four arresting wire and goes to the fantail.

When a pilot checks the maintenance log and signs for his aircraft, the maintenance chief can tell the pilot in which area to look for his bird, which saves the pilot a lot of time.

As Sweetwater was walking toward his aircraft, he reviewed his emergency procedures and went over the rules of engagement one last time. He knew only too well that if he wanted to fuck up his naval career fast, all he had to do was hit an unapproved target or deviate from his mission. Pilots used to be able to get away with it years ago, but not anymore.

Sweetwater's concentration was interrupted by a yell from Sundance. "Hey, Water, don't be getting all the action. Save some for the rest of us."

"Roger that. By the way, Sundance, can I have your Corvette and stereo gear if you catch a bullet?"

Sundance said, "Fat chance. You better watch your

six, hot shot.'' They both waved as they approached their aircraft.

As Sweetwater approached his aircraft, parked on the back left corner of the fantail, his plane captain, ordnanceman, and yellowshirt were waiting for him to get started. Master Chief Vic Terry ran the flight deck and was back in the Fly Three area to ensure everyone got started on time and was sent to the right catapult.

The Fly Three area was the most difficult and dangerous place to work, because of the close proximity of the parked aircraft. The most experienced yellowshirts were assigned to work this section. With seven of the fifteen go aircraft parked in this hot box, it made Sweetwater feel good to see Terry out there running the show. He was the best in the business. All the men who work the flight deck are worth their weight in gold. Master Chief Vic Terry was double platinum.

After checking the boarding ladder, Sweetwater climbed up into the cockpit and did a preflight of his ejection seat. He checked the SAFE/ARM handle in the SAFE position and then checked the rest of the seat. After the ejection-seat check was completed, he checked that all switches were in their proper positions, and put his charts and kneeboard in the seat, then got down to inspect the exterior of the aircraft.

The exterior inspection of the Hornet begins at the left fuselage and continues around the aircraft in a clockwise direction. The pilot must check that doors are secure and must look for loose fasteners, cracks, dents, leaks, and other general problems. Sweetwater inspected his ordnance load, gave a thumbs up to the plane captain, then climbed up and strapped in.

Radio silence was of the utmost importance, so when the aircraft was cleared to start, the air boss turned on the green launch lights positioned in front of and along-side the island. Once the yellowshirts got this cue, they started the go aircraft. The roar of the starting engines sounded like the start of the Indy 500. Once all the aircraft were started, they came up on a predetermined tactical frequency but would transmit only if they were in trouble or in a dogfight. Otherwise, there would be no talking.

Senior Chief Rob Tick had his men up all night making sure the catapults were up and ready to "smoke and poke." Nothing can delay a mission more than having problems with the cats at launch time. Tick and his men took pride in having the best working catapults and arresting gear in the fleet.

The E-2 and tankers would be shot five minutes prior to the main-strike aircraft. Each plane had a backup bird in case it went down for mechanical problems.

CAG Baland was leading the strike, so he was first off the cat. As Sweetwater approached the zipper track that led him up to and into the launching box, he could hardly see the end of the ship, because of all the lingering steam from Bullet Bob's cat stroke. The catapult shots were heavy ones because the Hornets were fully armed.

The cat shot in an F/A-18 was a lot different from that of an F-14. Instead of holding onto the stick, as in the F-14, and pulling the aircraft off the deck at the end of the stroke, the pilot did a hands-off launch with the F/A-18. It was like a "C" ride at Disneyland: as the pilot, you would position yourself for the launch, put your right hand on the throttle and left hand on the upper-left handhold and wait till you were airborne, before touching the stick. This took some getting used to after having flown the F-14.

Sweetwater's cat shot was an aggressive one. It caged his eyeballs. He could barely make out the tape readings on his instrument panel because of the quick acceleration. But once the cobwebs cleared, he was off and flying.

After all the Hornets left the nest, they rendezvoused and headed for their designated targets. Preying Mantis was under way. Once the surface ships were passed the word, they were to start firing·on the oil platforms. Four Hornets were sent up to patrol the coastline near Bandar Abbas. Their mission was to shoot down any Iranian aircraft that came out over the water during the operation. Bullet Bob and his wingman were flying near the Strait of Hormuz while Sundance and Sweetwater were up north.

Five minutes into the shelling of the GOSPs, the USS *Wainwright* sent a distress call that it was under attack by Iranian boghammers. These were fast-moving, heavily armed surface boats that assisted in destroying ships transitting the Strait. Sweetwater and Sundance heard the call and headed for the *Wainwright*. Sweetwater broke radio silence and told Sundance to knock out anything south of the *Wainwright*, while he would take the northern sector.

As the aircraft approached the war zone, Sweetwater and Sundance had a lock-on on their targets of interest. These boats were no contest for the Hornets. It was like shooting fish in a fish bowl. They both selected MK-82 bombs and rolled in on the attacking boghammers. Sweetwater was at 350 knots at 10,000 feet when he rolled into a 30-degree dive. As his heads-up display triangulated the impact zone, he hit the release button on the stick at 5,000 feet and pulled his Hornet into a climb after the drop to avoid being hit with small-gun fire from the boghammer.

Sundance used the lay-down method and destroyed two fish on one pass with his Easter-basket drop. By this time, Sweetwater was level and 10,000 feet up. Sundance came up on tactical and said, "One's making a run for it. Do you have him?"

Sweetwater rogered that he had a good lock-on and was rolling in hot. Sundance climbed back up to ten grand to watch the show. Sweetwater rolled his Hornet over on its back 120 degrees, picked up the run-in line, leveled his wings, and pushed over into a 30-degree dive as he accelerated to 400 knots.

He hit his master arm switch to ARM, lights indicated the weapon was selected, and the fight was on. As Sweetwater approached five thousand feet, he said, "I'm your wiseman from the East, bearing precious gifts." At that point he hit the bomb-release button and pulled for the sky. The bomb came off the rack as advertised and destroyed the final threat to the surface ship.

Sweetwater and Sundance had used a lot of fuel while attacking the boghammers, so they headed for the KA-6 tanker orbiting at a predetermined sector.

While Sundance was plugged in and receiving fuel, Sweetwater was out to the left waiting his turn. Once Sundance was fueled, he broke off to the right and waited for Sweetwater. As Sweetwater plugged into the refueling basket, Bullet Bob came on tactical and said, "I have a tally on the target of interest."

Sundance asked him, "What's your posit?"

Bullet replied, "I am five nautical miles southwest of Larak Island. The Iranian ship is the *Sahand*, and is heading two-ten at twenty knots."

Bullet wanted to make a recognition pass to get a positive ID, so he pushed his Hornet out of fifteen thousand feet and headed for the deck. At two hundred feet and five hundred knots behind the ship, CAG came smokin' by. Bullet got his positive ID but caught a round while doing so. As he climbed back to altitude, his right-engine fire light illuminated and smoke started to fill the cockpit.

"Sonofabitch," Bullet said, as he came up on guard. "Mayday! Mayday! Mayday! I've been hit. I've been hit." Bullet shut down his right engine and opened a vent to clear the smoke out of the cockpit. Once the smoke cleared and the aircraft was stable, CAG called for his wingman to look him over and get a vector from the E-2 back to the ship.

By this time, Sweetwater and Sundance were hauling ass toward Larak Island. Once they hit the check point, they set up a ladder search trying to locate the *Sahand*. At the same time, the *Enterprise* gave the order to launch the second war-at-sea package.

CAG's wingman, Sidewinder, reported a large hole in the right underside near the right exhaust nozzle of his bird. Sidewinder asked CAG if he was having any control problems and CAG said, "She's holding her own." They had seventy miles to home plate.

Slick and his strike birds were on their way to relieve the birds up near Bandar Abbas and assist in finding the *Sahand*. After ten minutes of searching, Sweetwater picked up a contact and got a positive ID on his target of interest. Sundance joined him in a combat cruise position, a half mile behind and a thousand-foot vertical separation. Sweetwater said, "Cover my six, Sundance, we're going in."

Sweetwater armed his Harpoon, which was the most

deadly piece of ordnance he had on board. With his master arm switch armed, and ordnance selected, he started his attack on the Iranian frigate *Sahand*.

At 10,000 feet, 350 knots and 5 miles out, Sweetwater launched his weapon. As they timed it to the impact area, they saw a large explosion in front of them and rolled in for a better look. The Harpoon hit just below the bridge of the *Sahand* and leveled it. Sundance broke off and set himself up for a dive-bomb run. He had two MK-82 bombs left and he planned to put them to good use.

Smoke was billowing high into the air, which made the structure of the ship hard to see. The Hornet's weapons systems didn't care if there was smoke or hail. They locked on to the target and Sundance flew a bull's-eye pass, peppering the ship from bow to stern.

While all this was going on, the USS *Simpson* spotted the Iranian frigate *Sabalan* making a run toward the Muarak oil platforms. Slick broke his division up and sent two aircraft to assist in the sinking of the *Sahand*, and he and his wingman headed for the *Sabalan*. The *Simpson* gave them radar vectors to the fleeing ship.

Commander Morely set up for a dive-bomb run and told his wingman to fly cover for him. Weapons armed, Slick rolled into a thirty-degree dive and planted a laser-guided bomb down the smoke stack. The *Sabalan* went dead in the water. Slick's wingman rolled in on a lay-down pass and blew half the bow off with his MK-82 bombs. At this point, Slick and his wingman were getting ready for their final pass when the word came from the *Enterprise*, "Disengage! Disengage! Get battle damage photos and return to the nest."

As Sweetwater and Sundance made their final pass

over the *Sahand*, Sundance said, ''Have a nice day, assholes.'' The ship sank within an hour.

The *Sabalan* was on fire and badly damaged as Slick and his wingman made their final photo run. The aircraft flying combat air patrol near Bandar Abbas didn't see any action. The terrorists wouldn't come out over the water to fight. They would take off, fly to the coastline, then head back inland. They may be dumb, but they weren't stupid.

CAG and Sidewinder made uneventful landings back at the Big E, and were up in the tower waiting for the rest of the strike force to recover. The F/A-18 not only proved itself in combat, but played a major role in the longest sea battle the United States had been engaged in since World War II. All aircrews landed without incident, and Preying Mantis went into the history books.

8

Rocket Man

Lieutenant Commander Stone swung his legs over the edge of his rack and sat up, ducking his head to miss hitting the bed above him. Rubbing his eyes, he opened them and gradually began to see the outlines of the furniture in his stateroom. Other than the light seeping in through the vents that went to the passageway, there was no light source in the room. Every time he awoke here, the darkness reminded him of where he was.

It just wasn't like waking up at home, where he could always see the room around him plainly, without straining. At home there wasn't the constant hum of machinery, the smell of conditioned air, or aircraft landing and taking off above your head. Living on a Navy warship was just not like home sweet home. The USS *New Orleans*, a landing helicopter assault carrier, had been Stone's hotel for three months with four to go before returning to the States.

What had stirred him from his sleep was his phone ringing on the desk nearby. He was thinking *Now what the fuck . . .* as he slipped out of the rack and grabbed the receiver to kill the noise before it woke his roommate. Nothing pissed him off more than to be awakened during a deep sleep by the phone or someone knocking at the door. He wondered, Who the hell is calling at this late hour? It's 0145, for Christ's sake. It better be good. He answered, "Lieutenant Commander Stone."

The familiar voice of his assistant said, "Sorry to wake you, Gordy, but the skipper wants to see you ASAP in his cabin. It looks like we may have a no-shit mission." When Gordy heard the word *mission*, the adrenaline started pumping, and the early wake-up call didn't matter.

He knew something was cooking, because Lieutenant "Mad Dog" Jones couldn't conceal the excitement in his voice.

"See you in five," Gordy replied. Trying not to wake his roommate, he gathered his uniform and, to his dismay, it wasn't wired up. All the collar devices showing his rank, his nametag, and the SEAL insignia over the left pocket, had been removed. "Goddamn it," he whispered. He had just gotten his uniform back from the ship's laundry and hadn't wired it up yet. He thought, "They'll have to accept me as is; sometimes shit happens." He pulled on a sweatshirt, threw on a pair of sweatpants and donned his Japanese "motorcycle boots," even though the rubber sandals were still damp from the shower. As ready as he'd ever be, he stepped out the door.

Stone had about a two-minute walk to the CO's cabin. While walking, he wondered what was up. He knew tensions were high in the Gulf and it was just a matter of direction that would set up an assault. The Marine guard opened the door as Stone approached, and looked at him with concern as to the way he was dressed. As he walked through the door, he saw all the department heads, senior Marine and, of course, the skipper. Their looks made it clear that his mode of dress was not quite right. But Gordy really didn't give a rat's ass, and neither did the skipper, which really burned some of the more senior department heads.

As his eyes passed the skipper's, he said, "Good evening, sir."

The skipper said, "How you doing, Rocket Man? Have a seat." The skipper had known Gordy Stone when he was on the Navy's parachute demonstration team, where he got his nickname.

"Gentlemen, we have a short-fused operation unfolding and Gordy and his SEAL team will play a major role in the success or failure of the mission. The operation will be called Broadsword and will start today at 0915. Several of our ships will take out the Iranian oil platforms Sirri and Sassan. They are offshore GOSPs. The Sassan will be attacked by the USS *Merrill*, *McCormick*, and *Trenton*. The Sirri will be attacked by the *Wainwright*, *Simpson*, and *Bagley*.

"These platforms have weapons on them plus communication gear to direct strikes on U.S. ships and assist in directing where to lay the mines. They are also being used to stage troops. There will be a warning for all personnel to evacuate the oil platforms before the ships begin shelling the dog shit out of them. Once the shelling has been completed, Rocket Man and his SEAL team will go in and finish the job by cutting the support legs off at the knees.

"The appearance of total devastation is desired, gentlemen. We want to send a strong message to the Iranian government.

"Rocket Man, the admiral wants you to make a high-altitude, low-opening assault at night."

Gordy thought, Oh shit, I wonder why he wants a

HALO jump at night? Oh well, that's what we get those extra bucks for, right?

"You will have two hours to do the job. I'll position the ship so that the CH-46s can get you out. We'll use the McGuire rig extraction. There is a possibility you may have company. The *Enterprise* will provide air cover until you get out.

"At 0900 we will fly your team into Bahrain and a U.S. Air Force C-130 will make the drop. The department heads will assist you in your planning, Gordy. You can use my briefing room once you get your team up and assembled. We don't have much time, gentlemen. Let's be professional and do it right the first time." He stopped, and everyone thought that was it, until he held up a hand. "Oh, by the way, let's kick some ass."

Everyone's blood pressure was rising. Stone told Mad Dog to get the men up and have them assembled in the briefing room by 0600.

"Yes sir," Jones replied, as he headed for their duty office to start getting the team together. The rest of the department heads forgot about how Gordy was dressed, knowing he was going to have to bail out at thirty thousand feet at night in hostile territory. Most of them thought, Hell, he can dress any goddamned way he wants, as long as I don't have to go with him. Gordy and the department heads who were crucial in the planning headed for the war room. The weather, ordnance and gear for the drop were some of the major areas which needed to be ironed out first.

At 0550 all the plans had been laid for Operation Broadsword. Gordy left the war room and headed for the skipper's briefing room. He had twelve men in his SEAL team. The team would be identified as Barbwire for this mission. As the men started to filter in, Rocket Man realized that the men in this room represented the most feared armed warriors in the world.

The team would be carrying C-4 high explosives and massive amounts of ammunition. The C-4 charges were already shaped for the supports of the oil rigs. With good intell, the team can have its C-4 explosives socked and designed for the mission prior to leaving the ground. This saves a lot of valuable time when in a hostile environment. They would have two automatic-weapons men carrying enough belted ammo to take up the slack in any firefight. Rocket Man's style was, "Go big or stay home," and, "When in doubt, overload." Each man had a rucksack which carried his ammo and C-4 charges. This sack hung below the parachute and followed the contour of the man's legs during the jump.

Once under the canopy, the sack was released on a line that hung below the feet. This was a safety feature in case they had trouble in the water. The sack had its own flotation device so that it wouldn't sink upon water entry. They also could release the lanyard and get rid of the extra weight if they had a problem during entry.

By 0600 everyone had been seated and Stone began his brief. "Gentlemen, we have a mission, code-named Broadsword. We will be making a HALO jump from a C-130 aircraft at thirty thousand feet. It'll be tonight, with a McGuire rig extraction two hours after we hit the silk. Our mission is to knock out what is left of two oil platforms. There is a good possibility we will have company, so we're going big and if you are in doubt of how much you're carrying, overload. Does everyone get my drift?" A loud "Yes sir," shook the room. He could see the excitement building in the eyes of the men as he talked. It had been a long spell for many since their last actual combat mission.

"We'll load up at 0900 on the flight deck and a CH-46 will fly us to Bahrain, where we will board the C-130 for our jump. Maps and final orders will be passed out before lift-off tonight. If there are no questions, start getting your equipment checked. And remember, a good preflight of all your gear may save your life. I'll see you up on the skid at 0900."

A night HALO jump is not the most enjoyable thing to do, especially when it's real dark and cold outside. And to do it into a combat situation will sober up even the most hairy-chested frogman. "If you are rowing the boat, you can't rock it," but things can still go wrong, so you must be in the right frame of mind. SEALs get into the right mind-set by not talking, just constantly reviewing the mission and their part in the operation.

The Barbwire SEAL team was set and ready to launch at 0900 from the USS *New Orleans*. The flight to Bahrain would only take about two hours. The team would have the rest of the day to go over last-minute procedures. Once the helo landed in Bahrain, the CH-46 was taxied to a large hangar and shut down. The team had special rooms inside the hangar that they staged out of until that night. Then they loaded onto the C-130, already parked inside the hangar.

While the war at sea was taking place, Stone could feel the tension as the men loaded into the cargo door of the C-130. The concentration of each man made the atmosphere still. As the aircraft lifted off the deck at Bahrain, each man was reviewing the procedures he was expected to perform in the coming hours. No matter how many times you review, you're always thinking about the "what ifs" and hope you are prepared.

Stone felt an extra amount of tension. This was the first combat mission where he was running the show. This was a no-shit, live-ammo, somebody's-gonna-shoot-back operation. The responsibility was major and he knew it.

High-altitude jumps were not new to Rocket Man. Of all the team members, he was the most at home in freefall.

He had a special talent for falling headfirst and picking up incredible speed before deploying his chute. His head and shoulders would make a hole in the air the rest of his body could fall through. He knew he was "in the tube" when he felt the back of his legs and feet banging against the wall of air which encompassed the vacuum his body was creating.

In this position, a wave of pressurized air would build up ahead of his body and cause the altimeter on his chest-mounted reserve parachute to read up to a thousand feet lower than he actually was. He had to be disciplined enough to fall a thousand feet lower than briefed, if he used this method of freefall. Otherwise he could overshoot his target.

Combat jumps and demo jumps are entirely different. Tonight, there was no crowd to thrill. This jump would be judged on how *few* people watched it.

Stone moved forward into the cockpit and conferred with the aircrew. A few miles from release point, the pilot said, "All set, Rocket Man?"

"Roger that," Gordy answered. "I'd better get the team ready to cheat death again. See you in the news." He headed aft and started rousting his men. "A few miles to jump zone. Hook up. I'll be by for final checks."

The red light flashed, signaling the jump run was

about to commence, and twelve hearts shifted into
overdrive. Standing back on the edge of the cargo ramp,
looking into the blackness of the night and feeling the
bone-chilling cold of thirty thousand feet made each
man wonder, *Do I really want to do this?* That last-
minute, gut-clenching anticipation/anxiety/fear combination always hit the jumpers, no matter how old and
bold they were. Right before the exit, your stomach is
full of hot lead, and your asshole is so tight, a sub-
atomic particle couldn't escape.

Green light! The spell is broken. Everyone charges
toward the night, and the chief is in the rear, pushing
as hard as he can trying to get as tight an exit as possible, so the jumpers won't be spread all over hell's
creation. Good tight exits are the key to getting a good
grouping during the freefall and landing, especially at
night. A sloppy exit can have your team spread literally
hundreds of yards apart on landing and at night it may
as well be miles. Regrouping at night is almost impossible.

As Gordy got into a stable freefall position, he looked
around for the rest of the Barbwire team. The small
chemical light each man had on his helmet glowed an
eerie greenish yellow in the inky blackness of the night.
He could see the points of light converging slowly toward one spot, and he worked his way toward the little
cluster of lights in the distance. At this altitude, and
with the combat loads they were carrying, maneuvering
was clumsy and much care was required in rendez-
vousing with the rest of the team.

Gordy glanced at the altimeter on his chest-reserve
chute and saw twenty thousand feet, still a long way to
fall. As Rocket Man approached the group, he could
make out their faces now. The men almost had an extra

expression, as a result of the air pressure on their faces. Some had an expression that appeared that of rapt concern, others looked like some kind of drug-crazed weirdos.

All except the chief. There he was across the circle, with tobacco spit trailing from the corners of his mouth. Grinning like a wildman, the chief jerked the hand of the man on his right. This brought the chief face-to-face with Rocket Man and the chief gave him a slobbering kiss on the side of his face. First night-combat HALO water-jump kiss over the Persian Gulf at eighteen thousand feet, thought Gordy, a new world record and a case of beer for all.

At four thousand feet the group began to separate, getting their spacing for the deployment of their chutes at two thousand feet. For this mission Stone had chosen the older-style Mark I paracommander chutes because of their low surge on opening, which decreased the chance of midair collision between jumpers right after opening. This mission did not require the square chutes, designed for a longer glide ratio.

Rocket Man could still see the greenish glow of the lights on his men's helmets as he pulled his rip cord. As the pilot chute came out and deployed the main chute, he felt the reassuring bump as the bag left his back and the lines started stretching out. When the chute deployed, it made a sound like paper being crunched up, a noise loud enough that someone on a clear night familiar with that sound could detect an aerial assault. However, this night was not a pretty sight. Gordy's feet swung below him as the canopy filled with air and broke his fall, slowing him to a rate of descent of about eighteen feet per second.

Looking around, he saw eleven canopies floating like

black weather balloons climbing toward the heavens. Once everyone had a chute open, they started twisting to converge for the landing. Everything looked good. All the men were reasonably close together and the water entry was going to be a mile or so from the oil rigs. They planned the water entry so they would be swimming with the waves as they homed in on their target.

The water entry went just as hoped—all their hard training had paid off. All the team members were out of their chutes with their rucksacks floating and weapons set for automatic. They circled up within ten minutes. The Barbwire assault team was sharp tonight. Stone wasted no time in dividing the team up. "You five men come with me. Mad Dog, you take the others."

The Sassan oil platform was where the extraction was to take place. The Sirri was about four hundred yards from the Sassan. "Mad Dog, get the charges ready. Set your timer for thirty minutes and meet us at the extraction rig. Remember, we only have two hours. Let's smoke some terrorists."

The men started swimming for their respective targets. It would take about twenty-five or thirty minutes to get to the platforms from where they landed. As the team laid on their backs to catch their breaths they could see the aircraft from the *Enterprise* circling high above the oil rigs. Each man had a rescue radio strapped to his left shoulder. They could call down the air cover at any time. This swim to the rigs was a piece of cake for the Barbwire team. They swam five miles at a whack just to keep in shape.

As Mad Dog approached the Sirri rig, he couldn't believe it was still standing. The ships had pulverized it to the point that half of one side was missing. He thought, This is going to be a snap.

There were no people on the rig as far as they could see. Once they got to the support legs, it was already preplanned that Mad Dog would hit the first pillion and the rest of the men would take a support post clockwise from him. Each man had his C-4 charges all socked and shaped for the supports on the oil rig. "Socked" meant that the explosives were sectioned in a socklike holder and sectioned to rap around the pillion evenly.

Finally, all charges were in place, and the trunkline was run to the primary pillion where Mad Dog capped in with the initiating charge and set the timer for forty-five minutes.

Rocket Man's section didn't have it so easy. As they approached their platform, they could see lights and could see figures walking around the top of the platform. Gordy made a call to the aircraft over head, "Barbwire to Broadsword, Barbwire to Broadsword."

"Come in, this is Broadsword, Barbwire. Go ahead."

"We have hostile contact on the platform. Will board, secure, and blow. May need some help. Will advise."

"Roger. Broadsword out."

As the men approached, they circled the wagons and Gordy went to Plan Bravo. "Okay, Chief, you take Smitty and work the charges. Once you're under the platform, give Mad Dog a light signal to let him know what we've run into. Have his team help set the charges when they get over here. I don't think they had any problems over on the Sirri. It looks pretty dark over there."

There wasn't much of a sea state that night, but there was enough wave action to create some water slap on the pillions to make some noise and mask the assault. Once the SEALs were all under the Sassan, Rocket Man and three others unloaded the C-4 from their rucksacks and made one central supply for the chief. The four men loaded their machine guns, overloaded with ammo, and waited.

Rocket Man wanted to ensure that they hadn't been detected before making the attack on the platform. Light communication was made and confirmed with Mad Dog's team. Now it was time to kick ass and take no prisoners. There were six support pillions on this rig, and the adjacent pillions had angle iron stepping up the side of the supports. They were used for checking the rig's pillions during heavy seas and tying up small craft so they could board the rig.

Looking at his watch, Gordy knew that he only had an hour left before his ride would be there. "Okay, men, let's go. Walters, you stick with me. Putt, you take Hutch and go up the other side."

It was a forty-foot climb to the top of the rig. As they started up the pillions, Rocket Man could feel his heart pounding. He knew the others could feel theirs, too. Once they reached the top and if they had not been detected, the game plan was to figure out how many Iranians were holding the platform. They knew this rig had the comm gear on it and they were to confiscate any material or coded documents.

Just then two men came out of what appeared to be the comm shack for a smoke and a joke. Walters and Stone moved down the pillion a bit as they walked by. They heard a muffled groan. What the fuck was that? Gordy wondered. As he peered up over the steel, he saw that Putt and Hutch had come across the platform and bagged the two unsuspecting men by slitting their throats.

With that threat out of the way, they headed for the comm shack. They were in a crouch as they approached the building. As they started to make their move, they were spotted and a steel door slammed in their faces. They shot a burst hoping to knock the guy out of the picture. Now they had to act fast before the sonofabitch called for help. Stone ripped two concussion grenades from his belt and headed for the glass window on the side of the shack. He told Walters and the other two to stay out front. Gordy went to the side, blasted out the window with a short burst from his machine gun, and threw the grenades into the building. The shack was like a vacuum. The open window helped, but the explosion blew the door off and blew the soldier right out of the comm station. When the door came off, Hutch and Putt leveled the place with machine-gun fire.

The fight was over, but with all the blasting going on an electrical fire had started.

Stone told Walters to head down the rig and get the others up on the platform. Just as he started down the pillion, the Sirri rig blew. "Holy shit," he whispered. The orange blast and smoke lit the sky up like a Christmas tree. The cat's out of the bag now, he thought. We better get our asses out of here.

The men below were just about finished when Walters told them it was time to leave. By this time the fire in the comm shack was out of control and things were starting to get hot.

Radio traffic got really intense at this point. Someone was yelling, "Bogeys inbound," and someone else was saying, "We don't want a confrontation."

"No confrontation?" Rocket Man screamed. "What

the fuck did they think this was going to be, Project Handshake?'' The E-2 Hawkeye aircraft was running the airborne part of Broadsword. Stone's voice began to rise a few decibels when he said, ''Get those McGuire-rigged CH-46s over here fast and call in some air cover.''

Sweetwater, Sundance, Slick and Bullet Bob had just finished tanking and were ready for some action if needed. They dropped down from twenty thousand feet to ten. They had a good reference point with the Sirri all in flames and the Sassan also ablaze.

Things were getting pretty tight on the platform. The fire was spreading, and parts of the structure were starting to weaken. It wouldn't be long before the whole upper structure collapsed. Off in the distance Gordy could see lights, which appeared to be his pickup helos. By this time the team was all together on the far side of the platform. It was about half the size of a football field, so there wasn't much room for the helos to make the pickup with a blazing fire going at the other end. Mad Dog handed Rocket Man the trunkline with the initiating charge.

Suddenly, the Hawkeye came up on the radio. ''Barbwire, Barbwire. You have four bogeys inbound, moving at a hundred and forty knots, about fifty miles out. The Hornets are rolling in on them.''

The air cover had radar lock-on and was proceeding toward the targets. Stone did a fast calculation and knew the bogeys would be on them within a few minutes. ''Broadsword, Broadsword. This is Barbwire. Have you got a fix on the extract birds yet?''

''Roger, they are on your zero-two-zero, four miles. You should be able to see their lights.'' Gordy felt a little better, because the lights he had thought were the bogeys were actually the recovery helos. The bogeys must be coming in black-horse, without lights.

The bogeys knew their cover was broken, so they split up and were going to make a four-point attack on the oil rig. The bogeys were Cobra-type helicopters. Sundance locked on his contact first and launched a Sidewinder. One bogey was history.

The others were having a problem locking up. Gordy forgot his radio discipline and started yelling. "Goddamn it, where in the fuck are those helos? We're going to get our asses shot off if they don't put some torque on." He told Mad Dog to get his men ready for the first helo pickup and Gordy and his men would extract on the second. A flare was set off on the down side of the burning platform so the helos could make their approach. By now the roar of the fire drowned out all other noise, so it was difficult to hear the radio. They had to go to hand signals almost completely now.

The first extract helo arrived and went into a hover about thirty feet over the platform. It dropped a one-hundred-foot wire which had hook-in points spaced down its length. The first man to the wire was Putt. He snapped in, gave the crewman a thumbs up, and the helo raised its hover so the next man could hook in. Mad Dog was the last of the first group of six. Once they were all hooked in, the helo lifted up and away they went. The only fear was that the helo pilot, in his excitement to get out of there, would not lift up high enough to clear all objects before they started their forward motion. If that happened, the last few men on the McGuire rig would impact the obstruction and ruin their day.

The second extract helo was overhead and Rocket Man was the last one to hook up. Just before he snapped in, he set the time for the charge to go off in two minutes. The timer was now set, Gordy was snapped in, he gave the crewman a thumbs up and away they went. As they got away from the platform, Gordy caught something out of the corner of his eye. An Iranian Cobra was rolling in on them. Just at that instant a flash, or a racing streak of light, went shooting towards the Cobra. Then came the prettiest sight he'd seen in a long time, a fireball in the sky. The streak was the smoke trail of the Sidewinder, which blew another helo out of the sky.

Sweetwater and Bullet Bob never got a shot off. The other two Cobras must have fled when the first one got hit, because Sweetwater and Bullet never even got a lock-on after their initial contact. Once the helos were out of trouble, the air cover climbed to ten grand to watch the fireworks. Within seconds, the Sassan blew and Broadsword was coming to a close for the Barbwire team. Now they just had to make it back to the nest safely.

As the helos flew towards their mother ship, the *New Orleans*, Rocket Man began to feel the fatigue. It was a different kind of fatigue than the one he felt after an arduous training exercise. But there was an exhilaration he'd never known before, a sort of heightened awareness which seemed to give him a great sense of clarity. He felt totally in control. Maybe this is what the mystics referred to as satori, he thought, or maybe I've had the biggest adrenaline fix in the universe. Just then he heard one of his men scream out, "It's Miller time!"

And that put it all into perspective.

Steel Beach

The E-2 Hawkeye was the last aircraft to recover from the mission. All aircrews involved in Operation Broadsword were to report to CVIC, the ship's intelligence center, for debriefing. The film from the aerial shots was taken to the lab for processing and the write-ups for the actual attack and destruction of the oil rigs began. These debriefings would take most of the pilots into the early morning, before they would be able to finalize their write-ups.

On the first day of the stand-down, at 1300, there would be a formal debrief with the battle-group commander on board the USS *Enterprise*. Commanding officers of ships in the battle group and the SEAL team officer in charge (OIC) would also be present for the debriefing. After a big mission of this sort the carrier and most of the ships in the battle group would take two days off the line and get caught up on maintenance. Although there is no flying on these off days, the carrier must always have a ready catapult and alert aircraft ready to go. When two battle groups are in the Gulf, one carrier can completely stand down on its maintenance days off. However, this was not the case for the

Big E, since there was only one carrier in the Persian Gulf.

The second day of the stand-down was a complete day of R and R. The ship's supply department would set up for a barbecue on the fantail of the carrier. The deck department would lay out staging for the ship's band to play on and set up various events: a 10-k run, skeet shooting, driving golf balls, wrestling and boxing matches. For those inclined toward less strenuous activity, there was good old sunbathing.

Sweetwater, Sundance, Slick, and Bullet Bob finished their write-ups at about 0200 and hit the rack. At 1300 they would debrief their part of the mission. A lot of lessons learned would be explored, and clear, concise briefs were of the utmost importance. The key to going into a debrief of this sort was being prepared.

During these nonflying days, the flight-deck personnel take advantage of the down time to scrub the flight deck. After several weeks of straight flying, the deck becomes extremely greasy. The fuel and hydraulic fluid are absorbed into the nonskid on the flight deck and the deck becomes dangerously slippery. The aircraft handling officer, who is in charge of all the aircraft, arranges the aircraft on the flight deck so the scrub team can clean certain areas. It takes several scrubbings before the whole deck is completed. The process may take weeks, depending on the flight schedule. During this entire evolution, one catapult must remain open in case some unwanted intruders want to play, and an alert package of aircraft has to be ready to take off at a moment's notice. The flight-deck scrub may take as long as ten to twelve hours. While the flight deck is being cleaned, maintenance personnel are working on aircraft that need long-deferred maintenance. On a two-day stand-down, the first day is devoted to a lot of hard work.

This stand-down day was a special one, because the battle group was working on its fiftieth day of sailing "in harm's way." During the Iranian hostage crisis, the U.S. Navy broke a two-hundred-year-old tradition by serving beer on board a U.S. vessel while at sea. Therefore, anytime a U.S. warship is at sea for more than forty-five days at a whack, each crew member would receive two cans of beer. Everyone was working especially hard knowing that tomorrow he could relax in the sun, listen to a few tunes and enjoy two cold beers—that is, unless he had the duty. The men who had the duty on the beer day got to enjoy their beer the following day at lunch or dinner.

As 1300 rolled around, the COs of the ships involved in Operation Preying Mantis started to arrive aboard the *Enterprise*. As each commanding officer boarded, the ship's bell would bong to announce his arrival. Some arrived by helo, others motored over to the carrier on their personal forty-foot boats. Their crafts would pull alongside the quarterdeck area of the carrier, where a ladder was rigged, and they would board the ship.

At 1300 Rear Admiral Mitchell, the battle-group commander, entered the war room. "Attention on deck" was called, and all officers came to attention.

"Good afternoon, gentlemen," said the admiral. "Please be seated. As you men might or might not know, history was made yesterday. Operation Preying Mantis was the longest U.S. naval battle at sea since World War II. It looks like the Iranian navy is almost nonexistent. Good show, gents. Now, let's get on with the brief."

The brief lasted for two and a half hours. Lieutenant

Commander Stone's assault team went into great detail, because of all the coordination that had gone into the planning of his entry and departure from the oil rigs.

Admiral Mitchell felt the operation blended smoothly into the overall plan, and he was especially proud of the people involved. He said, "There were a lot of youngsters out there who faced hostile fire for the first time in their lives, and they did a magnificent job. Make sure they get the word how we feel about them." In closing, the admiral congratulated everyone on a job well done, and finished by saying, "Gentlemen, remember we will be ready to counter the threat anywhere, anytime. And if and when we fight, we will win."

Sweetwater and Slick went down to the wardroom to get some bug juice and crackers before the evening meal. Sweetwater liked to put mustard on a dry cracker. This innovative appetizer almost turned Slick's stomach every time Sweetwater ate one.

"Come on, Slick," said Sweetwater, "it's not that bad. Besides, it makes the main meals seem like a treat. By the way, what do you have planned for tomorrow's Steel Beach party?"

"Our squadron has entered the round-robin basketball tournament. Does your squadron have a team?"

"What do you mean, Slick? We won the last tourney, remember? We'll be out there throwing them up with the best of them."

Slick asked Sweetwater if he was playing and Water said, "They don't call me Glide-the-Slide Sullivan for nothing. How about you Slick?"

"Not my sport, but I'll help in the coaching department."

The basketball court was set up in the hangar deck

and the tournament would start at 0900. It was a double-elimination round-robin which would go on all day.

This day of fun in the sun meant more to the morale of the troops than one could believe. Just to have twenty-four hours to do as you pleased made life away from your loved ones a little easier. Working eighteen hours a day for fifty-plus days takes its toll after a while. For those who didn't participate in the activities, just the time to write a letter or sit and watch the waves roll from the wake of the ship was therapeutic.

Steel Beach got under way at 0600 with a 10-k run for all the jogging fans on the ship. Since the carrier deck was about four and a half acres, a course was set up in and around the aircraft. All runners got a T-shirt that read, ''I would run a mile to smoke a camel.'' The shirt had a nuclear blast in the background and a camel in the foreground with a set of cross hairs zeroed in over the camel's heart. The commanding officer of the carrier started the race by shooting a .45 pistol. After the race, the supply department started setting up the fantail for the barbecue.

Since the *Enterprise* was on the back side of the deployment, everyone wanted to come home with a little less weight and a great tan. Steel Beach Day was a perfect way to accomplish both. Sundance wasn't playing in the basketball game, so he volunteered to secure an area near the ship's rock 'n' roll band, where the airplanes wouldn't interfere with the sun's rays. Once the joggers cleared off the deck and the area for the barbecue was roped off, the rest of the space was first come, first served.

Sundance had been planning for this Steel Beach party since his last cruise. He brought a plastic blow-up swimming pool along with blow-up party dolls. A couple of pilots from the Fighting Redtails brought in some palm trees from Diego Garcia, which helped in the landscaping around the pool. Lawn chairs were arranged around the pool, and a couple of coolers with ice were provided to keep the beers cold as the day went on. Everyone tried to come up with something unique, something that would make Steel Beach an unforgettable day. Sitting in the pool with the blow-up dolls floating alongside him, and drinking a cold Bud, a guy—if he worked at it—could make it out to be a day on the beach in Hawaii.

Sweetwater and a couple of his squadron mates stopped by after their first basketball game. They looked as though they had been playing for hours. Dripping with perspiration, the tired ballplayers sat in the pool to cool down.

"Well," asked Sundance, "did you win?"

"No, we lost by one point. We got a bye for our second game and play again at two."

"No beers until you win," replied Sundance.

"Bullshit," said Sweetwater, "I'm ready for one now." Sundance handed out the coupons required to redeem the beers. By this time the grills were fired up and the steaks, chicken, hamburgers and hotdogs were being passed out. The lines to get the food were long, so there was no hurry to eat.

It was evident that Sweetwater's squadron, the Fighting Aardvarks of VFA-114, had the best party in town. Crew members from all over the ship came by to take pictures. Even the cruisebook staff took pictures for their publication. One photo showed the squadron skipper, sitting by the pool in his lawn chair, wearing his favorite plantation hat, with a cold beer in his hand and

feeling proud of his troops, who had shown the rest of
the squadrons how to do it up right.

At 1330, the boxing and wrestling matches began.
Some of the boxers and grapplers were pretty good, so
it was a show not to be missed. Most of the matches
were in fun, but there were a few fellows who had a
score to settle and this was a fair way to clear the air.
Although gambling was not allowed or tolerated, some
bets were being placed before the fights. Sweetwater
and Sundance watched a few matches before the next
basketball game. The Aardvarks had to win this one or
they would be eliminated. Slick's team won its first
game, so it didn't have to play until later in the afternoon. As two o'clock rolled around, Sweetwater headed
for the hangar deck. Sundance said he would be down
after he watched a few more matches.

The Aardvarks were playing the Redtails, and at the
end of the first period the Aardvarks were leading by
six points. Playing on nonskid was not as easy as one
might think. The nonskid had a slight profile on it to
help keep the planes from skidding. So when someone
dribbled the ball, it might not have a true bounce. If a
player fell, he usually got a pretty good cut. It behooved players to wear long sweatpants or something
to protect their legs. At half time the Redtails were
leading by three points. There wasn't much ventilation
in the hangar bays, even though the bay doors were
opened, so the short rest the players got at half time
was well deserved. Most of the players on the Aardvarks had played organized ball before. Sweetwater had
played guard for the Black Bears at the University of
Maine, so this was no new sport for him. With two
minutes to go, the game was tied. The score went back

and forth down to the final seconds. The hangar bay was filled, and the noise from the fans was deafening.

With twelve seconds left and the score tied, the Red-tails had a one-and-one foul shot. The first one was good. As the second shot went up and bounced off the rim, Sweetwater broke for the corner. The Aardvarks' big center ripped the ball off the boards and fired out to Sweetwater. Water took the ball to half court and had a two-on-one at the other end. As the opposing player came out to meet him, Sweetwater whipped the ball behind him to his teammate driving toward the hoop. The pass was perfect and the lay-up was made with ease. The game was over and the Aardvarks were headed for the finals.

After the game Sundance came up and congratulated the team. He gave Sweetwater a slap on the back and said, "Goddamn, Water, where did you learn that move?"

"Oh, that's how we play up in the Northeast," Sweetwater laughed.

"Hope you have something left for the final game."

"I best get some fresh air and a rest or else I won't be worth a tinker's damn."

"Say, what time is the game?"

"It'll be at eight tonight. I guess we'll be playing the winners of the Redcocks and Indians game."

"Do you want to watch them play so you can scope out your competition?"

"Hell, no, I'm going to go up and sit by the pool and just relax for a while."

It was almost four o'clock when Sweetwater got up to the flight deck. People were beginning to clean up after the day's activities. He walked over to the area where his squadron had the pool, but it had already been drained and removed. However, the palm trees were still blowing in the light breeze across the flight deck, which gave the effect of being on the shores of a distant island. There were a few beach chairs still around and Sweetwater sat down and watched the golfers hit balls off the fantail.

As he sat and watched the sun slowly begin its descent, he began to think about Nancy and how much he wanted to see her again. Although they hadn't spent much time together, there was something about her that really intrigued him. She was an upbeat person, full of fun and happiness. He needed to be with someone like that.

At that point a young sailor said, "Excuse me, sir. We're starting to clean the deck and I'm going to have to ask you to move these chairs."

Sweetwater said, "No problem." He got up and collected the remaining three beach chairs and took them down to his ready room. After dropping them off, he went back up to the flight deck to help the troops clean up around where his squadron had its pool party. A lot of the pilots and sun worshipers helped in the cleanup. It takes an all-hands effort to clean up the flight deck. The littlest foreign object left on the flight deck can cause damage to a jet engine. These items, called FOD for short, can even destroy a jet engine and possibly put an aircraft and pilot into the water. Accordingly, it was in everyone's best interest to do his part in helping clean the deck for the next day's flight schedule. As the flight-deck crews were hosing down the fantail, where most of the action had taken place, Sweetwater heard a voice say, "Are you ready for the Persian Gulf All-World Basketball Championship?"

As he looked around, there came Slick the lobster

man. Not only was he burnt, but the sun had fried his brain. "Well, I guess by that, jester, we're playing you limp dicks for the championship."

"You betcha. We beat the Indians, but lost our last game by three, so we'll be seeing you at eight."

"I'm supposed to be worried, I guess?"

"That's right, Sweetwater, and you won't get away with that fancy passing with our boys." Then Slick asked how he was doing. When Water told him rigor mortis had set in about an hour ago, Slick started to laugh.

"Say, you better get some lotion on that skin. How in the hell did you get so burnt?" Sweetwater asked.

"I worked one of the grills for a while."

"I guess you did. Are you sure you didn't flop on one?"

"I'm going down and take a shower and write a couple of letters before the game."

"I'll see you at tip-off time," Sweetwater said.

Meanwhile the aircraft handler and the flight-deck crews started putting the aircraft back into the "go spot" for the next day's flight schedule. This re-spot evolution would take almost three hours to perform. All the aircraft that had been put up on the bow to allow room for the Steel Beach party had to be put back in place and the whole area checked over again for any foreign objects that might cause a problem. The duty crew, who couldn't enjoy their two beers until the next day, had the pleasure of performing this task.

At seven-thirty, Sweetwater went down to the hangar deck to start warming up for the play-off game. As he entered the bay, it looked like Boston Garden. The place was packed. Men were sitting on aircraft, the band had

moved from the roof to an area near the basketball
court, and it had the atmosphere of a real-live championship ball game. The adrenaline started pumping and
the soreness went away. Now, Sweetwater thought, all
we need is some real-live female cheerleaders.

Slick's team was a little taller than Water's, but didn't
have as much talent or college-ball experience. The first
half was a run-and-gun type of game, and although very
physical under the boards, it was a clean game to this
point. Slick's team was up by five at the half. The
second-half game plan was to work on open shots, not
make mistakes, and stop their fast break.

The third period was relatively slow, since both teams
were worn out. But when it ended, Slick's team was
up by eight. As the game came down to the final two
minutes, the Aardvarks' strategy began to work. The
Redcocks were making mistakes and throwing the ball
away. With two minutes to go, the lead had narrowed
to three.

At thirty seconds left on the clock, Sweetwater stole
the ball and made an easy lay-up. After the basket, the
Aardvarks put on a full-court press and forced a jump
ball at their end. Slick's team called time out, with five
seconds left. The Aardvarks' only chance was to get
the tap and put it in.

The fans were going wild as the two teams circled
up for the jump. The ref tossed the ball in the air and
both men leaped high after it. They hit the ball simul-
taneously and knocked it into the Aardvarks' basket.
The buzzer went off and no one could believe his eyes.
The crowd went crazy. The Fighting Aardvarks had
done it again.

Slick stood on the sideline, shaking his head in disbelief. The day ended with a bang and everyone had forgotten about the troubled area they were in, for a few hours anyway. The next day, business would be back to normal and protecting the sea lanes would be the priority.

10

The Tanker

The pilots for the 0100 launch filed into the VFA-22's ready room for the 2300 flight brief. Commander Slick Morely was the flight leader and he briefed the mission. It was the first night of flying after the raid on the oil platforms and the sinking of the Iranian frigate *Sahand*. Everyone was still riding high, ready to kick more ass if called on to do so.

As the brief began, Morely explained, "Tonight's mission is not a particularly demanding one. However, gentlemen, the weather is probably going to be our worst enemy and we'll be operating 'blue water.' As you know, that means that we don't have any divert fields available . . . we *have* to land back aboard the ship. We have been tasked to search for more Iranian mine-laying ships. Intell has information that an area north and south of the Strait of Hormuz is going to be mined. Sweetwater and Sundance, I want you to set up a search north of the Strait from two-seven-zero to zero-nine-zero. Gunny Leonard and I will cover the south portion. Lieutenant Commander Boots Costello will fly the refueling tanker. Boots, I want you airborne five minutes prior to the launch. Climb to seven thousand feet above the nest and get a good system-package check from the off-going tanker. If you can't pass gas we will launch the stand-by tanker. Once we know the tanker is sweet, we'll refuel overhead before we go on the mission. With the weather the way it is, I want to ensure we can get back and have a couple looks at the deck before we have to tank again. Recovery time is 0300. Be in the recovery stack ten minutes prior to push. Boots, after everyone is aboard you will then be cleared to land. Conserve your fuel while you're waiting for our return. Any questions?''

"What are the tops and bases of this weather?'' asked Sundance.

"Reported tops are fifty-five hundred and bases are eighteen hundred around the nest. The thunder-bumpers are near the Strait, tops are thirty grand. All the Hornets are configured for FLIR tonight. There are thunderstorms near the Strait and there is no visible horizon. It's going to be dark as a well digger's asshole out there tonight and I don't want anyone flying into the water. Check your radar altimeters. I don't want anyone below one hundred feet. Understood?''

A loud "Yes, sir" came from the flight crews.

"Okay, gents, we have an hour before man-up. Get your nervous head calls out of the way and give your flight gear and aircraft a good preflight. Remember, we're professionals, so let's do it right, but most of all let's be safe. See you in the air.''

Sweetwater and Sundance went back to their squadron's maintenance control to look over the logbooks for the aircraft they would be flying that night. Each pilot-in-command must review all discrepancies in the logbook for the aircraft he is flying. Once satisfied the plane is in an up status, he signs the white acceptance sheet acknowledging responsibility for that aircraft.

Boots Costello and his bombardier/navigator went to mid-rats to get some food. Slick and Gunny went to intell to see if anything had changed their mission. The mission was still the same, but on the way out of CVIC they ran into Black Cloud, the ship's weather guesser. He said, "The weather is getting worse and the ceilings will get down to two hundred feet at times throughout the night."

"Thanks," Gunny said. "You just made my day."

Slick looked at Gunny and said, "That's why we get those extra flight skins. We live by chance, and love by choice."

At 0015 the crews were in flight-deck control, putting their weight sheets in the catapult officers' in-boxes. The weight sheets tell the cat officer what weight the aircraft is, so he can set the proper steam pressure to get it airborne. It is the responsibility of each pilot-in-command to have the correct weight figured. An incorrect weight setting selected for the catapult steam pressure could put an aircraft in the water.

As the Hornet drivers walked to their machines, Boots had already lit the fires on his KA-6 tanker. The "K" in front of the A-6 meant that this aircraft was configured as an in-flight-refueling bird. As the pilots were strapping in, Boots was taxiing to the catapult. Checklists were being reviewed and completed as their launch bar entered and locked into the shuttle which would take them from 0 to 170 knots within two and a half seconds. As they sat in the box waiting for the steam to build up enough pressure to sling them into the black night, the cat officer held his right leg off the deck and shook it.

"Oh shit," Boots said to his B/N, "this cat shot is

going to be a kick in the ass, so hang on, partner. It's going to cage our eyeballs.''

"What do you mean, Boots?'' the B/N, who was a first-tour nugget, asked.

"Whenever you see a cat officer do that, he's telling you it's going to be a heavier than normal shot.'' Just as Boots finished explaining, the cat officer gave the signal to put the tanker into tension. The procedure was similar to cocking a gun. Boots told his B/N, "Check your spectacles and testicles, we are about to get our dicks knocked into the dirt.''

As the cat officer signaled for the firing of the catapult, the two crew members positioned their heads firmly in the ejection-seat headrest to absorb the recoil. Within two seconds, twenty tons of steel and flesh went hurtling down the deck. For that two and a half seconds, Boots and his B/N were in the hands of God. At the end of the catapult stroke, you are either flying or you're not. And there's no doubt in your mind which one it is. If you're flying—well that's what was meant to be. If you aren't, you eject. No hesitation, or you probably won't live to tell about it. "Holy shit,'' the B/N gasped, "you were right.''

She was a beauty. As the aircraft climbed out, Boots raised the gear and climbed overhead to relieve the off-going tanker. The off-going tanker examined Boots's refueling system and all systems checked out. The Hornets launched, rendezvoused overhead, got their extra gas and headed off on their missions.

One of the tanker's missions is to provide fuel if needed during the recovery of aircraft aboard the carrier. Normally, tanking is done over the carrier at seven or eight thousand feet, where it is fairly comfortable. But if during the recovery one of the aircraft has a problem getting aboard the ship, he soon becomes critically low on fuel. The tanker, circling overhead, is then directed to descend to an altitude where he can see the aircraft in trouble and "hawk" or closely watch his next approach.

If several attempts to get aboard fail, the pilot is usually down to emergency fuel and will need a drink. On his last approach, the controllers will say, "Trick or treat," to the pilot in the troubled aircraft. This tells the pilot that if he doesn't get aboard, then his signal is to plug into the tanker and get some gas.

It is the responsibility of the mission tanker pilot to have his refueling drogue out and to fly just ahead and to the left of the troubled aircraft, so that if he misses the arresting wires—called boltering—he can fly up and start tanking expeditiously. If not, the possibility of running out of fuel becomes very real.

As Boots drilled holes in the sky and watched the lightning flashes in the distance, 0245 had arrived and the first Hornet checked in with Marshall. By 0255 all recovering aircraft were holding and awaiting their push times. At 0300 the first aircraft left Marshall and headed home to the nest.

By monitoring the approach frequency with his second radio, it wasn't hard for Boots to tell that the weather was having a devastating impact on the Big E's normally high boarding rate. Several of the aircraft were having problems and getting low on fuel. He was instructed to descend to twenty-three hundred feet to hawk one of the F/A-18s. "Okay, Wrongway, we're going to get busy. Keep an eye on me and don't let us fly into the water."

"Roger," Wrongway answered, not quite concealing the concern in his voice.

As expected, he was still in the clouds at twenty-three hundred feet, so he descended to eighteen hundred feet, to monitor the aircraft approaching the ship. Let there be no doubt in anyone's mind, flying at eighteen hundred feet, on a moonless and overcast night, is damn low, especially when you have to be aggressive with the aircraft to get into position to aid the plane that needs fuel.

Boots was flying a racetrack pattern out to the left of the ship, while he extended his twenty feet of refueling hose. Wrongway was monitoring the radar altimeter, listening for the buzzing warning if they went below a preset altitude, in this case two hundred feet. One wrong input to the stick at this low altitude could put you, and the aircraft trying to tank, into the water.

Boots told Wrongway to call the ship and advise it that they were forced to tank at eighteen hundred due to weather. You can rest assured that the transmission got full attention. At that point, Boots was ahead of the approaching Hornet. The aircraft he was hawking boltered and now he was a problem. He needed gas, and he needed it now!

After boltering, the Hornet climbed, and approach control told him to switch to tanker control. As the Hornet driver checked in on Button 17, Boots noticed concern in his voice. Tanker control told the Hornet to tank and that his gas station was at his ten o'clock position. He rogered, with a "Tally ho," to signal that he could see the tanker, and started heading for the lights.

Knowing that the refueling hose and basket were already trailing behind the tanker, he slipped out to the left side of the tanker and started his rendezvous on the tanker's position lights. Since the tanker's bottom anticollision light is green, and all other aircraft's bottom anticollision lights are red, the Hornet driver knew he was cuing on the right plane. He wouldn't be able to see its silhouette until he was within fifty feet of it.

Within minutes the Hornet joined on Boots, who gave him a circling motion with a flashlight which shone red. The signal told the Hornet driver he was cleared to start tanking. At this point, he maneuvered his machine behind the refueling basket, which was lit up with white lights. The Hornet made his approach to the basket, plugged in, and started receiving gas. In those few minutes Boots's workload tripled.

Flirting with stark terror, Boots was momentarily reminded of a childhood dream of being chased by an unknown assailant. His legs, of course, were filled with cement. The transfer of two thousand pounds of gas was going painfully slow. It finally ended, as all good horror shows do, and the F/A-18 broke off and returned to the ship's control for a subsequent successful recovery.

Feeling fairly relieved, Boots retracted the hose and basket and started a climb back up on top of the weather. His fuel at this point was just enough to make it back to the ship at the regular recovery time with the normal reserve fuel to spare. No sooner did he level off, than he got the call to hawk another aircraft. "Sonofabitch," he told Wrongway, "those fuckers are going to drink us dry, if this shit keeps up."

Now the pucker factor really began to come into play, because if this plane needed gas, Boots would be giving the Hornet his own reserve fuel. As he descended, Boots monitored approach control. He could hear the landing signal officer talking to the aircraft on short final.

"Looking good. Hold what you got," followed by "Bolter! Bolter! Bolter!" He knew the aircraft had missed the arresting wires. Lieutenant Commander Bobby "Bug" Roach was the LSO on the platform, located on the back left corner of the ship's fantail. Bug was one of the best LSOs in the business. He could talk a scared pilot down, even with a thirty-foot pitching deck in a blizzard. After the Hornet climbed, Bug came up on the radio.

"Hey, Sweetwater, check and see if you have your hook handle all the way down and the red light in the handle is out."

As Boots was circling out to the left hawking the Hornet, he thought to himself. "If Sweetwater Sullivan is having trouble getting aboard, things must be dogshit out there tonight."

Boots's blood pressure started to increase thinking about his fuel and second-guessing his ability to get aboard on his first pass.

Sweetwater had boltered twice, when he should have trapped on both passes. His hook had skipped over the wires, causing him to miss. The air boss, who controls the aircraft around the ship, called down to the LSO on the platform and asked what Sullivan's problem was. Bug, the senior LSO, said he thought his dash-pot hydraulic pressure, which holds the hook down, might be low. If this was the case, the impact of the hook on the deck would start it bouncing, causing it to skip over the wires.

By this time Boots's blood-pressure skyrocketed and his fun meter was pegged to distress as he circled out to the left.

Approach control told Sweetwater if he didn't get aboard on the next pass, his signal was to tank. Boots was monitoring the frequency so he started setting himself up again in case Sweetwater boltered. Approach control turns the landing aircraft over to the LSO at three-quarters of a mile behind the ship. When Sweetwater called the ball, and the LSO rogered his call, Boots rolled in just ahead of Water's approaching aircraft and was a quarter of a mile out to the left. He heard Bug tell Water, "Looking good, keep her coming." Immediately, the good news was followed by the bad. "Bolter! Bolter! Bolter!"

As Sweetwater lifted off the deck, Boots was just ahead of him so that he could roll in and get some gas. *My gas!* Boots realized. While he was transferring gas to Water's plane, some amazing things were taking place on the flight deck.

The air bos'n, a rough, tough sonofabitch known to everyone as "Moose" Morgan, had seen this happen before and the solution to the problem was a relatively simple one. He ran off the flight deck like a raped ape and headed for the nearest bathroom. Everyone thought he had a bad case of diarrhea. But a few moments later, he returned to the flight deck with eight rolls of toilet paper. He called the air boss and told him to foul the deck for three minutes.

Moose and a couple of crash crewmen ran out in the landing area and put a roll of toilet paper two feet left and right of the center line under each of the four arresting wires. This raised the wires off the deck so that if Sweetwater's hook skipped again, he would have a better chance of latching on to a wire. As the air bos'n cleared the flight deck, he gave the air boss a thumbs up. The boss made a call on the 5-MC, "Clear deck, land aircraft, land aircraft."

By this time Sweetwater had finished taking on fuel and was being vectored around by approach control for his next pass. Boots was told to stay below the overcast and he would be cleared to land once the Hornet was aboard. Sweetwater had taken all the gas Boots would need if he boltered. Now Costello was faced with a "one look at the ship" fuel situation, after which he would need gas. Nothing like a pressure situation! The ship was now frantically trying to get another tanker ready to launch, if Boots had problems getting aboard.

As Sweetwater approached three-quarters of a mile, the controller said, "Three-quarters of a mile, call the ball."

Sweetwater said, "102 Hornet ball 2.5."

Bug said, "Roger ball. Bring her home to the nest, Sweets." After several bolters, Sweetwater's confidence was shaken a little. He was informed by approach control what they thought the problem was and what had been done to help him out. The sweat began to pour off his brow, stinging his eyes, making it hard to see. He could also feel the sweat dripping from his armpits. When this reaction starts, you know you're uptight.

As the aircraft approached the fantail, Sweetwater kept repeating to himself, "Fly the ball. Fly the ball." He pulled it off, with a little help from Morgan's trick. It was an okay three-wire pass with "whistling shit paper" flying all over the flight deck. Knowing that the mission tanker was low on fuel, the crash and flight-deck crew cleaned up the t.p. in record time and made a ready deck for the last recovering aircraft.

By now, Costello had maybe two looks at the deck before he would need some gas. Normally, when you make a night approach to the ship, it's a somewhat controlled and timely evolution. The approach lasts about ten to thirteen minutes from the time you push out of altitude until you trap aboard. That gives you time to get mentally prepared for ten full minutes of varsity flying, where minor deviations to an approach can turn your approach into your worst nightmare and just "pretty good" flying makes you a statistic. In this case, the "minor deviation" had the potential for becoming a major disaster. There wasn't a tanker airborne to bail Costello out if he didn't get aboard the first time. He knew he had to fly the best approach of his life, or it could literally be his last.

The ship was well aware of Costello's situation. He was immediately vectored to turn to a heading of 180 magnetic and directed to descend to twelve hundred feet and dirty up. He did as he was told, put his gear and flaps down in preparation for coming aboard. He had no mental preparation time . . . he had to do it right the first time or else.

A former skipper used to describe his physical apprehension about flying aboard the carrier at night by saying, "Your asshole is so tight that you can't drive a knitting needle through it with a sledge hammer." Without too much modesty, Boots can honestly say that now he could fully appreciate that description as an accurate one.

Within a few short minutes, he was lined up on the final approach so quickly that he could see why abbreviated approaches breed mistakes: like forgetting to lower your gear or drop your hook. But Boots didn't forget. He was ready and flying the best approach of his life.

As he approached the ramp he started to go high. Boots lowered his nose and pulled off some power, then came right back on with power to catch his sink rate. His hook skipped over the two and three wire and latched onto the four. As he slammed onto the deck and decelerated he thanked his lucky stars. But a second later he had the most sickening feeling a carrier pilot could experience: he started to accelerate when he should have been stopped. The wire had broken and he was headed off the deck into the water.

"Eject . . . eject . . . eject!" he screamed. As the plane was going off the angle deck, he pulled the lower ejection handle. As the ejection sequence started, everything seemed to hit slow motion in his mind. He could feel his legs being pulled back against the seat by his leg-restraint harnesses and his life history started flashing by him, hitting all the major events right up to that moment.

As the seat started to ride up the rails, the top of the ejection seat broke through the canopy and Boots had the sensation of sitting still as the plane and ship pulled away. After one swing in his chute, Boots hit the water.

Captain Frost, the ship's commanding officer, was sitting on the bridge. He yelled to the helmsman, "Hard right rudder! Plane in the water!" He was trying to turn the ship so as not to run over the crew. The flight deck had men down who had been hit with the parting cable.

The air boss called for the plane guard helo which was circling to the right of the ship. "Plane in the water, port side," he shouted. The helo was then vectored to the area. Medical was called to aid the injured men on the flight deck and the helo started its search pattern for the survivors. By this time Boots was trying to cut himself free from his parachute and get away from the ship before it dragged him under. He had been shot out to the right of the ship during the ejection and Wrongway appeared to land in the water in front of the carrier.

Costello's automatic life-vest-inflation system worked as advertised, so he had one thing going for him. As he looked up, he could see the dark silhouette of the ship's port side pass by him. Within minutes things got real quiet. Once free of the parachute, Boots started to inflate his one-man raft, which was in the seat pan attached to his bottom. He could hear the helo in the distance, but his main concern was to get the seat pan off his bottom, inflate his raft and get into it. Once safe in his raft, he could get a strobe light and flares out of his survival vest and start signaling for help.

Tom "Garters" Kistler was the pilot-in-command of the rescue helo. The air boss was giving him vectors as to the approximate area where the men were last seen. The LSO threw a couple of flares in the water to help mark the spot. Within fifteen minutes, Commander Kistler spotted a strobe light at his ten o'clock position. Boots had made it into his raft and gotten his strobe light out and flashing.

But there was still no sign of Wrongway.

The helo headed over to the light and prepared for the pickup. With the helo's search light beaming into the water, the search-and-rescue swimmer in the back of the helo could see Boots waving that he was all right. This meant the swimmer was not needed in the water. Boots got out of his raft and swam away from it. The helo will not hover over you if you are still in your raft, for fear the raft might get blown up into the rotor system.

The survival hoist was lowered and Boots was brought up into the helo. Once aboard, the crewman asked if he was all right and, after a thumbs up from Boots, put a blanket around the soaking pilot. Costello asked if they had picked up his B/N. When he was told they were still searching for Wrongway, Costello felt a sickening tremor race through his stomach.

The ship and helos searched the rest of the night and half of the next day. Wrongway was presumed dead and declared lost at sea. The parting cable had killed two flight-deck crewmen and injured five more. Costello was kept in sick bay overnight and released in the morning.

The nightmare will be with him the rest of his life.

11

Channel Fever

After ninety days in the Persian Gulf, everyone on board was ready for some liberty in Australia. But the *Enterprise* could not leave the area until it had a face-to-face turnover with the USS *Ranger*. The *Ranger* was about a day out and all the department heads on board the *Enterprise* were preparing their briefs, so that the turnover with their counterparts on board the *Ranger* would go smoothly. Once the turnover was completed, the *Enterprise* was relieved of its duties and cleared to head south. The briefings would last most of the day, and at 2030, the Big E would be cleared to leave the Cash Box operating area.

While all the heavies were preparing for their turnover, there was a lot of behind the scenes politicking going on within the air wing squadrons as to who was going to fly off early to Perth, Australia. The personnel selected to fly off early would set up the arrival parties and establish a shore patrol that would be located at fleet landing, where all the liberty boats would dock. Sweetwater, Slick and Sundance were just a few in the running for this grand opportunity.

Perth is a beautiful city in Western Australia, an area which looks a lot like southern California. Its climate is mild, with temperatures averaging in the mid sixties. And the women are gorgeous. The *Enterprise* had been steaming in the Western Pacific for two decades, but had never made an appearance Down Under, so you can imagine the excitement aboard.

The ships would arrive at the port of Fremantle, a terminal outside Perth. The larger ships would anchor out in the harbor, while the small boys would get to tie up at the terminal. There would be a total of twelve ships arriving with more than ten thousand sailors. The enlisted crewmen in their crackerjacks—their dress uniforms—and chiefs and officers in service dress blues, would be hitting the beach during the four-day stay.

The advance liaison party's job is to get the liberty boats contracted out from the locals, ensure there are enough buses lined up to transport the officers and men from fleet landing to the city of Perth, and set up the shore patrol at fleet landing in Fremantle. Although being on the advance party is a good deal, there is a lot of work to be done and not much time to complete all assigned tasks prior to ship's arrival.

A man would sell his soul to be on the advance party, especially to be in Perth several days before the herd arrived. So, the long days and extra bullshit he had to put up with were well worth it. Most of the squadron XOs are assigned as the senior shore-patrol officers. The most senior XO gets to pick the port he wants, and so on down the line. Slick Morely was the senior XO, so of course he picked the primo liberty port to stand shore patrol, and he was ninety-nine percent sure of getting his first pick. Now come the helpers.

Sweetwater and Sundance each had a foot in the door early for this little boondoggle. Standing double duty in less desirable liberty ports put them in the front for

a good deal. It also doesn't hurt to have the senior
shore-patrol officer ask to have you as his assistants.
The list would be posted on CAG's office door as to
who would be going in early. From Cash Box to Perth,
it would take six days of steaming and the advance
party would leave the following day on a US-3.

The US-3 detachment was based out of Diego Garcia, a small British-owned island in the Indian Ocean
leased to the United States. They would fly to and from
the ship until it reached Australia and support the battle
group until out of their operating range on the return
from Down Under.

Once the port call was over in Australia, the Big E
would head for the Philippines, where it would make a
brief stop to pick up stores for the long journey home,
and debrief Seventh Fleet on the operations that occurred in the Persian Gulf.

When the USS *Ranger* arrived on station, the whole
area was a beehive of activity. There were helos flying
from ship to ship picking up and dropping off people
to be briefed and debriefed. The escort duties for the
super oil carriers were about to begin, so there was a
lot of pass-down information that had to be given to the
Ranger battle group, in support of this mission.

The flag officer and battle-group commander on board
the *Ranger* was junior to Rear Admiral Mitchell, so he
would fly over to the *Enterprise*, along with the commanding officers of the ships in his battle group, for the
turnover brief. The briefing would last most of the day,
and when the last senior officer was bonged off the ship,
that would be the signal that the Big E was cleared to
head south and the *Ranger* had assumed duties at Cash
Box. But prior to departing, PR pictures of both battle
groups steaming side by side had to be taken. It was an

impressive sight to see. Once the photos were completed, the Big E's battle group made a sweeping starboard turn and headed south.

As night began to fall in the Persian Gulf, Sweetwater and Sundance began to get a little uneasy, because the advance party list had not yet been posted. The flight to Perth was scheduled to depart at 1000 sharp. Slick was pretty confident that his request would be honored. As a matter of fact, he was so confident that he was down in his stateroom packing. To make matters worse, the sonofabitch called Water and Sundance down to his stateroom to rub it in.

The ship depended on the advance party to have everything set up upon arrival. Among the items to be completed were shore patrol and city police liaison set up, transportation to and from the ship scheduled, bus transportation into Perth arranged, battle-group party set up, tours and sporting events scheduled, hotel rooms reserved for as many officers and men as requested them, and any incidentals that might come up. God forbid if things did not get done because of lack of attention to detail. You may have been the first off the ship, but you would be the first to return, and if it were toward the end of a cruise like this was, you probably wouldn't see land again until you hit the States.

At 2230 that evening, the list was posted: Slick, Sweetwater and Sundance were on it. There was no time to lose; packing was the first priority. You also must try to be as humble as possible, because a lot of your shipmates are pissed that they were not selected to go. After Water and Sundance were packed, they went down to mid-rats in Wardroom One for late chow and to try to avoid catching the dreaded disease called Channel Fever.

Sundance came over to Sweetwater and asked, "Can you feel it?"

Water knew exactly what he was referring to and replied, "Yeah, I think it's started to hit me, too."

By going to mid-rats and having a couple of hamburgers—better known as sliders—and some bug juice, they might hold off this infectious disease. But it didn't work. The fever hit them both like a fart in a space suit. In case you're wondering what Channel Fever is, it's the anxiety that builds up prior to pulling into port. The longer the at-sea time, the more severe it gets. You can't sleep. You can't even lay down and rest. The ship will have movies on all night because most of the crew will be up anyway.

Channel Fever usually will set in the night before you pull into port, but pulling into a port that you have never been to before makes it even worse. For some, it may strike two to three days prior to pulling in. Anyone who says he never got Channel Fever is either lying or more full of shit than the bottom of a bird cage.

The morning never seems to come quick enough when you have Channel Fever. Normally at daybreak you can see land, and the ship will start entering port. A lot of the crew will pace the flight deck to relieve their tensions. If the ship is pulling into a foreign port and tying up at pierside, then it's a whole different story.

The flight deck will have its aircraft in what is called a *show spot*. The airplanes will be prepositioned around the deck to look impressive. And the ship's company, both officers and enlisted men, will man the rails as the ship pulls in. If the ship anchors out, like it would in Perth, then it wouldn't require manning the rails. It's just ship protocol, and depends on a commanding officer's wishes as to how he wants to enter port.

At 0900 two US-3 aircraft landed aboard, and at 1000 the advance party of eight loaded aboard for the six-hour flight to Perth. But first they had to sit through a cat shot with someone else at the controls. This was not a beautiful thing to behold. The palms of their hands were sweating, their armpits were dripping, and a very uneasy feeling came over all the aviators along for the ride. The US-3 doesn't have ejection seats, so if you get a "cold cat shot"—not enough steam to get you airborne—there's a pretty good chance you will not survive the crash. The only good thing about this evolution was that you only had a few seconds to worry about making the big muster in the sky or surviving, because things happen real fast.

The supply officer was in the plane with Slick, Sundance and Water. The US-3 could hold four passengers, one crew member and a pilot and copilot, for a total of seven. As they were taxiing up to the catapult, Sweetwater leaned over and asked Slick, "If we crash and you don't make it, can I have your 450SL?"

That was all it took to turn the supply officer green. He had never had a cat shot, so he was already pretty uptight. Just prior to hookup, the stew burner filled his box-lunch container with vomit. Rather than making it unpleasant for everyone, the pilot decided to be pulled off the cat and sidelined while they got the mess cleaned up. The right engine was shut down, once the aircraft was chocked and chained to the deck.

At this point, the flight-deck coordinator and flight-deck chief did not know what the problem was. However, once they opened the door and got a blast of fresh puke smell, it became real clear why the pilot wanted to be sidelined. After the mess was cleaned up and the aft section of the aircraft was aired out, they started the evolution again. The door was shut, number two engine was lit off and they headed for the cat. After several hundred cat shots, you pretty much know what to expect. But for the supply officer, it was all new and his facial expressions showed it.

As the plane went up and over the box into the shuttle, Slick told the stew burner, "Stand by for tension." At this point the aircraft had been taxied into position to be shot. The box is a big steel housing about four feet long that holds the wedgelike shuttle that will hook into the launch bar on the nose of the aircraft and pull the plane down the cat track when the steam is released. When you go into tension, the aircraft goes to full power and the catapult is cocked like a hammer on a gun. Once the aircraft is looked over by the catapult officer and all the observers give a thumbs up, the cat officer will drop to one knee and touch the deck with his hand and the deck-edge operator will fire the catapult. At this point you are going away whether you want to or not, from 0 to 150 knots in two and a half seconds. You could have the parking brake on and be standing on the brakes, but all you'll do is blow both tires and make a mess on the deck. You will still fly down the cat like nothing happened.

When the stroke down the cat track began, Sundance let out a blood-curdling yell, and the supply officer just about went through the overhead. Once the aircraft was safely airborne, Slick leaned over and said, "It wasn't all that bad, was it?"

The supply officer just looked at him and said, "Bullshit, I just pissed my pants." Sure enough, you can't hide urine stains on a pair of khaki pants.

The flight was uneventful for the next five hours. But as they approached the coastline of Australia, the aircraft joined up and got permission to fly over the airport and break at the up-wind numbers. The adrenaline started pumping, because within a few short minutes they would be on solid ground, in a choice liberty port, where they had wine, women and freedom without the whole battle group to compete with. Most men would drag their balls through forty miles of broken glass just to get a few days' liberty in Perth. That's how popular this port is. Some sailors cruise for twenty years and never get to pull liberty in Australia. It's all a matter of timing.

As the US-3 taxied up to the ramp, they all started to unstrap and wait for the engines to be shut down. When things got quiet, the crewman cracked the door and started to get out, but was quickly met by an agriculture inspector, who asked him to step back inside. Once the crewman got back in, the inspector popped his head in and said, "Welcome to Australia, mates. We must debug you before you deplane."

This evolution took a couple of minutes, and then the members of the advance party got out and stretched their legs. Customs inspectors were waiting when they got out, so they filled out the appropriate forms, then got their baggage. Sundance would stay with the aircraft until it was refueled, to make sure it had no problems prior to its departure. Slick and Sweetwater went to get a rent-a-car and check on their hotel reservations. The supply officer got his men together after they cleared customs, got their car and headed for town. He didn't have much to say to the air-dales. Supply officers are like elephants anyway, nice to have around, but you don't ever want to own one!

By the time they had confirmed their reservations and gotten their car, Sundance had the US-3s refueled and their engines turning. The crews were pretty unhappy, because they wanted a night's liberty in Perth, but their orders were to return to the ship after the drop off. Once they were safely airborne, the advance men changed out of their goatskins, slapped on some civilian clothes and checked that spectacles, testicles, watch, and wallet were in place. Then they headed for town: Perth, Australia.

This was an opportunity that comes one's way maybe once in a naval career. They were ready to light their hair on fire in this port. Once they arrived at the hotel, they signed in and checked into their rooms. Slick and Sundance started making calls to let people at the embassy know that the advance battle-group party had arrived safely and to set up a time to meet.

Sweetwater had to unwind before he got down to business, and whenever he got off the ship for liberty call, he did the same thing he had been doing for fifteen years and six deployments. The first order of business was to get a bottle of scotch and a local newspaper, then fill the tub with hot water, add his favorite bubble bath, and relax in peace and quiet for an hour. No planes taking off or landing over his stateroom, no loud machinery humming, and no orders to take or delegate. Complete solitude. The only command he wanted during this wind-down period was command of his scotch and the bathtub. As he sat in the tub sipping on his scotch, he began to unwind for the first time in weeks.

The real work would begin in the morning. Message traffic had been sent to the embassy providing the names of the senior shore-patrol officer and the supply officer, because they were the key players during this in-port period and the local officials had requested the names for their files. Once all the calls were made and everyone knew the advance party had arrived, a mini cocktail party was set up in the hotel's lounge at six o'clock so that the advance party could meet with its host. Dress code for the night's festivities would be service dress blues. To wear this uniform in Perth is to get the key to the city.

The community of Perth welcomes U.S. sailors with open arms. Perth loves to see Yanks in uniform, and United States servicemen feel proud to wear their uniform on liberty. In most foreign ports, it is unsafe to wear the uniform, for fear of being shot.

Sundance and Sweetwater shared a room, while Slick got one by himself—rank has its privileges. By five P.M. everyone was wiring up his uniform, shining his shoes, and ensuring that pants and jackets were well pressed. Sweetwater, true to his nickname, put on his favorite cologne.

As usual, he smelled like a French whore.

12

Dial-a-Sailor

They all converged on the lounge about the same time, and it was a beautiful sight to see. Three naval aviators in service dress blue uniforms, standing tall as wedding cocks as they entered the lounge, turned a few heads. The host had not yet arrived, so they went to the bar and ordered. As they started to pay for the drinks, a voice from behind them said, "Their money's no good in this lounge. I'll pay for their drinks."

They tried to pay but the man was persistent. As they stood there, several distinguished-looking women approached, and the lady in the lead extended her hand toward Slick and said, "Good evening. My name is Tania Christie, this is Maryjane Evans and Marialyn Susi. We are with the West Australian Chamber of Commerce and we will be assisting you in setting up the battle-group ball."

Slick made the formal introductions and quickly gave the ladies his companions' nicknames so they didn't have to be so formal. After a few more drinks, they asked the ladies to dinner and the women accepted graciously. The hotel had a nice restaurant with perfect atmosphere.

As they sat around the table, the eye contact and

body lingo being traded back and forth was setting the stage for later entertainment. These "birds," as they are referred to Down Under, were very attractive and had influence in the community. It was tattooed over everything they brought up. Prior to finishing dinner, Tania asked Water if he and Sundance would like to join her and Marialyn for drinks at one of the local night clubs. Being their first night in town, the invitation was music to their ears. Slick and Maryjane looked like they didn't need any coaching. As a matter of fact, they were already carrying on as though they had known each other for years.

The ladies excused themselves and headed to the powder room. Their timing was perfect, because it gave Sundance and Water the opportunity to decide who was going to make the run on whom. Both men knew that that was exactly what the ladies were discussing in the powder room. Slick was oblivious to what was going on around him. His brains had already made the transition to his lower extremities, and Sundance and Sweetwater were both so horny that the crack of dawn got them excited. The evening was taking a decided turn for the better.

When the women returned, the quartet moved to the lounge for an after-dinner drink, while Slick and Maryjane stayed at the table. Sweetwater told him they'd meet him for breakfast at 0600. Slick gave a thumbs up as the others left the dining room. After they ordered drinks, Tania asked if they liked fashion shows.

"Well," Sweetwater piped up, "it depends on what's being shown."

Marialyn said, "You'll like what we have to offer. I guarantee it."

Water said, "What do you mean?"

Tania answered for her. "I own a modeling agency and my girls are putting on a swimsuit fashion show at my club tonight."

It was obvious Water and Sundance had latched onto a pair of heavy hitters. It appeared these ladies were a couple of players.

With that invite, Sundance jumped on the bandwagon. "You ladies know that you're with a famous individual, don't you?"

"What do you mean?" Tania asked.

"Well, Sweetwater Sullivan is world famous for his leg shaving. He has shaved more women's legs without a cut than any other man in this universe. As a matter of fact, he is in the *Guinness Book of World Records*. He has shaved over fourteen hundred sets of legs, without a single scratch. He has summer rates and winter rates and he does occasional design work, mostly hearts and diamonds."

Marialyn jumped in and said, "You'll be in the right company tonight to boost your record."

That statement lit their hair on fire and they were on the step now.

As nine P.M. rolled around, Tania said, "We better go. The show starts at ten and I want you to meet some of the girls. Oh, by the way, would you gentlemen like to escort the ladies out onto the stage? I think it would add a special touch, with your uniforms and all."

Sweetwater said, without hesitation, "We would love to assist the ladies." And a smile spread across Sundance's face from ear to ear. The ladies made one last stop in the powder room while the men waited at the front door. When they returned, Sweetwater asked if they would like him to get their car and Tania said, "No, that's all right. My driver will be here shortly."

Well, this really was the cat's pajamas. Here they were, a couple of fly-boys on liberty, in a foreign country, being treated like kings. Who would believe them if they told the story?

By this time a big 500SL Mercedes rolled up. A driver got the doors, and they all headed for the club.

The drive was breathtaking. It took them along the coastline and in and out of the most prestigious estates in Western Australia. It lasted about twenty minutes. The fly-boys were awestruck by the time they reached their destination. As they pulled up to the club, Sweetwater couldn't believe his eyes. It was comparable to the most lavish nightclub in Manhattan. The girls were high rollers and it sure was nice to see and receive this attention, because within a few days, they would be back on haze gray and under way, and in their business, there may not be a tomorrow.

The doorman opened the car doors and gave a courteous good evening to the owner, Ms. Tania Christie, and her guests. As they entered, heads began to turn and Sundance and Water knew they were somebody now. Tania said, "Wait here, I want to see how things are shaping up for the show." While they were waiting, Sundance asked Marialyn what her position was and she replied, "I am Tania's personal secretary and the public relations representative for her agency."

Both women were in their early forties, but on a scale of one to ten, they were twelves. Within minutes Tania came out and asked the pilots to join her backstage. What Sundance and Water were about to experience would make a young man's heart stop. As they entered the backstage area, the models were all over the place, and half of them didn't have a stitch on. Talk about eyeball liberty, Sundance and Water were like a couple of foxes in a chicken coop. Tania gathered most of the ladies together, introduced the pilots, and told the girls that the men would be escorting them to the stage as they were called out.

The show lasted about an hour and a half, and it went very smoothly. In fact, it went so well that most of the audience thought the fly-boys were part of it.

After the show, Tania invited a select few in the show to a party at her house. Now that the formal aspects of meeting the ladies were behind them, Water and Sundance were hoping to let their hair down and relax a bit. They weren't disappointed. The party was already on when they got to Tania's place. It was a beautiful home, on a hillside overlooking Perth.

Marialyn said, "You hotshots said you liked to shave legs. Well, you have several pairs of the hottest legs in Perth here tonight, so let's see just how good you are, Sweetwater. By the way, what does your friend do while you're shaving?"

"Sundance is my assistant. He prepares the legs with hot towels and applies the shaving cream. After I've completed shaving, he makes sure that I didn't miss any areas, then rubs the legs down with hot packs, and applies Vaseline Intensive Care lotion. See, most women will cut themselves around the ankles, kneecaps and shins, but I have perfected a stroke which allows a safe, sensuous shave."

After that little sales pitch, Marialyn said, "I want to be first."

And before the night was over, Water had shaved fifteen sets of legs. Water and Sundance played it cool. They didn't get grab-ass with the clients, which established their credibility. And, not coincidentally, set the stage for the nights to follow.

As two o'clock rolled around, Tania said, "I'll have my driver drop you back to the hotel and we will see you at 0800." They were a little disappointed she hadn't invited them to spend the night, but then again, she had to keep up an image for her employees. But she had that look in her eye, and the groundwork had been laid.

The hour 0600 came mighty early. It hardly paid Sundance and Sweetwater to go to bed. Slick appeared to be fresh, but his eyes gave him away. They looked like a couple of piss-holes in a snow bank and he wasn't talking too much. The first night in Perth had taken its toll, but they had work to do, and figured they best get some breakfast before the ladies showed up.

At 0800 the ladies walked into the lobby. The pilots said their good mornings and got down to business. Slick told Sundance to work on getting the reservations set up. Sweetwater was to work with Tania and the other women on the battle-group party, and Slick would meet with the police chief and set up the transportation and security. They would all meet back at the hotel at four-thirty and discuss the day's evolutions.

The day went by so fast that when 1630 came around, they all wondered where it had gone. Once they all got a drink, they went around the table discussing the day's progress. Everything seemed to go well except for the invites to the battle-group ball. Over seven hundred invitations had to be mailed out, and the postal service had gone on strike that morning. This was a serious problem because the battle-group ball was the highlight of the in-port period, and the only way one could attend was by invitation.

Maryjane said that a plan was being put together to hand-carry all the invitations, and calls would be made to the guests outside the area. That meant that the following day most of them would be delivery boys. Messages were coming into the hotel by the hour: "Set up a tennis match for the navigator." "The skipper wants a tee time at 1000 every day we are in port. Try to arrange." "Set up a soccer and rugby match." And on and on the list went. It was a busy time, and if they didn't get any one of these requests fulfilled, they'd better have a good reason why. At 1800 they had completed all business and it was time to party.

Tania said, "Gentlemen, I have a mission for you tonight. If you wish to accept, it might prove worthwhile. Sweetwater, I have volunteered you as a judge in a beauty contest. The rest of you would be escorts for the women during the show. What do you say?"

Naturally, they all jumped at the opportunity. Even Slick was up for it. The party afterwards had to be better than just sitting in your room waiting for 0600 to roll around.

Slick said, "Sounds great. Where do you want us to meet?"

"Be at the Eagle Club at nine o'clock. And one more thing. Be sure to wear your uniforms."

"No problem, see you then." They escorted the ladies to the door and headed upstairs to get ready. Slick said, "Let's meet back here at 2015 and we'll take a cab over to the club."

"Roger that," replied Sundance. And they were off.

They all shit, showered, and shaved and were set to go at 2015. The cab dropped them at the Eagle Club with time to spare. Tania had someone waiting at the door for them when they arrived and they soon realized that this was not your fly-by-night beauty contest.

Everyone was dressed to kill. The men were in tuxedos and the ladies were in evening gowns.

"Say," Sundance said to their escort, "what's this all about?"

The escort replied, "This is the Miss Pierre Water beauty contest. It's like your Miss America Pageant."

Holy shit, Water thought, this is big time. He said, "Tania's done it to us again. She doesn't mess around when she lines something up."

At this point, the escort asked, "Which one of you gentlemen is Commander Sullivan?"

Water said, "I am, sir."

"Ms. Christie would like you to join her in the judges' booth down in front. The rest of you, please follow me."

The club was as large as the new convention center in San Diego and Water began to get butterflies as he walked toward the judges' booth. As he approached, he realized he was the only Yank, the others all knew who he was from Tania's description. After all the introductions were made, he pulled Tania aside and said, "I don't know anything about judging a beauty contest."

"Don't worry, Sweetwater, just comment on the ladies and the different categories they're in. You'll be magnificent. What would you like to drink?"

"You can drink in the booth?" he asked.

"Why sure, mate. You're in Australia," replied Tania. "We do things a little differently Down Under." At nine-thirty the curtain went up and the show began. For a minute he began to feel like Bert Parks.

Slick and Sundance were naturals. The people behind the scenes gave them their cues and they performed like pros. They lived up to the Navy motto, "Performance, not excuses." By the time the swimsuit category came around, Water was under way. He had a comment about each girl who walked in front of the judges.

One judge would say, "What do you think, Sweetwater?" and he would say, "She carries herself well, but her smile seems forced," or "Her evening gown isn't in her color scheme." That was the way the whole night went in the booth. As the judges were selecting the winner, Sweetwater asked Tania what the winner would receive. She said, "A two-hundred-and-fifty-thousand-dollar scholarship, a million-dollar modeling contract and a trip for two to Paris." Water just shook his head. He couldn't believe that he was part of the pageant.

Everyone was headed for the Tugboat Saloon to party after the closing ceremonies. Tania was working his mind a little while he was in the booth. He wasn't really sure whether she was a player or not, so he wanted to be absolutely sure before he made a move. Sundance had a woman under each arm when he left, so it appeared as though he was occupied for the evening. Although Slick met several women backstage, he had Maryjane in tow when he left the club. He didn't get his nickname by being a loser.

Something was a little different in the way Tania talked and acted as they were saying good-bye to the others in the booth. It wasn't until they got to the car that Water knew the cat-and-mouse games had ended and the ball game was about to start. When he went to open her door, she looked him straight in the eyes and said "Let's skip the party and have our own at my house."

She asked him to drive. She knew what she was doing. She had planned it from the start. As they drove away, she snuggled close to Water, loosened his belt and started zipping down his fly. Then she slid her hand under his boxer shorts, feeling him rise to her touch.

He told her it wasn't a good idea, driving on the wrong side of the road as they do Down Under, half-lit and hornier than a half-fucked fox in a forest fire.

He said, "Let's wait till we get to your place."

She said, "Don't worry, I'm just getting you warmed up."

By the time they reached Tania's home, Sweetwater thought the top of his head was going to blow off. It had been over four months since he had been close to a woman and the foreplay while driving sent him into orbit. Tania knew it and planned it that way. That was one of the things Water liked about older women. When they want something, they go after it. And, like all good sailors, he believed there was no muff too tough to conquer.

As they entered the house, Tania asked Water if he would personally shave her legs, since she had watched while he and Sundance did their magic the night before. He said he would be more than happy to. Tania said, "Meet you up in my bathroom. I'll get some champagne."

"Okay," Sweetwater said, and headed for the bathroom. He stripped down to his shorts and gathered all the tools of his exotic trade before Tania came upstairs. When she entered the bathroom, he pulled her close and started kissing her neck, which sent her into overdrive. As he wrapped his arms tighter around her, he pulled her dress up and slipped his hands around her firm little derriere.

Gradually he moved his hands to the front of her panties and felt her wetness as he pulled them down. By this time they were on the llama-skin rug by the bathtub. He removed her panties, and buried his face between her hot, wet thighs, tasting and licking her until her breath came faster, her muscles tightened and she climaxed while gasping for air.

"Oh, God," she said, "don't stop, don't stop."

Never one to disappoint a lady, Water picked her up and carried her back to her king-size water bed, ceremoniously removed the few clothes she still wore and slipped under the sheets. He drew her close so she could feel how hard he was and entered her without effort. She tightened her muscles, pulling him deeper inside her and he popped almost immediately. They played hide the bologna all night long and her legs never did get shaved.

The next morning Tania said, "Take the car and I'll see you at the four-thirty meeting, that is, if I can still walk."

Tania had the body of a teenager, and she had put Water through his paces. It was a beautiful thing, but he felt like hell when he got back to his room at 0500. Sundance wasn't there, so Sweetwater assumed he had gotten his ashes hauled as well. At 0600 all the players were present, not feeling too chipper but remembering that if you are going to hoot with the owls, then you'd better be able to soar with the eagles the next day.

This was probably the most important and busiest day of the in-port period, because the ship was pulling in the next day and there still were a lot of loose ends to be tied up. The invitations all had to be delivered, and last-minute checks on the band and tours had to be confirmed. Slick had a deal going with the local TV and radio stations and if he pulled it off there would be some happy sailors by the end of this liberty period. He would brief them that night on its outcome. They ate and went their separate ways to get their assigned tasks completed before the day's end.

At 1630 all were present except Slick, so they started without him. All the reservations had been made, ninety percent of the invitations had been delivered, and the rest would be completed prior to noon the following day. The wine-tasting tour and harbor cruise had all been arranged. The battle-group ball was all set now and they could relax and enjoy the in-port period. Slick arrived at five-fifteen, smiling from ear to ear.

"Okay, Slick," Water said. "What have you set up?"

"Well, let me start with the transportation. Everything is set to go. The ship is scheduled to anchor at 1400 local time outside the Fremantle Channel. I've hired four hydrofoils and ten buses. Now the big treat. The phone company has set up forty phones at fleet landing. The TV and local radio stations will start advertising Dial-A-Sailor tomorrow at ten o'clock."

"Dial-A-Sailor? What does that mean?" asked Tania.

"What that means is, anyone in the area can call fleet landing and invite a sailor to their house for dinner or out for the evening. I just finished sending a message to the battle group laying out the ground rules for an invite to someone's house or committing to go on a tour. The bottom line is, if you sign up you better show up. Anyone abusing this privilege won't see land again until we reach San Diego."

"Sounds like a real good way to keep people busy."

"We'll see what happens."

Everyone was pretty burned out from all the partying, and the following day the city would be wall-to-wall sailors. Most of the advance party got a light dinner and hit the rack early, so they could face the challenges that might arise tomorrow. Tania wanted

Water to come over, but he declined. His body was crying for rest.

They were all up early, had a big breakfast and headed for the fleet landing in Fremantle. As they got close, they could see the Big E off in the distance. Her size was awesome as you looked at her silhouette on the horizon among the rest of the battle group. Small boats filled the channel and were motoring out to meet the battle group as the ships made their way toward their anchoring positions. This is a very uneasy time for the skippers of these big warships, for fear they might hit one of the small boats that came out to greet them. You only hope they keep their distance when they get close.

At two o'clock the ships that tied up at the pier had their brows over and sailors were hitting the beach. The larger ships that had to anchor out took more time to set up the camels against which the hydrofoils could dock before passengers could embark. But by three o'clock the invasion was in full swing. The Dial-A-Sailor program seemed to be working. The phones were continually ringing, and the lines to answer the calls were five deep.

When Slick felt things were going smoothly, he told Sundance and Sweetwater they could head back to the hotel. He thanked them and said he would see them at the ball that evening. When they got back to the hotel lobby it looked like Grand Central Station. It was full of naval officers and men ready to unwind and enjoy some well deserved liberty. A few guys in Water's squadron were in the lobby checking in and had to give him and Sundance some grief, saying, "You guys look like shit. Did you do any work while you were in here, or did you just party?"

Sweetwater gave them the canned answer. "Hell, yes, we worked. We hardly had time to play."

They said, "Right," as Water and Sundance waved good-bye.

Sundance said, "Let's get a couple of beers and kick back in our room while the herd checks in."

When they got up to the room, the red flashing light on the phone was blinking, indicating one of them had a message. "Get that, Water," Sundance said. "I have to drop some centerline ordnance."

"Roger that," replied Water, as he called the front desk.

"Yes sir, I have some messages. Just a minute, I'll get the slip. Oh yes, Ms. Christie called twice and would like you to call her."

"Thank you very much." Sweetwater had a feeling it had been she.

Sundance asked, "Who was it?"

"Tania."

"I wonder what she wants."

"Probably an escort to the ball, but I don't want to be tied down to one person tonight. I want to be able to roam, you know what I mean?"

"Sure do," Sundance said. "That's why I told the girls I was with that I had to police the area and ensure everything ran smoothly."

"Good call. How do you know they'll even be there?"

"Use your head, Water. Any gal that had any smarts at all got an invite. They'll be there, believe me. Those two are like those broads in *An Officer and a Gentleman*. New meat in town, they'll be around. What are you going to do about Tania?"

"I guess I'll call her and tell her I'll see her there. I

have to make a few announcements before the band
starts, so maybe I can dodge her that way.''

''But what about dinner?''

Sweetwater thought for a moment. ''I got it! You call
her and tell her I had to go out to the ship and will see
her at the ball.''

''Good idea, Water. I can make it happen.''

Sundance made the call, and it sounded pretty con-
vincing on his end, but Sundance wasn't sure she bought
it. They had some time to kill before they had to get
dressed for the ball, so they decided to go over to the
admin suite in the Sheraton, up the street a few blocks.
For its admin, each squadron collects money from its
own officers to rent the suite, to have a place where
people can come and go, shower and leave gifts without
having to go back to the ship every time they had to
drop something off. Some of the younger officers
couldn't afford a room each night in port, so this was
a way to cut the cost. There was a duty officer on around
the clock, who made sure messages were passed and
his shipmates were safe while in a foreign port. It also
allowed the squadron to party as a unit.

When Sweetwater and Sundance got to their admin,
guys were already under way. Their hair was lit and
they were in full afterburner. The stereo was blasting,
the booze was flowing and they had found some women
to liven up the place. When Water and Sundance blew
in, they were mobbed with questions about what went
on since they'd arrived and all the hot spots to go to.
After an hour of telling tales, some taller than others,
they headed back to their rooms to get ready.

They had to be seated for dinner by seven P.M. The
receiving line began at five P.M., followed by a cocktail
party that went till seven. The receiving line consisted

of the carrier group commander, all the commanding officers of all the ships in the battle group, and all the dignitaries in Perth. With everyone assembled, it was quite impressive.

Water and Sundance wanted to be fashionably late, so they arrived just before six P.M. The admiral and the carrier's commanding officer were the first two in the receiving line. As Water passed by them, they both commented on how nicely things were set up, and that was the best accolade he and Sundance could have received. If their superiors felt the job was done right, then the word was out that they had completed their mission with flying colors. They both were flying high when they got to the end of the reception line. They treated themselves to a well-deserved drink.

Keeping an eye out for Tania was a thorn in Water's side. Since he had to make some key announcements after dinner, he couldn't let loose until the band started up. Just prior to sitting down for dinner, he met her face-to-face in the salad line.

"Hi, Matt," she said. She hadn't called him that since the first night, so he figured she was a little hot. Sweetwater said good evening to her and commented on how nice she looked. She asked if she would see him later and he told her he would probably close the party down and they'd be able to dance before the night was over. As his eyes followed her back to one of the front tables, he noticed an attractive girl sitting to Tania's right. She was tall, with thick black hair tucked under in a sleek page-boy style. She was wearing a T-length, black strapless gown with a black ostrich-feather trim. What a dish she is, he thought. The only problem was that he thought he knew her.

All through dinner, Water couldn't keep his eyes off

her, and a couple of times she caught him staring at her. He knew he'd met the woman before, but couldn't put it together. As the meal came to an end and the desserts were almost gone, he got up on the stage and introduced the senior officers present and some of the dignitaries from Perth, one of whom was Tania. As he was making his closing statements, he was looking directly at the woman he'd been staring at all evening, and it finally came to him. It was Nancy, the nurse in Bahrain, who worked at the Gulf Hotel. He couldn't believe his eyes. What in the world was she doing here?

It wouldn't be long before he found out.

While the band was setting up, he went over to her table and broke the ice.

"Excuse me, miss, are you Nancy? From the Gulf Hotel in Bahrain?"

She said, "Hi, Sweetwater. I was hoping I'd see you tonight. Please, have a seat." She introduced him to the others at the table, and they reminisced about their previous meeting.

"What in the world are you doing down here?" Water asked.

She said she had vacation time coming and got word that the battle group was coming to Perth, so she decided to take a week off in hopes she would see him again.

Sweetwater was speechless, and that didn't happen very often. He asked if she was with anyone in particular and she said, "No, I was hoping to be with you."

This woman was a knockout, and he really wanted to be with her. But when he looked over to where Tania was sitting, she was giving him the death stare. Water didn't want to miss this opportunity to be with Nancy, so he excused himself and went over to Tania's table and told her that Nancy was an old friend. He explained that he wanted to spend some time with Nancy and promised to dance with Tania later. Tania was a class act and she didn't put him on the spot, but he could tell she was hurt.

As the night progressed, Nancy got closer and closer during the slow dances. He was quickly reminded of how attracted to her he had been. It seemed almost as if they were meant for each other. During the next break, Nancy went to the ladies' room and Water located Sundance and asked if he had seen Tania. Sundance said he'd seen her leave about an hour before. Water figured she was a big girl and would get over it. Besides, she could buy and sell him many times over if she wanted. His radar was locked on to Nancy and he wasn't going to let this little princess get away.

They danced several more dances and Nancy asked if he would mind walking her home. She was staying at the Sheraton, just up the street from the Hilton, where he was staying and where the party was being held. As they walked, she asked if he wanted to go on a wine-tasting tour with her tomorrow, and he told her he would love to.

"What time do we have to muster?"

"It's an early one. 0630, in the parking lot of the Sheraton. Do you still want to go?"

Looking at his watch and seeing 0220, he had second thoughts, but he couldn't let her get away, so he promised to be there. When they got to her room, she thanked him for escorting her to her hotel, gave him a passionate kiss and sent him home. He really had feelings for this woman, so it was a nice way to end a fun evening. Besides, she probably thought more of him because he didn't try to push staying overnight. The battle group still had three more days in Perth, so if it were to be, then things would take their course.

The next morning came quickly. It seemed to Water like he'd never gone to bed. When he got up, it was pouring rain and he didn't have an umbrella. He could see himself catching one hell of a cold. As he looked down into the parking lot, he could see three tour buses and people standing around waiting to board. He bought a newspaper and put it over his head and ran for the closest bus. When Water got inside, he didn't see Nancy and he thought she had overslept.

He looked in the other buses and there she was, sitting in the back on the third one.

"Is it wet enough for you, Sweetwater?" she asked. "Have a glass of wine. We can't let you sober up."

The people who put on the tour provided each bus with eight gallons of wine and plenty of cheese. The buses left at 0700 and most everyone was under way before they got to the first stop.

The tour lasted all day and Nancy had fallen asleep in his lap on the drive back. They had gone up the Swan Valley and toured most of the vineyards along the way. They all had drunk themselves sober by the time they hit the last winery. Nancy woke up just as they entered the parking lot at the Sheraton. Once she got her bearings and realized they were home, she asked if he would like to come up to her room for a while. At that point, he just wanted to lie down and get some rest, but didn't let on just how tired he really was. It was about 8:00 P.M. when they got up to the room. Water asked if he could take a shower.

Nancy said, "Sure. I'll order us some snacks."

He was hoping she would offer to shower with him, but that was as likely as a screen door in a submarine.

After the shower and a little snack, they turned on the TV and played kissy face, huggy bear for a while until they both fell asleep.

About 0230 Water was awakened by the hum of the TV. He got up to turn if off, but couldn't believe what his eyes were translating to his brain. At the bottom of the picture, a sentence was flashing, "Recall! Recall! All officers and men attached to the USS *Enterprise* return to the ship immediately. Ship is getting under way at 0830." By this time, Nancy was up and wondering what all the panic was about.

Water said, "Something's wrong. The ship is leaving tomorrow. I have to get back ASAP."

"When will I see you again, Sweetwater?"

"I don't know. I'll write. Wait, I don't have your address. Here, write it down on this wine label."

In his hurry to leave, he barely said good-bye.

13

The Party's Over

When Sweetwater got back to his hotel room, Sundance was almost packed. The first words out of Sundance's mouth were, "What the fuck is going on?"

Sweetwater replied, "You got me. Let's get our asses checked out of here, get to fleet landing, and see if Slick can give us an update."

The whole lobby of the hotel was bustling with *Enterprise* officers trying to check out and get transportation to fleet landing at this early hour in the morning.

The streets of Perth were awakened by the loudspeakers of police cars making announcements. "All personnel attached to the USS *Enterprise*! Return to the ship immediately!"

While Sweetwater was checking out, Sundance went outside to flag down a cab. By this time the word was out to all cab companies that there was a recall, so more cabs were becoming available by the minute. Just as Sweetwater headed toward the phone after checking out, Sundance came running into the lobby shouting that he had a cab and room for two more heading to fleet landing. Matt grabbed Sundance and told him to hold the cab, and he'd be right out. Sweetwater then ran to the phone booth and called Nancy's hotel.

"Sheraton Hotel, may I help you?"

"Yes sir, room 304, please."

"Just a minute." There was a hum and a click, and then the operator said, "There you go."

"Thank you." As the phone rang two then three times, Sweetwater began to wonder where she was. A sleepy hello came over the line.

"Hi, Nancy. It's Matt—Sweetwater."

"Oh, Matt, what's going on?"

"We aren't sure yet. I just wanted to call and tell you how much fun I had and I want to see you again soon."

Nancy confirmed how much she enjoyed their time together and checked to make sure she had his correct address.

Matt said, "I have to run, Nancy. Please write."

"I will. Take care of yourself," she replied.

Water gathered up his bags and headed for the door. The guys in the car were hot, so when they asked where in the hell he had been, he told them he was making sure all bills were taken care of. He was embarrassed to tell them he called Nancy to say good-bye. The guys bought his story and they were off to fleet landing.

When the taxi reached the pier, it looked like Times Square on New Year's Eve. People, cars, and confusion was the scene. Sundance spotted Slick, which in itself was a miracle, with all the chaos going on.

"Hey, Sweetwater, I see Slick. Get my bag and I'll meet you at the liberty boat."

"Roger that."

Slick was all business when Sundance got up to him. Slick was on the ship-to-shore phone and the alligators were nipping at his ass. When he hung up, Sundance said, "Hey, Slick, what in the hell is going on?"

Slick said, "Looks like the USS *America* hit a Greek freighter and put a hole in her side. The word is we're going to cover for her until CINCLANTFLEET gets another replacement. Look, I've got to run. Talk to you after this goat fuck is over."

"See you on the ship." Sundance headed for the line where the next boat pickup would be. Officers and enlisted men were sharing the same liberty boat. During normal boating to and from the ship, the officers had their own boat. Once on the boat, it was about a twenty-minute ride to the ship.

As they got out of the small inlet to the harbor of Fremantle, they could see the Big E. She was lit up like a Christmas tree. There was a lot of activity going on. There were water barges, food supply barges, garbage barges, and liberty boats all around the ship. When something like this happens, it is truly an all-hands effort to get all crew members back aboard, get the proper supply ships out to the carrier, and get under way in the designated time frame.

The boat ride seemed to take forever. Everyone on the liberty launch was talking up a storm, trying to figure out what was up, and where they were headed. Sweetwater and Sundance were a couple of hurting puppies, because of their lack of sleep. As they got closer to the fantail, the liberty boats were backed up two deep, so it would be another twenty minutes before they got their turn to pull up to the camel and off-load. The camel was like a floating barge secured to the stern of the ship, which allowed the liberty boats to pull up and off-load their passengers. There was a railed ladder that ran from the camel to the aft end of the jet shop on the hangar deck. The climb up this ladder was steep and if the ship was moving around, you'd better have both hands on the rails or you might fall into the water.

When their turn came to off-load, it looked like cattle being herded up the ladder. Sundance and Sweetwater just wanted to get to their stateroom and get some rest, because something was up and they probably would be flying. It behooved them to get some sound sleep. Guys were dropping their ID cards as they went up the ladder, holding the line up and causing several fights. Before a man could get aboard, he had to show his ID. Rather than wait till they got to the top to pull the cards, guys would have them in their teeth. With the boat rocking and rolling, they would drop the cards, and if someone didn't catch them, they'd fall down to the camel or, if it just wasn't that sailor's day, all the way into the drink. This slowed boarding considerably. Once aboard, they went to their ready room to find out what was really up.

At three-thirty in the morning, the ready room looked like Grand Central Station. Everyone was checking in to find out what the real story was and what the ship's plan of action would be. The part about the collision between the *America* and a Greek freighter was true, but the freighter actually had hit the *America*. The carrier was working in the Gulf of Sidra and the freighter lost steering and hit the carrier just forward of number one elevator on the starboard side. It put a twelve-foot hole in the side of the carrier and buckled the starboard catapult.

Ten crew members had been injured, but no one had been killed. The duty officer said it looked as though it would take several months before they could repair the damage, and intelligence indicated the ship would have to head back to Norfolk to be repaired. If this were the case, the *Enterprise* could be on the line for two months before it got relieved.

"Hey, guys," the duty officer said to Water and Sundance, "that ain't all that happened."

"What do you mean, Burner?"

"I heard the spies talking at evening chow that things are real hot in the Mediterranean. Seems Khadafy has a plant near Tripoli that's producing chemicals that could be hazardous to national security, if you get my drift."

"Ha! But how do we know that?"

"Pictures . . ."

"What do you mean 'pictures,' Delaney?"

"The guys said we caught the fuckers red-handed, with the SR-71."

"Now you're making some sense."

"All the squadron commanding officers will be briefed tomorrow morning by the admiral and then we'll be updated. Better get some sleep. We may not see much shut-eye if we start going around the clock."

As Sweetwater and Sundance picked up their bags and headed for their stateroom, Sundance said, "Hey, Burner, you just didn't make a swag about what is going on did you?"

"What do you mean by making a swag?"

"What I mean, Burner, is, did you just make a scientific wild-ass guess as to what is going on or is this no shit?"

"Hey, kiss my ass, Sundance. Get out of here and get some sleep."

Sweetwater and Sundance laughed as they walked and Sweetwater said, "You always got to bust somebody's chops, don't you?"

"Hey, anytime I can get in Burner's shorts, it's a pleasure."

Bill Delaney got the nickname Burner the first week after he checked into the squadron. His first flight with Water's squadron was almost his last. After a hot start, he tried to start up too soon and didn't let the engine cool down. That set the whole back end of the aircraft on fire. He'll never live that one down.

At 0830, the phone awakened them and it was the duty officer. "Sorry to wake you, Water, but there is an all-officers meeting at ten A.M. Make sure Sundance gets the word."

"Thanks, see you in a couple." Sweetwater hung up. "Hey, Sundance," he called out to the upper bunk.

"Yeah, what do you want?"

"We got an all-officers meeting at 1000, we better get up."

"Roger that."

The ship had only been under way for an hour or so. It would be a while before they found out who missed movement. Water was hoping none of his troops did, because there is a lot of paperwork and follow-up if someone missed the ship's getting under way.

With the ship expeditiously leaving port, there is always the chance someone won't get the word. Accordingly, a plan is set up to transport the stragglers to a midpoint where they can meet the ship. What they didn't know at the time was that Diego Garcia was that midpoint. They would be stopping there for twenty-four hours to pick up stragglers, replenish stores and on-load some sensitive cargo. When something like this occurs, thousands of people have to work around the clock, to get cargo and stores to a midpoint docking station, so that the mission can be met.

The trip from Perth to Diego Garcia would only take five days, because it would be straight steaming time, no flying. They would soon find out from the brief what their mission was and what the plan of action would be for the next few weeks.

At 0945 the ready room was filled with officers and senior enlisted personnel. The CO entered at 1000 on the nose and everyone came to attention.

"Please be seated. Okay, men, what I am about to tell you is classified and anyone not holding a secret clearance please leave the room."

A couple of senior petty officers only had a confidential clearance, so they excused themselves and the skipper got on with his brief. "Well, gents, the good news is all our squadron mates made it back. We have only twenty or so who missed movement, but we should see them in Diego Garcia. Yes, we're going to Diego, but only for twenty-four hours. It's only a short way out of our projected route to the Med.

"What I'm going to brief you on was passed out in the flag brief this morning. As of right now no one, and I mean *no one*, is to write home until further notice. That's right! No mail will leave the ship until this mission has been completed."

Sweetwater looked at Sundance with raised eyebrows, as much as to say, Something big is going down and it looks like we may see some action. The skipper confirmed that the *America* had been hit by the Greek freighter and would be out of commission and that the *Enterprise* would be taking her mission in the Med until another carrier relieved her, which might take several months.

"We have three reasons for stopping at Diego Garcia, gentlemen," he continued. "We will pick up the stragglers, replenish the ship and pick up a top-secret load. I don't even know what it is. We will be briefed on that at a later date. Things are real sensitive in the area we're headed for. There have been confirmed photos that a chemical plant in Libya is producing some sort of poisonous gases that could be used in chemical warfare. Khadafy is vowing to defend all waters within the Gulf of Sidra and has declared a 'Line of Death' across the mouth of the Gulf. Which means he may want his ass kicked again if we happen to get too close to this line.''

A wave of chuckling swept through the room. ''It looks as though things could get hot over there, so get into the books. Know your systems and be prepared if we must fight. That's all I know for now. We won't start flying until after we leave Diego Garcia. Are there any questions?''

A hand in the back was raised. ''Yes sir,'' the skipper said, as he pointed to the master chief in the back.

''Skipper, what about our families back home? We were supposed to be home in a few weeks.''

''Good question. Through Navy channels, the media and families and friends will be informed as to our extension and kept updated as information becomes available. Okay, men, get into the shops, get the aircraft ready to fly and most of all let's do it safely. We start flying after we leave Dodge, so get your minds on the business at hand. That's all.''

The XO called attention on deck as the commanding officer departed. Once the CO left the room, the XO said, ''Carry on,'' and the room emptied.

The mood was set throughout the squadron. They had been through this prep earlier in the cruise, getting ready for Operation Preying Mantis. Even though they

were being extended for a month or so, everyone was
pumped up and ready to turn to if needed. The commanding officer of the ship would brief the ship's company at 1200 noon on the ship's TV, but it wouldn't be
as detailed.

The transit to Diego Garcia was a good time to get
the ship and air wing into shape. The outstanding gripes
on the aircraft that took lower priority would now be
fixed, and those aircraft down for parts could be repaired and put back into an up status. Maintenance on
the catapults and arresting gear could be done without
interruption, as could the cleaning of the flight deck.

The pilots and aircrews would spend their time in
briefings, getting up to speed about the area and mission that might be assigned. The ship was scheduled to
pull alongside Alpha Pier at Diego Garcia late Saturday
afternoon. Only two duty sections would be allowed
ashore at a time. The rest of the crew would be loading
stores and equipment aboard during their duty cycles.

Like most of the aircrews, Sweetwater and Sundance
were in briefs most of the transit. Friday afternoon the
word came that all squadron COs, XOs and operations
officers were to report to the war room at 1400 for a
secret briefing. At this point they had a good idea that
something big was going down and they were to be
some of the major players.

By 1345 the admiral's flag space was filled and the
flight crews could feel the anticipation permeating the
room. At 1400 the chief of staff for the admiral barked
out, "Attention on deck." As the admiral entered, all
came to attention.

"Please be seated gentlemen," said Admiral Mitchell. "Gentlemen, I have received a secret message from
the Joint Chiefs of Staff laying out our mission. When

we get to Dodge tomorrow afternoon, we will be picking up some equipment and personnel who will brief us on our mission. Do not ask any questions until we are under way. We want as little talk and information spread at Diego as possible. The quicker we get in and out of there the better. What I can tell you is that our mission deals with a chemical plant in Libya and Colonel Khadafy. I want this in-port period to be short and productive. The captain and I are discussing whether or not to cancel liberty.''

At this point you could see a lot of faces sink. ''Yes, I agree,'' continued the admiral, ''I wanted a little liberty myself, but the success of this mission is dependent on secrecy and surprise and I can't afford to have anything leak out. We will brief you tomorrow as to whether we will have liberty or not. That's all.''

Everyone came to attention and the admiral departed. A voice from the rear said, ''Carry on,'' and the room was vacated.

Sweetwater and Sundance went back to their stateroom. Sundance kicked the door open with a ''sonofabitch'' to follow. ''Goddamn it, they take our liberty in Perth and now we can't get off the ship in Dodge. Fuck me.''

''Hey, Sundance,'' Sweetwater said, ''don't forget we spent four days in Perth while the rest of our shipmates were under way.''

''Yeah, you're right, but I had big plans those last few days. We might have been in there early, but we worked our asses off to make it right for everyone else.''

''Hey, shit happens. Roll with the punches. Who knows, we may get a chance to smoke some of Khadafy's cookies.''

A smile crossed Sundance's face, as he replied

"Yeah, you may be right. Hey, by the way, what ever became of that nurse you met?"

"She's a real sweetheart. I hope I get to see her again. There's something about her that I really am attracted to, but I haven't figured it out yet."

"Listen, let's go up and do some roadwork on the flight deck. I need to burn off some energy before chow. By the way, what are we having tonight?"

"The menu said seagull and trail blazers."

"We better run an extra mile to make room then."

After their run and evening meal, Sweetwater and Sundance spent a few hours writing letters home and to their girlfriends. Sweetwater wrote a long letter to Nancy, telling her how much he enjoyed her company in Perth and that he would like to meet her in Hawaii on his return home. The word was passed that the last mail call would be in Diego Garcia. Letters could be written and mailed in Dodge, but would not leave the island until the mission was completed. This meant that it might be weeks before anything was transported from Diego Garcia.

The night before the ship pulls into port is usually fun and an exciting time, but this night was quiet and very sobering. Everyone was wondering what might lie ahead and what the outcome would bring. Many thought they were going to war, and some thought this was just another show of the flag; but Sweetwater told Sundance as they laid on their racks, "Something big is in the making and we are going to be in the middle of it all."

"You know, Water," replied Sundance, "I think you're right. My gut tells me something's going down."

Being in the defense business as long as they had, they recognized certain signals. They knew there was more to this than just showing the flag.

The night was a restless one for Sundance. He was up at the crack of dawn and headed to flight-deck control to see how the night maintenance went on two of his aircraft that needed high-power turns. He was the maintenance officer for the squadron. The night handler was in the chair when he entered flight-deck control. "Morning, Handler," he said. "How did things go last night?"

"Not worth a fuck," said the handler. "We were at darken ship most of the night and all moves came to a halt. Don't worry, Mr. Karnes, I'm going to get your birds up at first light and get them turned."

"Thanks. Those are my last two problems before we pull into port today."

Sweetwater had a good night's sleep and was full of piss and vinegar when he saw Sundance at morning chow. "What's up? Did they get your problem children taken care of last night?"

"No, but they should be up and up by noon."

"Good. Let's go up on deck and get some fresh air."

"No, you go ahead. I have some paperwork to complete."

"Okay," Sweetwater said, as he left the wardroom. When he got to the flight deck, it was a hot humid morning, but clear as a bell. Off in the far distance, Sweetwater could see land, so he walked to the bow to relax and see if he could see any porpoises playing near the ship. It was quite a sight to watch them diving in and out of the bow wake as the *Enterprise* churned toward Diego Garcia.

By 1400 the last line was over the side and the Big E was tied up alongside Pier Alpha. But the word had not yet been passed to whether liberty was going to be granted. At 1430, the ship's captain came up on the 1-MC, an intercom which could be heard throughout the ship. "Gentlemen, I am going to grant liberty. Two duty sections at a time will be allowed off for a six-hour period each. One and three will be first and two and four will follow. Liberty will expire at 0230 and we will be getting under way at 0600. Do not talk to anyone about where we are going or confirm any rumors. If caught passing information you will be court-martialed. That means no phone calls to the States. We have a lot to do while in port. Have fun and be safe. That is all."

As the brows were being put up and Elevators Two and Three were lowered, the activity on the *Enterprise* and on the pier looked like that of an army of ants. A legion of nearly one hundred Filipino longshoremen worked frantically to get the first wave of sailors off the ship and start loading fresh foodstuffs and miscellaneous logistical supplies aboard. The surface line black-shoe officers and chiefs orchestrated this evolution as if it were a symphony orchestra. They were the experts at running the real Navy and were responsible for many of the unglamorous jobs that really made the ship–air-wing team click.

Since Sweetwater and Sundance were in duty section four, and wouldn't get off the ship until 2030, they decided to get a couple of hours of shut-eye. As Sweetwater lay in bed, he figured there was probably going to be a confrontation with Khadafy. Drifting off into a sound sleep, he kept rolling a phrase over in his mind. "There are fighters, and then there are targets."

At 2000 the alarm sounded. "Sweet mother of Jesus!" Sweetwater exclaimed. "Get that big sweet ass of yours out of the rack, Sundance. Let's get to the club and light our hair on fire. We may as well go for the gusto, because there may not be a second time around.''

Sweetwater sprang out of his rack and landed on Sundance's rowing machine in the middle of the room. ''Sonofabitch,'' he said, as pain crippled his right foot. ''How many times do I have to ask you to put this piece of shit up when you're done using it?'' Sweetwater limped over to the sink and switched on the light over the small stainless steel, prison-style washbasin. ''It's a wonder you can fly, Sundance. You're so fucking absentminded at times. I'll move it in a flash.'' He threw some water in his face and hair.

The staterooms were small and you had to rotate around the room to get cleaned up and dressed. Within twenty minutes, Water and Sundance were ready to hit the beach. As the two walked to the officers' brow, which was on the hangar deck between Elevators One and Two, they saw cranes moving tons of supplies aboard, and several busy work parties. Sundance said, ''I think we may be gone for a while by the looks of all this shit they're loading aboard.''

Sweetwater agreed. Although the carrier can go for many weeks without being resupplied, the skipper obviously wanted to be prepared for the worst. But picking up food supplies was not the primary reason for the one-day port call. They would find out soon enough.

14

Line of Death

A top-secret message had directed the diversion of the *Enterprise*, a nuclear carrier that could easily sail around the world several times without a port call. A top-secret message typically made things happen, and this one was no exception. It read like a mystery, and the admiral thought we would be picking up a "spook" unit or Delta Force team. The mission always involves spooks when the message traffic gets ambiguous like this.

As he was talking to the ship's captain, the admiral was interrupted by the phone ringing. "This is Admiral Mitchell," he said, picking up the receiver.

"You have some visitors, from the State Department."

"Okay, escort them to my in-port cabin."

As the admiral hung up, he said to the ship's CO, "What in the hell would State Department personnel be doing in Diego? Something big is up, Captain, and I've got the feeling we are part of it."

A few short moments later, a brisk knock on the in-port cabin door announced the arrival of the admiral's guests. "Enter," he said.

"Good evening, Admiral. I'm Special Agent Tom Kaplan and this is Special Agent John Milligan."

"Come in and have a seat. Would you gentlemen care for some coffee?"

"Yes, that would be nice."

"Steward, please get us some coffee and snacks," the admiral said. Kaplan and Milligan were muscular men. They looked more like recon Marines than special agents.

"Now, what can I do for you?" asked the admiral.

"Sir, Agent Milligan and I are here to brief you on the special cargo you'll be bringing aboard tonight. You will be loading a top-secret experimental aircraft which is en route from the States as we speak. It will be arriving in about twenty minutes. I have orders here from the President and I have been instructed to ensure you receive them and that the aircraft is loaded aboard. There is another group which will brief you on the particulars."

"Will this group appear as mysteriously as you did?" asked the admiral.

"No, sir, they will be with the aircraft, when it arrives."

"Just what kind of aircraft is this machine I will be loading aboard?"

"I am not at liberty to say," Kaplan replied. "The crew with the bird will brief you."

Sensing a classified cold shoulder of sorts, the admiral bid the gentlemen a good evening and had his orderly escort the special agents to the quarterdeck and off the ship.

The admiral asked the captain to leave his in-port cabin while he read the presidential portfolio. The cover letter was brief, concise and signed by the President. The enclosures were top secret. They were the operational plans for a mission with the code name "Golden

Rule.'' As the admiral read the standing orders, goose bumps covered his entire body. He almost could not believe what he was reading. The intelligence community had confirmed that Khadafy was producing chemical nerve, blood, and choking agents for use in a series of calculated terrorist attacks against several European cities and three metropolitan areas in the United States.

A conference was planned to be held at Colonel Khadafy's desert hideout near Tripoli. Abu Nidal and other high-ranking international terrorists were expected to attend this meeting. During the meeting, it was believed, orders were to be issued for execution of this planned attack on the West. Soviet complicity via Syria was a key, in that the Soviets intended to attack Israel after the West had been disrupted by the chemical attacks. By holding American and European people as hostages with the threat of exploding other strategically positioned chemical weapons, Khadafy could divert world attention just long enough for the Russians to overrun Israel with armored divisions deployed in Syria.

The Soviets knew that Libya might take a nuclear hit, but the winds were right and the United States certainly would not nuke Israel after a deep Soviet penetration. They would strike with too much mass and speed to be stopped by the Israelis, and Khadafy was expendable. The time was right.

The involvement of the USS *Enterprise* was to be twofold. The JCS (Joint Chiefs of Staff) had formulated a strategic master plan that would save Western civilization from Khadafy's mad dogs and stop the communist invasion of Israel. First, the *Enterprise* would place itself just north of Khadafy's Line of Death and conduct normal military maneuvers in international waters.

On June 8th the warship would launch a strike that would be heard around the world. The second mission would be the destruction of the chemical plant, before the chemical weapons could be manufactured. The admiral's thoughts raced as he read on . . .

After these two critical strikes were completed, the Soviets would be forced to abort the invasion plans based upon their loss of tactical surprise. Furthermore, back-channel "red phone" negotiations would be attempted to avert the aggression against Israel while the *Enterprise* was making her strikes. The big stick was the threat of a counterstrike against Soviet forces in Syria by submarine-launched cruise missiles, which would be stationed in the eastern Med.

The admiral sat in silence and contemplated what would be best to do first. He recalled the ship's captain and CAG and directed them to set up a tactical department-head meeting once the ship was under way.

As the sun was setting over the small island of Diego Garcia, the C-5A transport plane carrying its top-secret cargo landed. Sweetwater and Sundance were sitting outside the O club having a couple of cold ones on the picnic tables when the huge aircraft flew over. Sundance yelled to be heard over the big plane's engines. "I wonder what that trash hauler is carrying tonight."

Sweetwater replied, "Probably more food." They laughed and continued to get shit-faced.

As the C-5A's huge fuselage was opened, to everyone's surprise, there sat a large tandem-rotor helicopter. The crew chief and ground crew had the helo off-loaded and on the carrier's hangar deck within two hours. The helo was covered with a large tarp and Marine guards were placed around it until the ship was under way.

The officers and men with the helo were greeted by the ship's captain once the bird was secured. "Gentlemen, welcome aboard." At this point, the Marine Major stepped forward and introduced himself and asked the captain if he would like a brief on what this helo's mission would be. The captain said, "There will be a flag brief at 0900 in the war room. You can brief everyone at that time. Liberty expires at 0230, and the ship gets under way at 0600. Go to the club and get some dinner. It may be a while before we can see land again, the way things are shaping up."

"Yes, sir," replied the men.

The Marine Major asked, "Captain, have you seen Sweetwater?"

"No, not lately, but if I know him, he'll be at the club raising hell. How do you know Sweetwater?" asked the captain.

"I briefed him on the mission in the Persian Gulf when you first got over here. Major Lott."

"Lott . . . Lott . . . now I remember. You played a big role in the capture of the mine-laying ship."

"Yes sir," replied Lott.

"Good show. Get some liberty, it may by your last for a while. See you at the brief."

By the time Lott and his crew got to the Officers' Club, Sweetwater and Sundance were under way. They had taken over the shuffleboard table and had had four straight wins. Major Lott walked through the swinging door to the bar and started singing the "Marine Corps Hymn."

Sweetwater looked up and couldn't believe his eyes.

As they began walking towards each other, Sweetwater started in on him. "What in the hell are you doing here, you one-eyed trouser serpent?"

"Hey, Water, I couldn't let you have all the fun."

"Jimbo, I thought you left the fleet for shore duty."

"I did, but was selected for some special projects in Delaware. I'll brief you on the ship. This desert is pretty dry, so where can a Marine get a drink around here?"

"Come on over and meet Sundance. He's all liquored up, but he is one hell of a shuffleboard partner. Sundance is my roommate."

"Hey, Sundance, meet Major Lott."

"Nice to meet you," replied Sundance.

"Hey, Gunny, take my place at the table. I'm going to talk with Major Lott for a while."

After some small talk and three sliders, Jimbo was ready to party. But the fat lady was about to sing. The club was about to close and they had to head back to the ship. Sweetwater asked Jimbo if he had his room yet.

"It was supposed to be all arranged with the flag sec," Jimbo said.

"Flag sec?" replied Sweetwater, "Are you racking it in flag quarters?"

"I guess so."

"Why you sonofabitch! I have to live with Sundance for seven long months, walk a mile at times to shit and shower and you come aboard for a week or so and everything is at your fingertips. That's bullshit. And to make things worse, I'm senior to you. Get into the van and let's get back to the ship."

The *Enterprise* was about three miles from the O Club. They could walk it, but the transportation was available, so they made use of it.

Once back on the ship, Lott and Sullivan parted, after deciding to meet at morning chow at 0800. The night went by fast and reveille came quickly. As the two were sitting in the wardroom, Water asked Lott what in the hell was up. Jim told him part of the mission and said, "I'll tell you the rest at the flag brief this morning."

At 0845 the flag war room was packed with all the major players for a tactical briefing. This was becoming a common occurrence on this deployment. At 0900 sharp, Admiral Mitchell entered. Everyone came to attention and he called for all present to take their seats.

"Gentlemen, we have a large task ahead of us and we don't have much time to prepare, so I will turn the floor over to Major Jim Lott. Jim?"

"Good morning, Admiral, Captain Frost, and officers of the *Enterprise*. As you know, it takes us Marines a while to get started, so I thought I'd kick off with a little joke. Does anyone in the room know how the phrase, 'you've got to be shitting me' originated?"

No one raised his hand. Lott thought, good, this will set the tone for a good brief. "Well, it seems that when George Washington led his troops across the Delaware River during the Revolution, he needed a place to quarter two hundred troops for the night. The first farmhouse along the road was approached and the farmer said he could only house one soldier. General Washington called up Corporal Peters and ordered him to spend the night. Continuing down the road with the remaining soldiers, General Washington came across a large brothel. When he asked the madame if she had room for any soldiers, she replied, 'How many do you have?' General Washington answered, 'I've got a hundred and ninety-nine without Peters.' The madame said abruptly, 'You've got to be shitting me!' " The war room erupted with laughter.

"Gentlemen, this briefing is top secret. My previous assignment was the Special Operations Tactical Response Element. After my tour with Spectre, I was selected to be the test pilot for a new helicopter built in Delaware. This helicopter is a medium-lift tandem-rotor all-composite stealth assault helicopter capable of lifting a fifteen-thousand-pound payload and flying more than two hundred and fifty knots. It operates on a fly-by-optics automatic-flight-control system and is capable of many aerobatic maneuvers. The key to this machine is it has been constructed with composite materials and is totally invisible on conventional surveillance radars. The blade tips have been drastically swept with modifications, which makes the machine very, very quiet. It has been painted flat, dark gray and has FLIR. It can in-flight refuel and has night-vision goggle, heads-up displays for night special operations. This helicopter has been equipped with an extensive navigation and communications package, and has the capability of shooting .50-caliber cannons and four Stinger air-to-air missiles. Gentlemen, this machine is in the hangar bay now and will play a big part in your tasking. The helicopter is code-named Nightstalker."

At this point the admiral thanked Major Lott, and continued the brief.

"Gentlemen, Major Lott has been selected to conduct a mission with CIA support, which will result in the destruction of selected storage tanks at the chemical nerve agent plant outside Tripoli. With the support of a specially selected team of CIA paramilitary operatives, the success of this mission will depend on surprise and air-strike support. A Libyan colonel on Khadafy's staff has been recruited, and will assist in the destruction of the storage tanks that house the toxic agents. When the agents are mixed, this is when you get your deadly force. These tanks and the plant must be destroyed by selectively placing remotely detonated devices in critical areas. The colonel will make this happen. Once the tanks and plant are blown, a strike of three F/A-18s will hit and eliminate twelve of the highest-ranking terrorists in the world, including Khadafy himself. Timing is a critical factor, the strike must be on the heels of Major Lott's egress with the CIA team departing the chemical plant.''

CAG caught the admiral's attention to ask, ''Admiral, how is the CIA going to get into the plant?''

''It appears they will execute a covert border crossing at night from Tunisia and the Libyan colonel is going to meet them as a partisan in the countryside. The colonel will escort them into the plant past the guards. This has already been accomplished on two occasions for site surveys by the team—they are true professionals. That's all for now. We'll keep you up to speed as information becomes available. The planned attack will occur on the evening of June 8th. We will test fly the Nightstalker between here and the ditch. We only have ten days before the strike. Keep your troops informed, but only to whatever degree their clearance will allow. I'm sure most of you sitting in this room are thinking the same thing I was after I read the President's orders, and that is, 'You've got to be shitting me.' Carry on, be safe, and let's be professional.''

Planning began for the strike right after the admiral's brief. The game plan was to have three aircraft on target in the desert, with three CAP birds circling over head looking for bogeys. A KA-6 would be used as the tanker and the EA-6B Prowlers would do the radar jamming, while the E-2C Hawkeye would oversee the whole mission. Major Lott, along with his copilot, Dirt Oliver, and SAR air crewman, would pick up the CIA operatives at time zero-zero, on the night of the 8th.

The Libyan colonel, along with one of the CIA agents, rigged a miniaturized version of the PPN-19 radar beacon forward air control in the spare tire in Khadafy's desert vehicle. The RABFAC was preset to start transmitting at 2330 on the night of the 8th. This would allow the F/A-18s to pick up final targeting info before weapons drop.

The aircraft on the strike would be loaded with two MK-83 one-thousand-pound bombs on Stations 2 and 8, an AIM-9M Sidewinder on stations 1 and 9, and a MK-77 napalm firebomb on each pylon at stations 3 and 7. This mixture of weapons was better known as "shake and bake." All strike aircraft, including the Nightstalker, would in-flight refuel overhead mother at eight thousand feet, then proceed to their stand-off points until Golden Rule went into effect.

Once the operatives were on board Nightstalker and the tanks started to blow, the code words "Let the big dog eat" were the cue for CAG, Sweetwater and Sundance to roll in on Khadafy's desert party. One pass was all each aircraft would get, then make a beeline for the ship. Once the 18s rolled in, it was everyone for himself and get back across Khadafy's Line of Death before any MiGs were launched. Nightstalker would act as combat SAR once the aircraft went feet wet. The whole mission would take thirty minutes once Golden Rule went into effect.

On the night of the 8th, the final briefings were completed at 2100. All aircrews were in their machines turning and burning at 2230. Launch was scheduled for 2300. Jimbo Lott would launch five minutes early along with the KA-6 and E-2C. The ship's captain maneuvered the ship as close to the target as possible. At most, the targets were sixty miles away. Nightstalker, the tanker and the E-2 launched at 2255. Each of the four catapults had an aircraft ready to launch, with the final two F/A-18s behind the jet-blast deflectors on Cats 1 and 3. The backup bird was in spot and would be pulled if needed. The whole launch was to take less than ten minutes.

At 2258 aircraft on Cats 1 and 3 were put into tension. At the stroke of 2300 two F/A-18s, grossing out at 41,000 pounds each, went smoking down the cat track at speeds of 160 knots. The catapult officers on the bow and waist cats turned around and put the aircraft on Cats 2 and 4 into tension and launched them. After the jet-blast deflectors were lowered, the yellowshirts directed the next two aircraft into position. Once on the catapults, the cat officers launched them in the same sequence.

The whole launch took five minutes and forty-five seconds. CAG had waived the thirty-second rule for night cat shots. Normally you had to wait thirty seconds between shots at night, for separation. But it was a clear night and they wanted the birds in the air as soon as possible. The launch went flawlessly. Now it was up to the men and their flying machines.

Major Lott would be flying to a large concrete slab three hundred yards from the chemical tanks. This slab was used for the trucks to pump the chemicals into tank trucks for transportation to the air fields, where they would be shipped. The operatives were to be there at 2350, pickup was at 2355, and the fireworks were to begin at 2400 or zero-zero.

Bullet Bob, Sweetwater, and Sundance hit the tanker overhead mother and were inbound to their holding point. The combat-air-patrol aircraft also hit the tanker and climbed to twenty thousand feet to await any unwanted guest. The Prowler made his run up the coastline jamming everything, and the E-2 was circling at twenty-five thousand, also looking for bogeys.

Nightstalker went feet dry, hitting speeds of 250 knots. Lott's heart was in his mouth. He had a 40-mile ingress into the country before he hit the pad. He had the latitude and longitude of the pad and his navigation equipment was guiding him to his target. The Libyan radar units, partially jammed by the Prowler, didn't have a clue that the inbound stealth helo was now only miles from the plant. Navigating with the Hughes FLIR and Litton AN/AVS-6 night-vision goggles made the approach look like day.

Lott flew a low-altitude, high-speed approach and set a 90-degree offset flare into the pad, decelerated to 150 knots and executed a safe, no-hover landing. The CIA team was there along with one extra passenger, the Libyan colonel. He had asked for political asylum in the United States. This request allowed Lott to fly him to freedom. The helo was back in the air within forty-five seconds. As the helo lifted, the one operative who carried the detonator touched off the fireworks.

Meanwhile, Bullet Bob and his section had locked on the RABFAC beacon in the desert and circled, waiting for the code word. Then, over the secure radio came the call, "Let the big dog eat. Let the big dog eat."

Back on the *Enterprise*, the flag war room heard the same call, "Let the big dog eat." At this point, they knew CAG was inbound to his target and that the chemical plant was up in smoke. Secure voice satcom to CINCLANTFLT passed the details as they were developing. CINCLANTFLT had a secure STU-111 telephone linked to the White House situation room. The President was on the hook for the duration, and the calls to the Soviet Union had begun. The American people were oblivious to the events unfolding in the Med and no news release had broken yet. While a free America slept, her best pilots, Navy and Marine aviators, were making things happen.

Bullet Bob had a lock on the RABFAC beacon and selected a zero range-and-azimuth-offset aimpoint. At ten thousand feet Bullet rolled in hot. Master arm switches on, Sweetwater and Sundance were in trail. With a thirty-degree dive angle and four hundred knots, the first two MK-83s left the rails. The sky lit up like the northern lights as Bullet headed for the coast. The war room on the *Enterprise* passed to CINCLANTFLT, "The heat is on."

Bullet pulled about six g's leaving the target. Sweetwater was a quarter of a mile in trail. As he picked up his thirty-degree dive angle, he transmitted over tactical, "Kiss a fat lady in the ass, Khadafy." Four thousand feet was the hard deck, so the procedure was pickle, pull and climb. This meant release your weapons at 5500 feet, then pull as many g's as it took to get climbing without going below four thousand feet. Sundance followed right behind. As Sweetwater was passing eight thousand feet, he heard a call from the Hawkeye, "Bogeys inbound."

"Oh shit, better hit the deck and run for it."

As Sundance pulled off target he made a battle assessment and it appeared to be six MK-83s on target, no survivors.

As Sweetwater was accelerating to six hundred knots, he heard Bullet call, "Feet wet," to signal he was over the coastline. Both Water and Sundance were on the deck trying to get to the water before the MiGs got a lock on. Just as Sweetwater began to catch his breath, he heard a loud explosion and his heart skipped a beat. Oh, fuck, he thought, now what?

The left fire-warning light started flashing, so Sweetwater brought the left throttle to idle. His right EGT was high and smoke and fumes started to fill the cockpit. At this point he started to transmit, "Mayday . . . Mayday . . . Mayday," and started squawking 7700, the emergency code.

The E-2 came up on the net and said, "We have you, Sweetwater. You're five miles to the coastline—can you make it?" There was no reply. By this time Water had his hands full. He secured the bad engine, lit the fire-extinguishing system hoping to burn the fuel downstream from the fuel-shutoff valve. He could see the lights of the coastline when the second explosion occurred. The aircraft became almost uncontrollable and it was time to give it back to the taxpayers. Sweetwater knew he had to slow down before he punched or else the wind blast would rip him a new asshole. He pulled the good throttle to idle and started to zoom climb to bleed off some airspeed. The Hornet started to roll right, and Water grabbed the stick with both hands to level the wings. He estimated his altitude at about 1900 feet.

Sweetwater reached for the lower ejection handle, positioned his butt and back as straight and as far back in the seat as he could, and released the stick. With one hand, he gripped the wrist of the other on the ejection handle, made sure his elbows were close to his body and pulled sharply up and towards his abdomen. His life started racing before his eyes. From childhood to his first piece of ass. His mother, father and Nancy were very distinct images before the wind blast hit him. From the time the canopy went until the wind blast hit was only a second and a half.

When he started to go up the rails, he only prayed that the chute would open. The drogue chute gun fired and the seat stabilized and decelerated. He got man-seat separation almost immediately, then his chute deployed and his training took over. Sullivan got his O_2 mask off, inflated his life vest and pulled the handle to release the seat pan where his raft was stored. Everything worked as advertised, except for the raft; it did not inflate.

On water entry, he got rid of his chute, and tried to inflate his raft, but to no avail. The CO_2 cartridge did not fire.

While all this was going on, the E-2 contacted Nightstalker, who was acting as combat SAR and vectored him to the area where Sweetwater went down. By this time two MiGs were in hot and it appeared they were locked on Sundance's aircraft. Sundance was yanking and banking to break lock. The E-2 vectored the CAP aircraft to the area and the fight was on. The MiG-23 carried radar-guided Apex as well as heat-seeking Aphid missiles. The Aphid homes in on a jet's exhaust, the Apex is most effective for its head-on shot.

Sundance broke lock and was down on the deck, turning and burning when the 18s jumped the MiGs. Once the MiGs realized they had aircraft on their sixes, they split and tried to make a run for it.

Wrong answer.

The two F/A-18s also split and the right wingman fired his Sidewinder. The first Libyan MiG exploded and ended up in a fireball plunging towards earth. The other MiG changed course and accelerated into a dive for the deck. The lead F/A-18 matched him turn for turn and dive for dive. As his missile locked on the MiG, and the trigger was squeezed, a voice transmitted, "The fat lady is singing."

The second MiG went down.

Sweetwater had a ringside seat for the whole show. But it only lasted six minutes. Now the shock of the ejection and hypothermia started to take effect. The water temperature was seventy-six degrees, but it was a cool night and Sweetwater knew from his training that hypothermia starts taking effect within twenty minutes in eighty-degree water. He started to conserve his body heat by getting into a fetal position.

Within ten minutes a helo seemed to come from nowhere. Normally, you can hear and see helos miles away. Nightstalker's night-vision capabilities made it easy to spot the pilot once the E-2 got a good cut from his emergency beacon. Sweetwater had enough sense not to put the strobe light on his helmet for fear the bad guys would have shot him out of the water.

As the helo hovered over Sweetwater, he gave the swimmer a thumbs up, to signal he was okay and didn't need any assistance. The hoist was lowered with the horse collar on it. Sweetwater wrapped it around his upper torso, gave another thumbs up, and Nightstalker pulled him to safety.

As Sweetwater came up the hoist and saw the load of pax aboard, his first words were, ''Thanks for the party, but where are the women?''

15

Seaweed Charlie's

After Sweetwater got the horse collar from around his shoulders, the crewman, PR1 Walters, wrapped him in a warm blanket. He began to shake and could feel the soreness from the ejection. Once he realized he was safe and really on his way back to the ship, he borrowed the crewman's headset to talk with the pilot.

The first words out of his mouth were, "Hey, Jimbo, it's a beautiful thing. Name your bottle."

That's Navy tradition. If a helo driver pulls you out of the drink, he gets the bottle of his choice, as do the riggers who packed your parachute and the mechanic who worked on your ejection seat. Hell, Sweetwater thought, I'll give these guys a bottle every Christmas for the rest of my life.

Major Lott responded, "Hey, Water, sit back and enjoy your ride. We'll get you home in one piece. It sounded like you guys made a smokin' hole out there in the desert."

"I can tell you this, Jimbo. There was a lot of dirt moving around, and if anything is still walking or floating, it will only be the dust."

At that point, strike ops on the ship called and gave Nightstalker a steer to the nest. Everyone else had already trapped aboard, and was waiting for Lott to bring in the final element. This was one of the most successful strikes and one of the smoothest ingress operations in U.S. naval history.

As Nightstalker approached the fantail, Sullivan could see hundreds of men awaiting their arrival. It almost looked like a dependents' day cruise, with all the crew members and their guests out on the deck. This was an awesome sight, and it sent shivers up and down his spine.

After the helo landed, Marine guards came directly to the bird and escorted the CIA operatives and defecting colonel to a secure area, where Admiral Mitchell would conduct a debriefing. The flight surgeon and some corpsmen jumped in the back of the helo and started to check Sweetwater over. He looked at the "combat quack," a nickname they gave Dr. John Moskowitz, one of their flight surgeons, and said, "Hey, Doc, it isn't time for my flight physical. I still have a month before my birthday."

"Shut up, Water," he said. "Now, roll over and let me check your back."

After ten minutes of inspecting, they helped Sweetwater out of the helo and made him get into a stretcher. He wasn't happy about it, but he lay down and was off to sick bay. The corpsmen carried him to the forward bomb elevator, between Catapults One and Two, and lowered him six decks to the medical ward. This was the fastest and most expeditious route without having to use any ladder wells.

They took vital signs and informed Sweetwater that he would have to spend twenty-four hours in the ward for observation. That fried his ass. He wanted to hit the ready room and tell his squadron mates what had gone on out there and what it was like to be blasted out of the cockpit of a Hornet. But no, he'd be cooling his jets on the ward in sick bay. He didn't even get a shot of medicinal whiskey like downed fliers used to during the Vietnam War. Times had changed.

But it wasn't long before Sundance, CAG and a few other buds were down to see him. Of course, his close personal friend, Sundance, had a little pick-me-up for the occasion.

After the visitors left, the combat quack gave him a shot to help him relax and fall asleep. Before he drifted off, someone was pulling on his arm.

"Hey, Water! Hey, Water, it's Jimbo. I'll be leaving in the morning. You take care of yourself and I'll see you Stateside."

"Where are you going?" he asked.

"A COD will be landing at first light to fly the CIA team and the colonel to Sigonella and I'll follow them. A C-5 will load the Nightstalker and us aboard then fly us to Washington for our debrief."

"Okay, Jimbo, I owe you one. See you back in the States."

"Roger that," Lott said as he left.

At 0545 the C-2 Greyhound, a twenty-four passenger, turboprop aircraft, slammed aboard the Big E, catching the one wire. After it taxied out of the wires, the yellow-shirt director parked it on the six-pack line, adjacent to the forward part of the island structure. As the back ramp was lowered, the CIA operatives and the defecting colonel were escorted to the plane and loaded aboard, along with several thousand pounds of mail.

While this was going on, Major Lott was awaiting lift-off. Once the C-2 was loaded up, the flight-deck crew launched Nightstalker and directed the C-2 to the catapult. At 0605, the C-2 hit the wind, going from 0 to 155 knots in less than three seconds, and was on its way to Sigonella.

That afternoon Sweetwater was released from the ward and returned to his stateroom. His ribs and lower back were very sore and he would be down from flying for a couple of weeks.

The next day, Sweetwater debriefed the mission to his squadron in the ready room and then went to the paraloft to find the men who worked on his chute and ejection seat. When he entered the shop, the men came to attention and said, "We drink Johnnie Walker Red."

They were into the third week of their second month after being extended. As he and Slick walked the deck after the evening meal, they could see their relief carrier, the USS *Coral Sea*, steaming toward them as the bright orange sun settled below the horizon. It was a beautiful sight, especially knowing they would be out of the area by the following noon and heading east to their loved ones and the good old USA.

Sweetwater was still feeling the aftereffects of his ejection. His back was still not one hundred percent healed, and he was to exercise daily, to help him recover more quickly. The flight surgeons had him on an aggressive program, and were optimistic that he'd be back flying before he got to Hawaii. While in a down status, he had plenty of time to get all his paperwork done and write lots of letters. The days really seemed long when you didn't fly.

The ship had had several mail calls since the strike, but Sweetwater still hadn't heard from Nancy. He was hoping to hear from her before going through the Suez Canal, since the mail would be held up because of the ship's movement from one coast to the other. By the time the mail was rerouted to the West, it could take almost a week. He figured he would send one more letter asking her to meet him in Hawaii, and if he didn't get a response before the *Enterprise* entered the Malacca Straits, he'd have one of the COD pilots call her from Diego Garcia and pass the message.

The ship was to be docked at Pearl Harbor on the twentieth of July. In his letters to Nancy, he had asked her to meet him at Seaweed Charlie's, a favorite bar in Lahaina on the twentieth at twelve noon. He also asked her to reserve a room for him at the Maui Westin on Kaanapali Beach, hoping she would share it with him.

Seaweed Charlie's was a famous aviation bar. Charlie Gorthy, better known as "Torch," was a retired Navy captain, who got hurt during an ejection and was medically grounded. After twenty-three years of service, he had decided to retire and open a bar, something he had always wanted to do. This bar was a class act, as was its owner. The restaurant and bar opened at noon, with live entertainment starting at nine P.M. in the Seaweed Room. The aviation memorabilia Charlie's friends had donated to the bar were a sight to see. Torch even had the ejection seat and parts of the chute that saved his life hanging behind the bar. Sweetwater felt this would be an ideal place to meet Nancy and rekindle the fire that had been lit in Perth.

The next day, the debriefs were completed and the *Enterprise* headed east. Sweetwater stood on the flight deck watching the *Coral Sea* get smaller and smaller, as many thoughts raced through his head. *Boy, I'm lucky to be alive. Thank God, I wasn't hurt in the ejection. Will I ever see Nancy again?*

The hours turned into days and the days turned into a week. They were almost to the Strait of Malacca and still no word from Nancy. He now feared he would not hear from her again.

While in a down status, the ship's navigator asked Sweetwater to research the battles that had occurred in the Strait of Malacca. On the day the ship transited the Strait, Sweetwater gave a history lesson to the crew members over the ship's intercom. The transit took several hours and the crew enjoyed the briefing.

The next morning, Sweetwater would fly his first hop since the ejection. The flight surgeons had given him an up chit and it was time for him to get back into the air. The flight was an uneventful one and he flew like he had never been out of the cockpit, according to his wingman. The ship would bypass the Philippines and head directly to Hawaii, where the crew would get some liberty. The transit time would be about eight days.

As the ship passed the Philippines, Seventh Fleet, a three-star admiral who had flown in from Japan, flew out to the ship for a debrief. Normally this brief was given in port, but since the *Enterprise* was bypassing Subic Bay, it was done at sea. Some of the sailors were disappointed that the ship was not pulling into port, and the people of Olongapo City were especially upset, because of the amount of revenue they would lose.

There would be very little flying between the Philippines and Hawaii. Each pilot would fly every two days, just enough to keep him day and night qualified.

The night before pulling into Pearl Harbor, Sweetwater still hadn't heard from Nancy. He still planned to take some leave and go to Maui. The captain wanted to be at the mouth of Pearl Harbor at sunrise, and be tied up at the pier by 0730.

As Sweetwater and Sundance lay in their racks, Sweetwater had a brainstorm. He jumped out of bed, threw on his flight suit and was out the door before Sundance knew he was gone. He headed for strike ops, where the flight schedule was written for the ship. Commander Bob Gillett, better known as "Razor," was putting the final touches on the flight schedule when Sweetwater came flying in.

"Hey, Razor, where are you picking up the harbor pilot tomorrow morning?" he asked.

"He'll be at Honolulu International."

"Can I hop a ride on that helo in the morning?"

"Sure, we got plenty of room."

"Put me on that bad boy. I'll get clearance from my skipper and it'll save me a hassle at the pier. I'm going on leave to Maui and I can catch the early flight over to the island if the old man doesn't have heartburn with me leaving early. I'll let you know within the hour."

By eleven that night, Sweetwater had gotten permission to leave early. Whenever a carrier goes into an unfamiliar port, the harbor pilot for that area will assist the commanding officer in getting the ship through the channel safely.

By getting off the ship early, Sweetwater would save hours in getting over to Maui. This really was a good deal. When he returned to his stateroom, Sundance got up.

"Hey, Sundance, what's the matter? A little Channel Fever setting in?"

"Fuck you. At least my little honey will be at the pier to meet me."

This wasn't the smartest thing to say. Sweetwater really got hot, but thought, Hey, I started it. Patience was wearing thin at this point in the cruise. They all needed a break from one another. As Sweetwater started packing, Sundance said, "Aren't we starting to pack a little early?"

"Don't worry about me, butt breath."

"Ooh, getting a little testy are we?"

Sweetwater continued gathering his liberty clothes and finished packing without telling Sundance he was leaving at first light.

At 0500 Sweetwater got up and out of the room before Sundance was awake. He had to be in flight-deck control at 0515 for an 0545 launch. The trip to the beach would only take twenty minutes at the most. The crew was up preflighting the bird when he got into flight-deck control. The night handler said they would send the flight crewman in when it was time to load up. The blades were turning at 0540 and Sweetwater was on board for the 0545 lift-off.

The flight was uneventful and he was dropped off at the fixed-base operator's helo pad just south of the Aloha Airlines ramp. The customs agent was awaiting his arrival and he cleared customs without delay.

With his travel bag in one arm and golf clubs in the other, he looked like a genuine tourist. The walk to the Aloha Airlines ticket counter was less than a hundred yards. Talk about door-to-door service. After buying his ticket, Sweetwater headed down to the gate. The first flight wasn't until 0730, so he had about an hour wait. The waiting area was empty except for the custodial service, which was cleaning the floors. Sweetwater found a seat close to the gate, dropped his bags and sat down.

By 0645 people started filtering in and the waiting area started to get crowded. By seven-ten there was standing room only. A flight from Hong Kong had just arrived and there were a lot of passengers off that flight going to Maui.

As Sweetwater started to get in line, his heart skipped a beat. He said to himself, "I'll be a sonofabitch." Off in the distance he saw a woman who looked like Nancy, but he couldn't get a clear view of her because she was looking the other way. The day was right and she could have been on that Hong Kong flight. He took a closer look. At that moment, the woman turned around and it was Nancy, standing tall and looking like the princess she was.

He started pushing people out of the way to get to her. Leaving his bag and clubs in the chair, he started to call her name and after the third "Nancy!" she spotted him. They met halfway and he picked her off her feet and swung her around knocking people left and right. Then he started kissing her and kept telling her how much he'd missed her.

"Matt, Matt, slow down," she laughed, "You're making a scene."

"If they can't hack the program, they shouldn't have signed up," he said. "How have you been, Nancy? I was afraid I wouldn't see you. When did you get my letter?"

"You mean letters."

"How many did you get?"

"I think it was seven, plus a phone call from your friend in Diego."

"Well it's nice to know you can depend on someone to get the job done. You look great, Nancy."

"You don't look so bad yourself, big boy. In one of your letters you mentioned you had to punch out. Are you okay?"

"I feel like a million bucks, now. I'll tell you all

about it. Let's get on the plane and relax. Did you get us a room?''

''Yes, Matt, I got you a room and I got one for myself.''

''Oh. I was hoping we could share the expense.''

''We'll see. I don't want to ruin a good thing, if you know what I mean. Besides, let's get to know each other again and take it from there. I'm going to need to take a nap once we get settled in. The flight from Hong Kong was a killer.''

After landing in Maui, Sweetwater got a rent-a-car, while Nancy got the bags. When he pulled in front of the open-air terminal, he couldn't believe his eyes. Nancy had five bags and a big trunk. He said, ''Are you planning to stay a while?''

''You didn't receive any of my letters?''

''No, I sure didn't.''

''Well, that explains it. I quit my job and am moving back to the States.''

After a short lesson in packing a car, they were on their way to fun in the sun. They would be staying at the Westin Hotel on Kaanapali Beach. There were several golf courses close by, and the hotel had sailing and fishing trips available. The place was just about perfect. The crowds were nonexistent and it was nice being away from all the hustle and bustle of Wacky-Wacky.

They were at the front desk at ten o'clock but their rooms weren't ready. Sweetwater asked Nancy to get them a table near the ocean and they would have breakfast while they waited for the rooms. She went to request a table and he talked to the receptionist. He had a bottle of champagne sent to Nancy's room along with some flowers and a note that simply stated, ''Thank you for making me the happiest man on earth,'' and signed it, ''Your big boy.'' Then he joined her for breakfast.

After they ate, the rooms were made up and they checked in. They were on separate floors and Sweetwater told her to call when she got up from her nap, and that they would go to Seaweed Charlie's for dinner. He had a little piece of aviation memorabilia he wanted Torch to hang in his collection of naval history.

While Nancy slept, Sweetwater went shopping and rented a sailboat for the following morning.

At four o'clock the phone rang and it was Nancy to say she would be ready to go at five.

''Great,'' he said, ''see you in the lobby at five.''

At quarter to five he was down in the lobby, waiting. When she walked in she turned some heads. She had on a flowery Hawaiian dress with no bra. Her pert breasts bounced rhythmically as she walked toward him. She threw her arms around him and gave him a seductive kiss that blew the top of his head off, then thanked him for the champagne and flowers.

They had dinner reservations for seven o'clock, but wanted to get there for happy hour, so Sweetwater could give Seaweed Charlie his gift. As they pulled up to the front of the restaurant, one of the parking valets opened the car door for Nancy and escorted her to the entrance while Sweetwater got his claim check.

''Hey,'' Nancy said when he joined her at the door, ''this is a classic place.''

''Only the best for my little princess,'' he said.

As they walked in, Charlie was standing next to the bar talking to some guest. He and Water really didn't know each other, but they had mutual friends. Once they made eye contact, Charlie knew he and Sweetwater were from the same mold. He extended his hand

and welcomed them to his bar. Before he could say anything more, Sweetwater said, "Charlie, how are you? I just came in on the *Enterprise* from an extended Westpac. This is my friend, Nancy."

Nancy extended her hand and said, "Hi, Charlie, I've heard a lot about you."

Sweetwater cut in to say, "Hey, Charlie, I have a little something for your collection."

"Great, what've you got?"

"I had to punch out over the Med and I want you to have the lower ejection handle that fired me out of my aircraft."

"Thanks. You guys really raised some hell over there. Glad you got out okay. It looks like you didn't get hurt. What outfit are you with?"

"VFA-114."

"Oh, yeah, the Fighting Aardvarks. Great squadron. How do you like the Hornet?"

"It's a mean machine."

"Listen, the drinks are on me tonight, your money is no good in here."

"No, no," Sweetwater argued.

"Hey, shipmate, I'm the boss in here."

"Roger that," Sweetwater said, as Charlie escorted them to one of the better tables with a view. He and Nancy drank and ate some of the finest seafood in Maui, then danced until the early morning. They couldn't thank Charlie enough for his gracious hospitality.

The ride back to the hotel seemed like it took forever. As they pulled up in front, the valet took the car and Sweetwater walked Nancy up to her room, hoping she would invite him in. But he wasn't going to push the issue if she didn't. They hugged and kissed, then those dreaded five words came out, "See you in the morning. Thank you for the gifts, Matt. I'll call you when I get up.''

"Okay. See you later." As he walked to the elevator, he thought, This gal is really special and I'm not going to let her get away.

The next morning, Sweetwater was awakened by the phone ringing in his ear. "Good morning," he said picking up the phone.

"How is my big boy doing this morning?" a sweet voice replied.

"Just fine, how about you?"

"I feel great! I just got back from a half-mile swim in the ocean. Boy, was that ever refreshing. Shall we go to breakfast?"

"Sure. Let me shit and shower—I mean, let me get cleaned up and I'll meet you poolside.''

"Okay, see you in thirty minutes.''

As he hung up, Sweetwater thought, Jeez, I better watch my language. Eight months at sea can make one's lingo pretty foul.

While at breakfast, he asked Nancy if she would like to go sailing. Her eyes opened as big as saucers. "Where? How?" she exclaimed.

"Well, I rented a boat for us at ten o'clock and we have it for three hours.''

"Oh boy, I've always wanted to go sailing in Hawaii.''

They had an hour to kill before it was time to pick up the boat. They walked around the shops looking for some gifts for Nancy's parents. She hadn't been home for two years and would fly home after she left Hawaii.

At ten o'clock they were standing at the rental booth for the sailboat. Sweetwater had reserved a sixteen-foot Hobie Cat, and one of the employees was rigging it while they got checked out on its gear. The waves were breaking rather close to shore, so the guy who rigged the sail helped them get out past the breakwater. Once past the breakers, they were off like a shot. The wind started to pick up and it was just a perfect day for sailing.

Sweetwater hadn't sailed a Hobie Cat for almost six years, but he didn't let on. Everything went well. They talked about their time apart and his close call. All in all, it was precious time. On their way back in, Nancy got close and gave him a hug and kiss and told him how much she enjoyed being with him and how special he was to her. This was music to his ears. There was something about this woman that he still hadn't figured out. Whatever it was, it made her special, more special than any other woman he had been with, even Ginny, who he once had thought was the girl for him.

As they got closer to the shore, he could see the waves were really big and if he didn't approach the beach correctly, he would bust the boat and their asses, not to mention blowing his image as a dashing seaman. Things must have been going his way, because as he started to make the approach, the guy who had rigged the sails waved him off and another couple started to swim out to the cat.

Great, he thought. Now, I just have to make a 360 and get close enough for them to get aboard. They made a clean transfer and he and Nancy jumped off to swim ashore. They thanked the rental people for a great time and headed for the pool.

They lounged around the pool for the rest of the day and decided to have an early dinner at the Rusty Harpoon, which was close by. He walked Nancy to her room so she could clean up for dinner and she asked him in for a drink. "Say, Matt, let's drink some of this champagne you sent up. And I have something I want you to open."

Sitting next to the flowers was a white envelope with Sweetwater written across the front. "Matt, this is your birthday gift."

"Birthday gift? How do you know when my birthday is?" he asked.

"Oh, I have my ways. Open the champagne and then you can open your present."

He walked over to Nancy, put his arms around her and started to rub her neck and nibble her ear as he guided her over to the bed. As the backs of her legs hit the side of the bed, he forced her to fall back on the king-size mattress. By this time the juices were flowing and he was so hard a cat couldn't get his claws into his erection. As they rolled around on the bed, things started to get really heated, but Nancy said, "Matt, we better stop."

He kept after her, but she pushed him back and he knew he better relax. They got up and he went over to open the champagne.

"Boy, you sure know how to get me going."

"Matt, I want to make love to you, but I need more time. I really care for you, and I don't want to be just another name in your book. The time will come when I feel right and our relationship will be more than a fling in Hawaii. Do you understand how I feel?"

"Yes, I do. And I respect you for your honesty."

Now that things were out in the open, he knew where he stood with her and didn't have to be totally frustrated, sexually and mentally.

As he grabbed the champagne bottle, he asked her if

she had ever seen a bottle of champagne opened with a knife.

"God, no!" she replied. "What are you going to do?"

"Watch this, my dear."

"Be careful, Matt."

"You take the bottle," he said, "and shake it up." Then he took a knife room service had left in the room to cut fruit with and whacked the neck off the bottle, just below the cork. A clean cut was executed, and Ms. Nancy stood in awe.

"How did you do that?" she asked.

"Shaking the bottle causes the pressure inside to build and when you hit the neck of the bottle the pressure is released so fast that you get a nice clean cut and no mess."

"Pretty slick," she said, "but I don't think I'll try it for a while."

Sweetwater poured two glasses full and reached for the envelope. "What do we have here?" he asked, pulling the upper seal open. He read the note inside, looked at Nancy in disbelief and said, "How in the world did you know I wanted to do this?"

She had given him a day of sport fishing. He had always wanted to do it but never could afford it.

"I knew you liked to fish from our talks in Perth. So tomorrow, my love, we both are going out on the high seas to catch the big one."

"How did you arrange this?" he said.

"I looked in the Yellow Pages, found where these sport-fishing outfits were located and went down to the pier this morning after my swim and set the trip up."

"You're something else. What time do we have to be there?"

"We sail at seven and will be back by five."

He downed his glass of champagne. "See you in thirty minutes and we'll go to dinner."

After dinner they walked around the shopping mall and picked up some food for the fishing trip. The excitement he was feeling reminded him of when he and his dad would go on their yearly fishing trip. Sweetwater knew he'd have trouble sleeping, thinking about the possibility of catching the big one. As they walked back to the hotel, Nancy asked if he wanted to stay over.

He said, "That's a stupid question. Of course I want to stay with you."

They put the food in the refrigerator and called the front desk to wake them at five. They had to be at the pier early or they wouldn't get a parking spot. It was going to be hard keeping his hands off her, but he knew the ground rules and if he wanted her respect, he knew he had better cool it. They hugged, kissed and held each other until they both fell asleep.

The phone rang at five sharp. Sweetwater jumped out of bed and told Nancy he was going up to his room to get cleaned up. He said he'd meet her in the lobby at five-thirty.

"Okay, Matt," she replied, "and thanks for being so understanding."

"Don't worry, Princess. It's easy when you care for someone," he said as he closed the door.

At 0530 they were in the car and on the way to the sport-fishing pier. They parked the car and went over to a fast-food store for breakfast. The boat launch was only a block or so away. By 0630 people started showing up. Nancy had said there would be three other fishermen along, for a total of five, plus two crew members.

The boat's name was the *Maui Surfer* and it was forty feet long. After everyone met and paid the balance of their bill, they loaded aboard.

The captain's name was Slim, for obvious reasons. He was about six-five and weighed about 160 pounds. His face was weathered and the long bill cap he wore fit the image. The first mate, who handled all the rods and reels, was a young guy in his early twenties. Once they were all aboard, the captain gathered them around to brief them on the day's events and what procedures would be used when a fish was caught.

The first item was to give everyone a number. Since Nancy was the only woman aboard, she received number one, Sweetwater got two, the man next to him three and so on, until all five had a number. "Once we get to the fishing area," Andy, the first mate said, "I'll put the lines out. When a fish hits one, I'll call out the number of the rod, and whoever it is, you get into the chair. You may be in the chair for ten minutes or three hours, depending how big your fish is. Are there any questions?"

Nancy asked, "What happens to the other rods when someone hooks a fish?"

"Good question, Nancy," replied Andy. "Once the individual is in the chair and I've given the rod to him, I'll reel in the rest of the rods. Then the fight is on. Whoever's in the chair, just listen to me and we'll get your fish aboard. By the way, has anyone been sport fishing before?"

One man raised his hand. "Okay, each captain likes to run his boat differently, so what I've laid out for you is how we'll operate today and we'll work out any problems when and if they arise. Okay, sit down and relax. We have about an hour ride before we get to the fishing area. Remember our motto. 'This is not a sight-seeing trip, we're out to catch fish.' '' At that point, the captain lit off the twin diesels, backed the *Maui Surfer* out of her slip, and headed for open water.

As the boat headed for the area they would be fishing, Andy started rigging the rods and the guests aboard got to know each other. They would be fishing on the back side of Molokai. Slim said that he hadn't been up there for a while and he had a feeling the fishing would be great.

As they got close to the fishing area, Andy started putting out lines. Nancy's went out first. The bait used was pretty interesting stuff. It had two large hooks lying one behind the other with red, white and blue streamers covering them. A three-inch, circular, clear fiberglass plug was in front of the hooks and streamers. The line was let out about forty yards behind the boat.

Nancy's rod was on the port outrigger, with Sweet-water's just forward of hers in a rod-holding apparatus. His line was out about sixty yards. Two other rods were set up similarly on the starboard side and one was rigged from the top of the navigation platform. The ride out to Molokai was fairly smooth, but as they turned to her windward side, it started to get rough. The swells were about four feet and getting higher. So far, everyone was doing fine.

After about an hour, they had traversed the back side of the island. The sights were spectacular. They saw three-hundred-foot waterfalls and views that would take your breath away. But they were there to catch fish, not sightsee. Slim wheeled the boat around and started another sweep of the area. He told Sweetwater that boats didn't go up in that section much because of the rough seas and the distance.

Within ten minutes after they turned around, all hell broke loose. *Snap! Zing, zing!* went the number two rod. The first mate started yelling, "Number two in the chair! Number two in the chair!"

Nancy slapped him on the back and said, "That's you, big boy, get into the chair."

Sweetwater jumped up and got into the chair, as Andy was handing him the rod. As he put his feet up on the support pedals and hooked himself into the chair, the rod went into the holder between his legs. He grabbed the blue rubber area in front of the reel with his left hand and reeled with his right.

As he made his first pull back on the rod, to get some slack to reel in, the fish came out of the water like a breeching whale. Boy was he big. Sweetwater could almost see the fish eyeing him, as if to say, "Okay, hotshot, let's see who tires first." Back in the water he went. Within twenty seconds, out he came again, this time fighting and twisting like a warrior. Then he went back into the water and dove like a detected submarine.

Things on the boat were hectic. Andy was reeling in the other lines, while Slim was maneuvering the boat to fight the fish. Within ten minutes all lines were in the boat and all attention was on the man in the chair. At this point, Sweetwater knew this was not a lake trout like he used to catch in Dexter, Maine. And it wasn't as easy as it looked on the TV show *American Sportsman*.

After forty-five minutes of pulling and reeling, Sweetwater thought his shoulders were going to be pulled out of their sockets. Andy was right beside him, coaching and supporting his efforts. Several times he wanted to let someone else feel the pain this big bastard was inflicting on him, but Andy graciously insisted, "You hooked 'im, you bring him in."

As time went on, he asked Andy what type of fish it was. Andy said, "It's either a striped marlin or a blue marlin. And the way he's fighting, it looks like a blue."

Slim knew it was a blue right off the bat. He'd been doing this for fifteen years and knew every trait of every sport fish. But each fish fought differently.

As the battle approached the hour mark, progress was finally being made. They were almost up to the forty-foot splice. When the line reached that point, Andy, wearing a pair of heavy gloves, would wrap the line around his hand and start pulling the fish to the surface. Once he got him close, Slim would jump down from the navigation platform, grab the gaff and gaff the fish.

Everyone on the boat had to stay out of the way because with the gaff in the fish, and Andy and Slim trying to get it aboard, things would be flying. Sweetwater was instructed to sit in the chair and man the reel in case the marlin made a run for it. You don't realize the power of one of these fish until you're trying to reel him in.

At one hour and ten minutes the splice was visible. Andy grabbed the line and Sweetwater said to himself, "Thank God." He was beat. As the fish came close to the surface, he could see the beautiful iridescent colors in its side and back. Suddenly, the marlin must have seen the boat: he made a run for it. Andy had the line wrapped so that if the fish made a run, he could release it without getting injured. Off he went and the fight was back on.

Sweetwater was thinking, I can't fight this sonofa-bitch much longer. Another fifteen minutes went by before he saw the splice again. Nancy and the rest of the guys aboard were cheering him on, but all he could focus on was getting that splice up to the point where Andy could grab the line.

At an hour and thirty minutes, Andy had the line and was pulling the fish to the surface. The call for Slim came and the pros were hard at work. The fish made a dive for the props to try to cut the line, but Andy hung on and got the fish at an angle where Slim could gaff him. Once the gaff was set, they pulled him alongside the boat and killed him by whacking him in the head with a bat. The other men in the boat helped pull it aboard, and after an hour and forty minutes, the big marlin was in the boat. Slim and Andy felt it would go close to three hundred pounds.

After all motion had stopped in the boat and the fish was incapacitated, Nancy jumped up and threw her arms around Sweetwater and gave him a big kiss. Then the rest of the fishermen and crew shook his hand and asked if it was Miller time yet. They popped a few beers and rested before putting the lines back in the water—minus Sweetwater's. He was done for the day. Not because he caught a fish, but because he couldn't have done battle again if he had to.

Within a half hour they were back fishing. It was about twelve-thirty and the sea was really beginning to rock and roll. Nancy was beginning to feel a little green, as was one of the other fishermen. Two hours went by without a strike and it was time to start home. This didn't bother anyone, because it was getting real roug-hand after almost eight hours of rocking around they all had had enough. The ride back to port seemed like an eternity; they pulled into the slip at ten to five.

On the way home, Slim had called ahead on his short-wave radio to let his boss at pierside know that they had caught a big blue. The more people he could have gathered around when the boat pulled in, the more advertising he received, thus helping him get future bookings.

As the boat tied up, a large crowd had gathered on the pier. Nancy got her feet on the ground and began to feel a little better. She never did vomit, but later admitted to almost losing it. The fish was hoisted off the boat and weighed. Three hundred and forty-four pounds, ten feet six inches long were the measurements. People were asking Sweetwater if he was going to have it mounted and he told them he wasn't sure what he was going to do with it. It was so big and would cost too much for him to have it mounted, so he asked Slim if he knew of anyone who wanted it. At this point Nancy said, "How about Seaweed Charlie's place? I saw a great place to hang it."

"Good idea, Nancy. Let's head over there for a drink and see if he wants it. Hey, Slim, give me an hour and I'll let you know if I'm going to keep it."

"Okay, but if you aren't back in an hour, the fish is mine."

"You got a deal." They said good-bye to the people they'd fished with, got a bunch of pictures taken and headed for Seaweed Charlie's just down the street.

As Sweetwater and Nancy walked toward the bar, Nancy said "Let's not stay too long. I want to get back to the hotel and get cleaned up. Besides, I don't really feel like drinking. I still feel like I'm on the high seas."

"You'll feel better once the vestibular apparatus in your inner ear settles down."

"How do you know that?"

"The same thing happens when you're flying and you get air sick. It takes a while for the vestibular apparatus in your semicircular canals to settle down. Once on stable ground, you'll be fine.''

When they reached the bar, Charlie was greeting guests as they entered. "Hey, Sweetwater. And Nancy." He never forgot a face or name he wanted to remember. "Good to see you again. Come on in and let me buy you a drink."

"No, Charlie, the drinks are on me."

"What happened, Sweetwater, did you two get married?"

"No, not yet," he said. A twinkle came into Nancy's eye.

"Then what's up?"

"You wouldn't believe what happened today. Nancy gave me a sport-fishing trip for my birthday and we went today. I caught a three-hundred-and-forty-four-pound blue marlin and we want to know if you would like to mount it in here."

Nancy said, "It would look great hanging over the entrance to the Seaweed Room."

"You know, Water, you've just made my day, and Nancy you must have been reading my mind. I was in the process of trying to find a sailfish or a marlin to hang and, my friend, you have solved my problems. Sure I'll take it."

"Listen, watch Nancy. I have to tell the guys at the boat that I'm going to keep it and get the name of the place where they do the mounting and put a deposit down. I'll write a check and you can pay me when I return."

Sweetwater felt a lot better now that someone could use the fish, otherwise it would be used for dog food, since blue marlin isn't good for human consumption. He went back to the slip, advised Slim of his wants and paid him for the mounting. He filled out the paperwork for where he wanted the fish sent once it was completed and thanked the guys for a great trip.

He also gave Andy a nice tip for his help and professionalism. Then he headed back to Charlie's place.

As he walked in, he could see a crowd of people gathered around Nancy. She was telling everyone the story about the big catch. He went over to Charlie, handed him the paperwork, and told him he would have his fish in three months. "How much do I owe you, Sweetwater," he asked.

"Twenty-two-hundred dollars."

"It doesn't surprise me. Those things don't come cheap. Let me write you a check."

After Charlie gave him the check, Sweetwater went over and put his arm around Nancy and asked her how she was feeling.

"Oh, much better. Let's go after you finish your drink."

As he downed his drink, Nancy leaned over and asked, "Do you think we really might get married one day?"

Sweetwater smiled.

16

Sex and
the Naval Aviator

Nancy and Sweetwater finished their drinks, and thanked Charlie for his hospitality. He thanked them in turn for the marlin and they headed back to the car. As they walked, Sweetwater couldn't stop thanking Nancy enough for the great birthday gift, an opportunity of a lifetime. They planned to get a bite to eat at the hotel and just relax, since this was to be their last night in Maui.

The next day they would fly back to Oahu to spend their last day together. Sweetwater had to be back at the ship by 0800 the following day, because the *Enterprise* would get underway at 1000. They had reservations at a hotel on Waikiki Beach for the night and Nancy would drop him off at the ship and leave Hawaii that afternoon for the mainland.

After dinner Nancy and Sweetwater walked on the beach arm in arm, watching the moon come up over the pineapple fields. It wasn't until then that he started to relax and unwind from the several months at sea. It usually took him a week or so to slow down and become a type B person. The stresses of deployment are overwhelming and it really takes a while to unwind and come back to reality. The evening was peaceful and very calm, a perfect night to spend their last hours together.

They arrived at Honolulu Airport at 1330 and were on their way to Waikiki Beach by two. When they pulled up to the hotel, the beach area was packed with tourists and *Enterprise* sailors. Sweetwater thought, Boy, am I glad we went to Maui. It wasn't so crowded and it was much more romantic.

The valet parked their car and they checked into the hotel. While standing at the counter, Sweetwater heard a loud voice yell, "Hey, Water, you one-eyed lizard." He didn't even have to turn around. He knew by the voice it could only be Slick, and sure enough it was.

When he walked up to them, Water introduced Nancy to Slick and asked him how his in-port stay had been.

"It's been great, but we missed seeing you do your famous dirty gator at the Blue Note." That was a small bar along the strip, where some of Sweetwater's legendary antics had taken place.

"What's the dirty gator?" Nancy asked.

Sweetwater was trying to wave Slick off, but it was too late. Slick was on a roll, and Sweetwater had to let him explain the dance to her.

"Well, Nancy, what the Water will do is find some nice filly who thinks she's God's gift to the dance floor and humble her a little by doing this unbelievable gyration with his body. What he will do is dance up a storm, then jump and go completely horizontal to the floor, land on his stomach, flop his hands and feet, roll over on his back, put his hands and feet in the air, move them up and down several times then get back up and continue dancing like nothing happened. The only problem is, everyone else is laughing so hard they can't believe what they've just witnessed, and the girl whothought she knew every dance step goes into shock. I've seen him humble many a woman with that dance.''

Nancy was grinning from ear to ear. ''Well, big boy, are we going to get to see this two-step tonight?'' she asked.

''Let's see how the night goes.''

Slick stopped laughing long enough to say, ''Hey, there's a big cocktail party on the twenty-second floor at seven. Why don't you and Nancy come?''

Sweetwater and Nancy looked at each other, gave each other the high sign, and Sweetwater said, ''We'll be there.''

''Great,'' Slick replied. ''A lot of the wives have flown over and Nancy can get to meet some of them.''

Their room was on the fifteenth floor overlooking Diamond Head, and the view was breathtaking. While they unpacked, Sweetwater ordered some food to enjoy with the scenery. At six they started to get ready for the gathering. The squadrons usually had a big party when they pulled in, but everyone was so beat that they waited until the last night in port. They would not be flying until the second day out, so everyone could enjoy themselves and have a good time.

They arrived at quarter to eight and the party was in full swing. It was great seeing spirits high again and harmony restored. After long at-sea periods, everyone just needs to be alone for a few days to unwind. Slick's girlfriend had flown in and Bullet Bob's wife was there. Sweetwater was looking for Sundance to apologize for his behavior before he'd left the ship, but he didn't see him. Slick introduced Mary to Nancy and they started up a conversation.

"Hey, Slick," Water said, "have you seen Sundance?"

"Saw him yesterday on the beach with two pelts that would have made you stand tall."

Sweetwater snapped around to see if Nancy heard that remark, and Slick said, "Don't worry, Sweetwater, they're out on the balcony."

By nine-thirty, everyone was having a ball. Sundance had showed up with his two lady friends and Slick was right. They were lookers. Sweetwater had time to make amends with loverboy before he hit the silk. When Sundance got some oil aboard, he was hard to outwit. Slick tried to introduce Mary and Nancy to him, but he was on a different cloud formation.

The classic was when he asked Sundance if he planned to marry one of the gals, and Sundance said with a straight face, "You know, Slick, there are three things you always rent in life."

"And what might they be, lover boy?" Slick asked.

Sundance replied, "Boats, planes and women."

On that note Sundance said, "Let's go dancing." He headed out the door with one girl on each arm.

Sweetwater and Nancy took a rain check. They wanted to spend some time alone and figure out when they might see each other again. He was becoming very attached to her, and still trying to sort out in his mind what made her so different from most of the women he'd dated, especially Ginny. Oh well, he thought, It'll come to me one day.

They said good night to everyone and went to their room.

After they got back to the room, Nancy said she was going to get comfortable and he might want to join her. As she went into the bathroom, she purposely left the door open a foot or so. From where he was sitting, he had a perfect view of Nancy. As he pretended not to be watching, she slowly unbuttoned her dress and slipped it down around her ankles and hung it behind the door. The hanging of the dress caused the door to close almost shut, but he had a straight shot to the mirror, which gave him a ballpark view.

As she slipped her bra off, he started to become aroused and wanted to go into the bathroom and attack her, but his better judgment told him this was a test. He felt sure she knew he was watching her, so he played along. She turned on the shower and climbed in. He thought he probably should have been the one taking the shower. After twenty minutes she came out refreshed and as beautiful as ever.

"Okay, Matt. Your turn," she said.

Sweetwater went in, took a quick shower, and was back with her in ten minutes.

They had some wine and talked about their future. He wanted Nancy to be at the fly-in when he arrived in San Diego. She had talked to Mary, Slick's girlfriend, at the party and Mary had offered to let her stay at her place until the day of the fly-in, scheduled for Friday morning, August 2nd, at ten A.M.

"If I stay," she asked, "will you fly home to St. Paul with me on Sunday, to meet my folks?"

He thought a moment, then said, "Sure, I'd love to meet your parents." He had over seventy days of leave on the books, and had never seen that part of the country.

"Good, I'll call Mary in the morning and let her know I plan to meet you on the fly-in. We'll rearrange our flights so that we can fly home together."

Things are starting to happen a little fast, he thought.

Go home to meet her parents? What does this woman have up her sleeve?

He didn't feel threatened, but he didn't want Nancy to get the idea that she had him wrapped around her finger. They talked till the wee hours of the morning and fell asleep about two A.M.

The wake up call came about six-thirty and neither of them really wanted to get up. But duty called, and it was time to get a move on. While Nancy was getting ready, he paid their bill and checked them out.

They left the hotel at 0730 and were at pierside by eight. As the farewells were being said, the tears started to fall. The pier was a madhouse with all the guests who were going to ride the ship back to Alameda. Getting to the officers' brow was almost impossible. Sweetwater was not one for lengthy good-byes, so he gave Nancy a big hug and kiss, and told her he'd see her in a few days. At that point, he heard someone calling her name. It was Mary, who had just dropped Slick off. She had been heading back to the car when she spotted Nancy.

At 1000, the ship's whistle blew and the call came, "Ship's under way. Shift colors." People standing on the pier could hardly tell the massive carrier was moving. The tugboats were pulling her away from the pier so she could make her way out the channel. Within a couple of minutes you could see it was pulling away from the pier and making way.

After he dropped his gear in his room, Sweetwater changed into his uniform and headed to the roof. He walked to the bow where he told Nancy he'd be as the ship left port. It took him a while to spot her in the crowd, but he finally saw her standing by the security gate, waving and throwing kisses. He didn't see Mary, so she must have headed back to the hotel. Nancy had never seen an aircraft carrier up close, so it must have been quite a thrill for her to see the *Enterprise* leaving port.

As they pulled out of the channel and he lost sight of Nancy, it began to hit him just how much she meant to him and that he really did want their relationship to go somewhere.

Once they cleared the breakwater and hit the open sea, Sweetwater headed to the ready room to see what was planned for the first day. They had an air-wing briefing in the wardroom at two o'clock. A flight surgeon and a highway patrolman were to be the guest speakers. At eleven-thirty, the commanding officer wanted to get the squadron together and talk with the men about the upcoming flight schedule and events that would take place before and after they returned home.

At eleven-thirty the skipper entered and the men all came to attention.

"Be seated please," he began. "Well, men, we are almost at the end of the most successful deployment in naval history. We have accomplished more on this deployment than five carriers have in thirty years. As you know, these next few days can be very dangerous, if we get complacent. There are a lot of guests aboard and many of you have your relatives here to enjoy the transit back to the mainland. We will be putting on an air demo day after tomorrow. For those of you who will be flying in that demonstration, use your heads and don't let your guard down. I don't want to lose anyone this late in the game. Be smart, watch out for your shipmates and their guests, and most of all, think safety. See you all at two for the air-wing brief. From what I heard, it is a great presentation. Carry on."

Sundance and Sweetwater went back to their state-room to unpack and tell tales about their in-port stay. Sundance was still a little pissed about Water's hasty departure, but it was cleared up as fast as it was brought up. That's one of the reasons they got along so well. If something was on one of their minds they would get it out in the open and discuss it and press on. People who keep things inside them on these cruises go nuts or have a bad attitude most of the deployment.

After an hour of bullshitting, they headed down to the Wardroom where the brief was to be held. Not all of the air-wing officers would be able to fit in the room, so a second brief was arranged for seven that evening for those who didn't make it at two. They were there twenty minutes early, and still almost didn't get in.

At 1400 the CO of the ship, Captain Frost, entered, and all came to attention. "Please be seated, gentle-men," he said. "Today we are privileged to have two gentlemen brief us on the effects of a Western Pacific deployment and how we can better prepare ourselves for our return to the States. The first gentleman to speak is Captain Spike Prescott, a California highway patrol-man. His topic will be 'The Westpac Swing.' Our sec-ond guest speaker is the Airpac head flight surgeon, Dr. Frank Shiney, whose topic will be 'Sex and the Naval Aviator.' So without any further ado, here's Captain Prescott."

A warm, welcoming applause greeted him as he walked to the podium. "Good afternoon, gentlemen. It's a pleasure to be with the elite of the fleet. You men sure have made your country proud of what you have accomplished over the past eight and a half months and my job today is to make you aware of what you are coming back to in relation to highway safety. Gentlemen, you may have been fighting terrorists overseas, but you are about to face a different breed of enemy and that is the drunk driver, the driver who is high on drugs, and your good old speeders. They are all out to kill you. Yes, gentlemen, kill *you*. You men have been away from driving for almost a year, and some of you probably haven't driven since you left on deployment, so listen to what I have to say today: it may save your life.''

Prescott went on to discuss some of the new rules and regulations that had been developed while the *Enterprise* had been deployed. He pointed out the importance of wearing seat belts and showed a film on highway accidents which really caught the audience's attention.

''Now, you gentlemen are probably wondering what the Westpac Swing is all about. Well, I usually save this for my closing. I've been giving these briefs all over California for the last ten years and I came up with the concept of Westpac Swing after observing sailors returning from extended deployments. What I'm about to divulge is what I've learned during many hours of standing on overpasses, observing drivers on Highways 805 and 5.''

Prescott paused for effect, sweeping the room once with his eyes before continuing. ''What I observed was that there are two distinct types of problem driver. One is the driver who had too much to drink. You could hear him coming a mile away. The way you knew this was it would be quiet for a while, then you would hear the thumping of the tires going across the lane dividers, then it would get quiet again. After listening to this for a mile or so, a rhythm would be set, and as the car passed under the overpass a call would be made to the chase car and he would pull the car over. Nine times out of ten the driver had been drinking."

The air-wing officers were paying close attention. Prescott had hooked them with his dramatic delivery. "Then comes the returning sailor fresh from a nine-month deployment. After all the kisses and hugs and all baggage and children are loaded into the car, dad has to show he is still the boss, so he hops behind the wheel of his big Ford station wagon and heads for his home sweet home. Well, gentlemen, this is where the term Westpac Swing came from. After dad is behind the wheel for a minute or so and he is over the Coronado Bridge, the stories and adventures of his trip start to flow. Eye contact with the wife and children is important and hand expression is most effective when giving detailed descriptions of events that took place. Therefore, his attention to driving is minimal at most. So, as I stand on the overpass, and listen to the tires crossing the lane dividers, I have to stop and think, 'Is this another driver that has had too much to drink, or has a carrier just returned from Westpac?' "

The men buzzed a bit. Prescott had nailed their behavior almost perfectly. They all knew it, and it made them a little uncomfortable. When the buzzing died down, Prescott smiled. "My point here, gentlemen, is let the wife, girlfriend, or a friend drive you home the first day of your return. We don't want you to be another California highway statistic. Welcome home and drive safely. Thank you."

A loud applause rang out in the wardroom as Captain Prescott left the podium. Captain Frost said, "Let's take a ten-minute break before Dr. Shiney speaks."

After the break was over, the CO introduced Captain Shiney, the Airpac flight surgeon. Again, the officers

gave him a warm welcome as he approached the podium.

"Well, good afternoon, gentlemen. I must say it's a
real treat to be here and especially to talk to such an
honorable group. My topic of discussion today is 'Sex
and the Naval Aviator.' Now, many of you may have
misinterpreted the subject of my lecture today, but by
the end of my talk I think you'll be reading me loud
and clear.

"As you look around this room, you will see a self-
selected audience. A group of men who enjoy what
they are doing, but pay the highest price tag for failure.
You are shit-hot people, you are sexy people, who do
sexy things, like fly high-performance jets off aircraft
carriers."

The audience interrupted with a loud "Right!"

Shiney smiled, but didn't let it faze him. "You bet
I'm right. Now, let me show you something about
yourselves. If I were to take a survey in downtown
Bangor, Maine, on oldest sons, how many people would
it take? Probably one in three would be your figure.
How many here are oldest sons?"

The men seemed confused. They laughed, but Shiney wasn't joking. He counted raised hands. "Aha!
Take a look gentlemen, about seventy percent of the
men in this room are oldest sons. Now, how many men
usually make the dean's list?" Again, the men were
confused, but Shiney was using it for a purpose. He let
them puzzle a bit before answering the question himself. "About five out of one hundred. How many in
this room were dean's list?"

Again hands were raised, and Shiney nodded. "Look
around, gentlemen. About sixty-five percent of you
were on the dean's list in college. Something is hap-

pening here. How many in this room played a varsity
sport that knocked the shit out of the opponent: wrestling, boxing, football, something like that?''

More hands this time. ''Look, almost eighty-five
percent. Okay, see what I'm trying to point out here?
You guys are self-selected overachievers. You are com-
plex weapon platforms and you are goddamn good at
what you do. By the way, do you know how you can
tell an F/A-18 pilot?''

The crowd answered, ''No!''

''His watch cost more than his suit. You know how
you can tell if a guy is an aviator?''

This time, he was greeted by total silence. ''He's
always trying to cash a check.'' The crowd exploded
into laughter.

Sweetwater leaned over to Sundance and said, ''This
doc has got our number pegged. Most of the items he's
touched on fit us to a T.''

Shiney continued, ''The chief feature that you gentlemen possess is that you like being in control of people and events. Just like your F/A-18. When you move
that stick and rudder to the right, that Hornet banks as
hard and long as you want it to, and when you want to
stop, you neutralize the stick and rudder and come back
to level flight. Right?'' the doctor asked. ''But, when
you're *not* in control, then you become uncomfortable.
This is when you build in calculated emotional distance. You gents are mission-oriented, compartmental-
ized, systematic and methodical to the point that you
are predictable.

''Now, the reason I'm pointing all these traits out to
you is because in a few short days you will be rejoining
your loved ones and you need to adjust your ways of
doing things. For example, when you are at the dinner

table, you don't ask, 'Pass the fucking potatoes, please,' and you don't stand in line ten minutes prior to dinner. You've been in an environment where you have been in control. Those of you who are married and are going home to families must remember, your wives have been running the household while you've been away, and you have to work your way back into the family style of living. You can't return home after nine months and expect to be the boss. Believe me, gentlemen, it won't work, and you'll have some rough times ahead if you take that route.''

Shiney had touched a nerve, and he knew it. Most of the men had been out before, and they had been through it. ''The one thing that is dreaded the most by a returning shit-hot overworked aviator, is the 'Post-deployment Talk' with your wife. She wants you to sit down and listen to all the hardships that occurred while you were gone, and God forbid you don't act interested. Remember, women carry an invisible trash bag over their shoulders. They put all the little hurts in it, to be pulled out and used against you at any time, and that bag never, never gets emptied. So you need to be sympathetic and understanding of her emotions. You must also remember, controllers marry controllers. That's why Navy wives are a special breed, and can carry the load while you're off protecting our nation's defense. You have an adjustment to make, gentlemen, and you need to start reprogramming.''

The room grew quiet, as Shiney held up a hand. ''The last item I want to touch on is the infamous carrier air-wing fly-off. For those of you who will be flying off to your home bases in a couple of days, don't become complacent. There are planes on this ship that have been hangar queens most of the deployment. If it isn't ready to fly, don't fly it. What this insidious carrier air-wing fly-off really is, is the 'Get-home-itis and the get-off-this-fucking-boat syndrome.'

"Remember, familiarity breeds contempt. You hot-shot war heroes feel you have the world by the ass because you've survived another Westpac without buying the farm. Take a moment and remember when you first walked out to that T-34B at Saufley Field. You were a humble student, who probably used more runway horizontally than vertically to take off your first several times and you probably almost puked on your PS-7 spin flight. But, as you became proficient in the T-34, you felt more comfortable and started to let your guard down, until you stood beside that T-2C Buckeye which had no visible means of propulsion and then you reverted right back to being overly cautious again. Have a flashback on me, gentlemen, before you strap on that machine for the carrier air-wing fly-off. Thank you for the opportunity to talk with you today." He was rewarded with loud applause. A standing ovation helped escort Captain Shiney back to his seat.

Captain Frost took the podium just long enough to say, "This concludes the briefs. Dismissed."

As Sweetwater and Sundance headed back to their stateroom, they couldn't get over how well both speakers brought them back to reality. They were both great presentations and, who knows, they may have just saved someone's life or marriage by pointing out a few basic rules.

The ship was a madhouse with all the friends and relatives aboard. You couldn't go fifty feet without someone asking you how to get back to where he started from. It was heartwarming to see the young sons of the pilots and crew members walking with their dads to the aircraft they fly or the shop they worked in. Sweetwater hoped one day to have his son walking alongside, as he showed him the plane he flew and the ship he lived on for nine months at a time.

The first two days after leaving Hawaii are fun for the guests, but then they start to get a little restless and can't wait to get off the ship. That's when the sailors bring them down to their short hairs, by asking, "How would you like to be on this floating hotel for nine months?" That usually gets them back on track real fast.

On the second day, the aircrews got back to the business of getting airplanes ready to fly. The third day would be the flight demo, which would show bombing of a target being towed behind the ship, in-flight refueling, high-speed flybys and a rescue at sea of a man overboard. The fourth day would be the air-wing fly-off. Eighty-seven airplanes would fly back to their respective home bases and the only aircraft remaining would be those that were hard down and needed more work and the helos that would act as channel guards for the ship when it entered port.

Sweetwater, Sundance, and Slick weren't flying in the air demo. They had flown in many before and wanted some of the junior officers to get the experience. None of the three had guests aboard, and they wanted those pilots who did to fly so their families and friends could see them perform.

At ten A.M. on the third day out, fifteen aircraft started their engines and the flight deck of the *Enterprise* was noisier than the Brickyard at the Indy 500. A lot of the guests were up on the 0-10 level watching as the flight-deck crew prepared the aircraft for the launch.

Once all aircraft were airborne, then the crew and their guests could come out on the deck to watch the show.

Bullet Bob, as air-wing commander, would lead the diamond formation flyby at six hundred feet to open up the air demo. Sweetwater, Sundance and a couple of the fathers whose sons were flying in the demo were standing on Catapult Four when the diamond of F/A-18s flew by. After the noise settled, an announcement for Lieutenant Commander Sullivan to report to flight-deck control was made on the 5-MC. He told Sundance, "Hey, I'll see what's up and talk with you in a bit."

"Okay, Matt," Sundance replied.

As Sweetwater entered flight-deck control, the handler said, "Water, the chaplain wants to see you." At that point, a sickening feeling swept over him.

He quickly exited flight-deck control and headed for the chaplain's office, located beside the ship's library on the O-2 level. As he entered the chaplain's office, Father Duffy was waiting for him.

"Come in, Matt."

"What's up, Father?" he asked.

"Matt, have a seat. I just received a Red Cross message that your father is very ill, and that your presence is requested at home as soon as possible."

"Did they say what happened?"

"No, just that he was gravely ill. Had your dad been ill, Matt?"

"His health wasn't good, Father. He has emphysema."

"He must have taken a turn for the worse. But I hope he'll pull through."

"Thank you, Father. I'll be flying-off tomorrow, so I'll head for Maine in the afternoon."

"Is there anything I can do?" the chaplain asked.

"Yes, Father. Would you send a message back to Airpac and have them make a plane reservation on Delta Airlines for an early afternoon departure on Friday? Destination will be Waterville, Maine."

"I'll send that off ASAP. Anything else?"

"Yes, Father. Please say a prayer for my dad. He's a great man. I only wish he could be here with me." Sweetwater's eyes started to tear up as he left the chaplain's office.

As he climbed the ladder well to the 0-3 level, he could hear the planes landing. He knew the demo was over and that Sundance would be down to see what was up. He really didn't want to see anyone. He just wanted to be alone, so instead of going to his room he went to the chapel. When he entered, no one was there, so he went to the front altar and knelt down. He made the sign of the cross and said a few prayers and asked, "Lord, if you're going to take my dad, please wait a few more days so I might see him one last time."

As he got up and started out, Sundance was standing at the back. As Sweetwater got close, Sundance came up and put his arms around him and asked if he could help, not knowing yet what was wrong.

Once they got out of the chapel, Sweetwater told him of his father's condition and they headed back to the room.

"Matt, if there's anything I can do, let me know."

"Thanks, Sundance. I just need some time alone."

"I'm going to chow. Do you want anything?"

"No, I don't feel like eating anything. Besides, I have to pack and figure out what I'll need to take back to Maine."

"Don't worry, there are enough of us flying off. We'll be able to get all you need to the beach."

At that point the phone rang. Sweetwater said, "Hey, Tom, would you get it? I don't want to talk with anyone."

"Sure." He answered the phone and it was the skipper of their squadron. "Water, he wants to see you in his stateroom."

"Okay, tell him I'll be right down."

As Tom hung the phone up, Sweetwater headed out the door. The skipper's stateroom was just down the passageway. When he knocked, the skipper said, "Come in, Sweetwater, and have a seat. Matt, I'm sorry to hear about your dad's condition. We'll get you off first thing in the morning."

"I'm scheduled to fly off with you, Skipper, at 0800."

"That's one of the reasons I called you down. CAG doesn't feel it would be wise to let you fly a plane with your dad on your mind."

"I'm okay. I just need to get in so I can catch that flight back to Maine. Besides, Skipper, my girlfriend will be there for the fly-in and I want to see her before I have to head home. Honest, I'm all right. I'll go see the flight surgeon and if he feels I can't handle it, then I'll find another way off."

"If he feels it's not prudent, we'll get you off in the S-3."

"You got a deal."

After an hour with the combat quack, Sweetwater finally had him convinced that he was capable of flying his aircraft. He felt fine; he just wanted to get on with it, and be with his dad before he died.

The night was a restless one. He didn't sleep a wink.

It was almost like he had Channel Fever. The flight in would only be an hour or so, since they were only a few hundred miles off the California coast.

The first wave of forty planes was to depart at 0800. Some were headed for Washington State, some to Lemoore, California, and the rest were headed to San Diego. The second wave would leave an hour later.

Sweetwater's emotions and state of mind were on the fly-off, because he knew if anything went wrong, heads would roll. People could get in trouble just for letting him get into a cockpit, no less fly off on probably the most dangerous evolution on the whole cruise. Of course, it wasn't the most dangerous flying they did, but because of the desire to get home and off the ship, some crazy things have happened and people have died.

Sweetwater was on Cat One and Bullet Bob was on Two. Sundance was on Three and his skipper was on Cat Four. The plan was to shoot them, then they would all join up in a loose diamond formation and lead the first wave into Miramar. They all blasted off on schedule and joined up. All systems were working as advertised and they were on their way.

Fifty minutes into the flight, CAG called San Diego approach control and got a nice welcome home from them as they gave them a vector to Miramar. They tucked it in, in order to look good coming into the break. By this time Sweetwater could see the runway at Miramar and Bullet came up on tactical and said, "Okay, let's look sharp."

At 400 feet and 250 knots, they flew over the hangars where they would park. Bullet told them there was quite a crowd gathered, since they couldn't observe while flying form on their lead. "Okay, let's step it up to three hundred knots, gents, and give them a good carrier break.''

Sweetwater's heart was pumping, because he knew Nancy would be there awaiting his arrival as would the loved ones of the rest of the men flying in. As they came over the field at the numbers, Bullet Bob kissed him off and broke left. Two seconds later, he kissed Sundance off and broke and he followed, as did his wingman. They all landed safely and taxied up to the line and shut down.

By this time the next division was coming into the break. There must have been two thousand people there to see the fly-in. They had a band playing as the pilots walked toward the crowd, balloons were hanging everywhere, and then Sweetwater spotted his little Princess.

She was decked out in a sundress that made her look like a million bucks. He couldn't wait to hold her in his arms.

The security force tried to keep the families in the hangar until the pilots entered, but CAG's wife and their two little girls started running as the men approached, and the rest of the crowd followed. Nancy came running out and almost knocked Sweetwater down as she ran into his arms. He starting hugging and kissing her and telling her how much he'd missed her when she said that she had heard about his dad's condition.

He asked her how she had found out and she said, ''CAG's wife called Mary and Mary briefed me.''

He thought, It's amazing how the wives and girlfriends find out information before the news is passed.

The Airpac duty officer came up to Sweetwater and said, ''Commander Sullivan, here are your tickets for your flight this afternoon. The flight leaves at one-thirty.

Your squadron paid for the tickets and you can reimburse them when you return.''

"Thank you, Commander Fletcher," Sweetwater said, reading his nametag while he was departing.

"Nancy, I want to call home and get the scoop. Would you please excuse me?"

He went to the phone in the hangar and called his sister's house. "Hi, Mary-Ellen, it's Matt. How are you doing?"

"Oh, pretty good," she replied.

"What's up?"

"Dad's not good, Matt," she said, starting to cry. "They don't expect him to make it through the day."

"You tell Dad I'm home and am on my way. Is he coherent?"

"Yes, and as feisty as ever. He's real weak though, and could go at any time."

"Tell him I'm on my way. Say hi to Mom and everyone. I leave at 1330 and will be in at eleven tonight."

"Okay. Be safe. We love you."

"Love you, too," he said, as he hung up. As he walked toward Nancy, he broke down and started to cry. She held him in her arms like a baby and said, "Get it out. It's okay, it's okay."

By this time the other planes had landed and he went to get the rest of his belongings. Everyone was drinking champagne and having a ball. Sweetwater was pretty sad, but Nancy made the pain seem not quite so bad. Mary said he could use her apartment to get changed and store his flight gear while he was home. All his belongings were in storage, since he rented his house out while he was deployed.

Nancy had rented a car while she was in San Diego,

and she drove him to the airport. On the way, he kept telling her how sorry he was that he wasn't going to be able to go home with her, but that they would get together after he returned from Maine.

"Hey, don't worry about me," she said. "Get home and be with your dad."

She wanted to come in and be with him before the plane left, but he told her not to bother, since he only had thirty minutes before the flight was to leave. As they said their good-byes, she said, "I love you, Matt." And he told her that he loved her too. They kissed and he headed for the gate.

The plane was scheduled to leave on time. As Sweetwater entered the plane, he took his seat, which was next to the window. He normally liked the aisle due to his long legs, but this would do fine. He just wanted to be home with his family.

As the 727 left the ground, and passed over Mission Bay, it struck him why Nancy was so special, and different from the rest of the women he had been with. She accepted him for what he was, and not what she wanted him to be.

NAVY JARGON

AILERONS—movable flaps attached to trailing edge of wing.

AIR BOSS—nickname for Air Department Officer on carrier.

AIR FOIL—surface of wing, aileron, rudder, or propeller blade designed to obtain reaction against the air through which it moves.

ALPHA STRIKE—a certain number of aircraft required to carry out a raid on a target.

ANGELS—altitude expressed in thousands of feet.

ANGLE OF ATTACK—the acute angle between the direction of a relative wind and the chord of an air foil.

ASAP—as soon as possible.

ATTITUDE—term used by Landing Signal Officer during landing of aircraft, to change the nose position of the aircraft relative to the Flight Deck.

AUTO-DOG—soft ice-cream which comes out of machines.

BAT PHONE—direct line to all critical personnel on carrier.

BATTLE GROUP—carrier with 5 to 7 escort ships.

BDS—battle dressing station, a small operating room on the Flight Deck near Flight Deck Control.

BIRD FARM—nickname for carrier.

BLUE SHIRT—person who chocks and chains aircraft on Flight Deck.

BOGAMMERS—Iranian fast-moving heavily armed surface boats.

BOGEY—enemy aircraft.

BROWN SHIRTS—plane captains.

CAG—Carrier Air Group, also nickname for commander of CAG.

CAP—combat air patrol.

CHARLIE—message from Air Boss clearing an aircraft to commence his approach.

CINCPAC—Commander-in-Chief, U.S. Pacific Fleet.

COD—carry/on board/delivery. A type of plane.

CRUISEBOOK—photo "yearbook" of a carrier cruise.

DIEGO GARCIA—small island owned by the British in the southern Indian Ocean.

DITCH—nickname for Suez Canal.

DOWN CHIT—temporary grounding for medical reasons.

5-MC—Flight Deck loudspeaker.

FO'C'SLE—bow of ship where anchors are kept on 02 level; also used for large meetings, weddings, etc.

FRESNEL LENS—optical landing system on port side of Flight Deck which indicates aircraft's relative position to the Flight Deck.

GREEN SHIRTS—catapult and arresting gear crew.

HELO—helicopter.

HOMEPLATE—nickname for carrier.

KNOTS—measurement of speed, slightly faster than miles per hour.

LOOSE DEUCE—two aircraft flying in a formation which provides each other support.

LSO—landing signal officer.

MARSHALL—a person you call while airborne to get landing instructions.

MID-RATS—a meal served after the evening dinner, usually served around 10 P.M. to 1 A.M.

MILITARY—maximum power, but without afterburner.

99 AIRCRAFT—message to all airborne aircraft.

1-MC—ship's loudspeaker.

PAX—passengers.

PLANE CAPTAINS—men responsible for care and maintenance of aircraft.

PLANE GUARD SHIP—escort ship which trails carrier a quarter to half a mile during night recoveries.

PLAT CHANNEL—pilot landing aid television camera, located on surface of Flight Deck, to aid in critiquing pilot landings.

POCKET ROCKET—condensed book for emergency procedures.

POGEY BAIT—candy, gum, etc.

PRIMARY FLIGHT CONTROL—where Air Boss controls aircraft within a 5-mile radius of the carrier and up to 3,000 feet during day visual flight rules.

QUARTER-DECK—officer's brow on carrier.

R&R—rest and recovery leave.

READY ROOM—briefing room for squadron pilots, also gathering spot during off-duty hours.

RECCE—slang for recognition, identification, or clarification.

RED SHIRTS—fire fighters.

RIO—radio intercept officer.

ROLLER—hot dog.

SEA CABIN—skipper's quarters at sea, just off the Bridge.

SEAGULL—chicken.

SDO—squadron duty officer.

SIGNAL DELTA—message to all aircraft to hold at a certain altitude.

SLIDER—hamburger.

TAC CAP—tactical air cover for attacking aircraft.

TALLY HO—message meaning the object or aircraft has been spotted.

TILLY—large Flight Deck crane for lifting damaged or overturned aircraft.

TOPPING OFF—refueling.

TRAIL BLAZERS—big hamburger meatballs, looks like camel dung.

TRANSVERSE G'S—gravitational forces applied to the front of body.

TRAP—an arrested landing.

WARDROOM—officer eating area.

YELLOW SHEET—Naval aircraft flight record.

YELLOW SHIRT—person who directs aircraft on Flight Deck.

ZONE-5—maximum power with afterburner.